WHAT DOESN'T KILL US

AN ENDS WORLD NOVEL,
BOOK 2

MERCYANN SUMMERS

Dear Reader:

Welcome to the other half of the Ends Duet. I'm sure you find yourself here in one of two camps: you loved book 1 and can't wait to find out what happens next, or you hated book 1 and you can't wait to trash it some more. Either way, welcome back to the Ends World, all are welcome here.

If you have not read *Ends of Being, Ends Duet Book 1*, I caution you to please read book 1 before attempting to read *What Doesn't Kill Us*, otherwise you will be lost to a considerable amount of the story. Or at the very least, go skim the last 35% of *Ends of Being* because, according to Goodreads, that's where I finally got my shit together and started telling the story rather than just fucking around being confusing. Oh, but don't miss out on chapters 13, 14, and the backend of 18 for all the extra spicy bits, unless you're looking for straight smut, in which case you should skip this series entirely.

WDKU is classified as romantic suspense with dark themes and, yes, a lot of jokes. Lots and lots of jokes. And as most of you know, I am unapologetically not funny.

If you have no triggers and have zero issues reading any kind of questionable content, please skip ahead to chapter one to not risk any type of spoilers. Even if you are seldom triggered, please read this note in its entirety, and make a conscious decision on whether this book will be a good choice for you. Your mental health is important. Always choose wisely for your own personal well-being.

TW/CW: There is some OW drama, but don't worry, it isn't dragged out. There's a considerable amount of dubious consent between the MMC/FMC as well as kidnapping, suppressed memories, hypnosis, human trafficking, organized crime, and perhaps other various forms of kinky fuckery. There is drugging/noncon/SA, though NOT between the MMC/FMC. There is BDSM, spanking, blood play, breath play, and more naughty words and graphic depictions of sexual acts and violence than I would care to count (366 fucks, 61 cocks, 51 dicks , 33 pussies).

This book is not suitable for persons under the age of 18.

Thank you for reading. I hope you're ready to fuck around and find out.

—Mercy

To the traumatized. The adrift.
The ruined. The aggrieved.
I see you.
Take my hand.

Chapter One

DARE

"WHAT THE FUCK, ANTOINETTE?"

If I thought that I had known pain in the past—this pain—far exceeds any agony I've ever known throughout my entire life.

Because if what I'm seeing is true, then everything I've ever believed was a fucking lie, and I may as well go out in a blaze of glory than pretend I can withstand this deep ache of betrayal.

My heart hammers in my chest, and a cold sweat coats my skin as nausea rolls over me in waves. My breath hitches in my throat, and I choke back a snarling laugh as I dig deep for control, my urge to snuff out what hurts me overwhelming any sense of self-preservation I possess when I'm obviously beyond outnumbered.

I shake my head, turning my focus back on the woman standing a mere ten feet from me. She frowns, then gives me a puzzled look, and the man beside her leans in and whispers something into her ear, and she nods before walking over to me.

She stops in front of me, looking up into my face, and my breath catches to have her so close. I lean forward, intent on being closer to her even as I feel my tethered sanity unraveling, and she doesn't flinch away or anything; she just continues to peer up at me.

I inhale deeply, needing to breathe in her scent in the hopes it will calm me, and that's when I realize something's wrong.

Her scent is off.

I take a closer look, and it's her face, but it's not her face.

The body is wrong, too, and the hair is different.

Finally, I focus back on those blue eyes that are so familiar but at the same time are so incredibly wrong, and I say, "You're not Antoinette."

One corner of her mouth turns up a little as she says, "How very astute of you, Darius Hughes."

The voice is different. It's not quite as husky, with just a hint of an accent that I can't quite place. I look her over some more and note that she's around the same height as Antoinette but also a bit slimmer. She's more angular, stiffer and more formal in her mannerisms.

Whoever this person is, she's obviously well-versed in the game, as her face gives away nothing. I look into her eyes again as I ask, "But who the fuck are you?"

This time, she smiles, and for a moment there, I see Lilith, and it causes a shiver to run down my spine. She steps back from me a bit as she answers, "My name is Agatha. I'm the third fucking sister."

I blink at her blankly for a moment before my eyes widen in horror, her words sinking into my tired bones and settling around me like an ominous cloud.

Then, I sigh heavily, suddenly overwhelmed by the need to sit down.

What the actual fuck?

Chapter Two

Toni

IT'S BEEN THREE MONTHS since Dare disappeared on that jet.

We spent the first week chasing down every lead we could come up with, only to end up at a dead end at every turn. We figured most of the leads were complete bullshit and some of them were most likely planted to throw us off, but considering how messed up the entire situation was, not following up wasn't an option. And so, we ended up spending a considerable amount of time spinning our wheels.

Lilith, of course, was her typical unhinged self and went "end of worlds" on the entire criminal underground, which means I've been learning a lot.

First, say no variation of "burn it all" to Lilith or Tony, because they'll have those torches lit so fast your head will spin. I've also learned the quickest way to end a life and the longest way. They're quite similar, but also very different.

Eventually, we all decide we should attempt a bit of normalcy to get our heads on straight, especially since none of the so-called hot trails ever ended up being hot. Which meant I went back to work. Everyone was perplexed about why I'd bother working, given my access to money literally had no bounds, but whether or not they understand it, this is my normal.

My first few weeks back behind my desk were torture. His absence was so intense that I had moments when I felt like I was caving in on myself. This was also when the past and present would collide, and it would overwhelm my mind with scattered memories that I rarely could make heads or tails of. Obviously, the most recent interactions were solid; however, some of the past moments that would blink in and out of my memory were disconcerting and, sometimes, problematic.

The boys were proving to be incredibly unhelpful in assisting me with sifting through fact and fiction. Tony doesn't seem to have anything concrete to add about any of it, but Matt's reactions are suspicious. I'm certain he knows more than he's letting on, but I also know he'll never tell me anything more than Dare would've instructed him to.

Complicating my inability to settle is the continuous influx of urgent information where I need to switch gears at the drop of a hat. The constant back and forth between accountant Toni and vendetta Toni is exhausting, but I keep doing it in the hopes our luck will change, and we'll get the hit we're desperate for.

And that's how I find myself at my desk late on a Thursday evening, scrolling through some gossip sites to take my mind off my woes. It's in the middle of said scrolling I pause and then slowly scroll back up. I do a double-take, then a triple-take.

What the actual fuck?

I take a screenshot of the page and forward it to our group message with a couple of question marks and exclamation points, and within seconds, they are pinging me back with the same *what the fuck* I had. Tony pops in, telling us it's time to rendezvous, and I pack up my shit and head out the door.

According to an international gossip rag, one Darius Hughes is currently in France on the arm of some slender brunette movie star. If that's the case, more than *his* head is going to roll.

When I get to the warehouse, the three of them are already waiting for me. Tony and Matt seem relaxed, but Lilith is pacing the floor like the raging bitch she is, cursing a blue streak, stomping around, and gesturing wildly with her hands.

She stops pacing when she sees me, then walks over and cups my cheeks as she asks, "Are you okay, Toni?"

I frown at her, shaking her hands loose and walking around her as I reply, "Yeah, I'm fine. Why wouldn't I be?"

She snorts from behind me and then follows, so she's standing beside me as I sit on the stool by the computer bench. She gives me a pinched look and says, "What do you think that picture's about?"

"How the fuck would I know? You're better off asking one of these fucking yahoos. They're friends with him."

Lilith turns her gaze on Tony and glares at him. "What do you have to say for your friend, Tony?"

Tony gives her an annoyed look as he retorts, "I don't think there's much I can say, considering I have no fucking idea what's going on."

Lilith narrows her eyes at him and steps closer until she's right in his face. "I have a really fucking hard time believing that. You all have been bosom buddies since you could barely reach the urinal. There isn't anything you don't know about each other."

"Kind of hard for me to know what's going on, seeing how I haven't seen the man in three fucking months. How about you get control of your fucking emotions for a minute and actually think about the big picture here."

She gasps in outrage, her hand coming up so she's pointing right in his face as she snarls, "You watch your fucking mouth."

Tony leans closer and whispers, "Or what?"

I roll my eyes as I stand up and push between them until they both step back. "Break it up, assholes. This isn't the time for your little pissing contest or mating game or whatever the fuck this is between the two of you."

"Good call, Antoinette. I've been listening to these two snarling at each other for the last twenty minutes, and it's getting us absolutely fucking nowhere," Matt says from behind me.

I turn to him. "So, how're we going to handle this?"

We all look at each other for a few moments as we ponder our options with the limited information we have. We certainly could rush over there with guns blazing, but since it was rather obvious from that picture that Dare was in no great distress, that option seems unnecessary.

I turn to Tony and ask, "Do you think there's any chance, any chance at all, that Darius has a relationship with whoever this woman is?"

Tony shakes his head, his arms coming up to cross over his chest as he replies, "Not a chance. Not one fucking chance, Nettie. There's definitely a far bigger picture here than what we see in that picture. There has to be."

I turn to Matt, knowing he wouldn't have spent the last hour twiddling his thumbs. "What do you know, Matt?"

"Not a lot. My initial feelers report back that he's going by his real name. The woman is a European actress, newly arrived on the scene by the name of Carolina Tennent. I found a short trail of them on some lesser-known red carpets. It seems like they've been working their way up the ranks slowly over the last few weeks. It's fucking weird and makes little sense at this point in this clusterfuck."

I frown, a little perturbed by this seemingly ridiculous scenario. The fucking guy has been missing for months, and then he pops up on the arm of some young movie star. Like, what the fuck kind of alternate reality am I in right now?

I raise my hands up in front of me in surrender. "All right, I got nothing here. So, you guys tell me what I'm gonna do, and then let's go do it because I'm fucking sick of this entire thing."

Tony and Matt smile at each other, and a small shiver of foreboding goes down my spine. They both turn their focus on me as Tony says, "Come on, Nettie. You know the old Darius Hughes motto."

I roll my eyes and groan as Matt snickers and adds, "We're gonna go over there, and we're gonna fuck around and find out."

I groan and shake my head at them. "Well, I guess we will, indeed."

It doesn't take long for our plan to take shape, and before I know it, we're on a plane headed to France. I don't speak French, but apparently everyone else does.

Watching the three of them put together a plan—and several back-up plans—was impressive. I meant to throw in a few tidbits here and there, but one thing Matt and Tony keep repeating is that if Darius is playing a role with a certain endgame in mind, getting him to crack publicly will be nearly impossible.

They've reminded me so many times, it's getting fucking annoying, so when Tony brings it up for the millionth time, I finally snap back at him, "Yeah, Tony. I fucking get it already. Why don't you lay off?"

Tony frowns at me and then leans forward in his seat. "I don't think you get it, Nettie. Darius is not some amateur hack who randomly turns his back on the people he cares about without a word, unless it's for a very specific reason. And whatever that reason is, he will not break character out in the open. You need to have your game face on and keep your cool. And for the love of all that is holy, when our man on the red carpet comes up to you, you gotta play the part."

I roll my eyes, unable to keep the petulance from my voice, as I mutter, "Yeah, fine. I can pretend to be enamored by a random, attractive man. Not a problem. I got this."

Lilith snorts beside me. "Oh, yeah. She's totally fucking got it."

"Shut up, Lils." I snark, showing her my middle finger.

She grins at me, reaching out and giving my arm a pinch. "That's no way to speak to your elders, Toni. I know you think you're ready for all this, but I worry you underestimate how shocking it's going to be to see him with his hands on another woman. Especially given the memories that have come back recently."

I sigh and swallow past the lump in my throat. She's not wrong. As time has gone by, more and more bits and pieces have come together to make me see a bigger picture of my life. It appears as if the memories come back in reverse order, and a lot of them have to do with the period when we didn't have a romantic relationship; however, they show how the frequency and intensity of our dalliances increased. I feel that it's a safe assumption for me to believe if that incident in the warehouse hadn't happened, we would've ended up together much sooner.

Thinking about it makes me sad and a little angry, given there are still so many pieces of my previous life I don't remember. Lilith helps me fill in some of the gray areas around the solid pieces, but she never gives me too much information for fear she'll create false memories.

Tony's voice startles me from my thoughts. "So, tell me one more time, Nettie. What are you gonna do when you see him?"

I take a deep breath, straightening in my seat as I stare back at him. "I'm going to do nothing. I'm going to stare right through him like he doesn't exist."

This was a mistake. Standing on this fucking red carpet in this stupid fucking dress with sweat rolling down my fucking back is not my idea of a good time.

This was supposed to have been choreographed perfectly so we would cross paths at the exact right moment, but so far, there's no sign of him or the whore he seems attached to.

Yes, that's right. Whore. Whore. Whore.

My three comrades are waiting in the wings where they can observe what's happening without being easily spotted by Dare whenever he saunters down the red carpet with that whore.

I give my head a small shake, centering myself on the mission at hand. At some point, Darius is going to appear. Then, strategically, some dashing man named Peter Thorne will strut in and literally sweep me off my feet. Tony assures me his old military buddy will have zero issues maneuvering the scene appropriately, regardless of how I manage my own emotions.

Still, I swallow down some nausea at the thought of having to pretend to be enamored by some fucking stranger, but a job is a job.

It's fine. Everything is fine. I can do this. No problem.

I sense him before I see him, as the fine hairs on the back of my neck prickle, and I attempt to glance around inconspicuously. From the corner of my eye, I catch sight of him, then I avert my gaze, staring in the other direction toward the theater entrance. Inhaling deeply, I straighten my spine, raising my chin to prepare for what must be done.

My gaze roams over him again and then shifts to the woman standing next to him. She's tall and stacked, her dark hair shiny, and her full red lips smiling seductively.

I want to punch a hole through her chest, rip out her heart, and fucking eat it.

I push the violent thought down and let my gaze slowly shift over him, and I see he's staring in my direction. I raise my eyes to his face, meeting those golden eyes briefly before moving on, not wanting to focus on him for too long for fear I'll lose my focus. But I feel his eyes on me still, and I can't stop the physical reaction as my skin tingles, and I feel the heat rise in my cheeks. My heart swells in my chest, almost choking me, and my breath stutters as I turn back toward him, my eyes lifting slowly until I'm staring into golden orbs that are practically burning a hole right through me.

Out of nowhere, a man rushes from behind Dare, skirting around him as he continues in my direction. I do a double-take, genuinely shocked by what I see. He's taller and broader than Darius, with an exquisitely chiseled jaw, his dark hair perfectly styled, and all of those muscles rippling under his tailored black tux. If I were any other person in any other life, my panties would melt right off.

I'm gaping, so I snap my mouth shut and take a few small steps toward him before he's on me, sweeping me up in his arms. A little squeak of surprise falls from my lips as he lifts me, and then one of his hands moves into my hair, and he's pressing his lips against mine in a rather demanding public display of affection.

I do my best to relax, my arms coming up over his shoulders and my hands tangling in the soft tendrils of hair at the nape of his neck.

He purrs, a little growl of appreciation vibrating against my lips as he pulls back, smiling into my eyes as he says, "There you are, pet. I've been waiting all day for that bit of sugar."

His subtle British accent washes over me, and I find I'm tongue-tied for a moment, something I'm not at all used to. I have no idea who this person is. He's no movie star I've ever seen before, but the amount of sex appeal and charisma oozing from his pores should be illegal. Peter finally lowers me back to my feet, then takes me by the hand and leads me down onto the red carpet.

He appears to be popular here, considering the number of photographers, reporters, and non-celebrities I see waving at him, trying to get his attention. I say nothing; instead choosing to duck my head as I do my best to keep up, infinitely grateful that my panties haven't disintegrated.

Peter releases my hand to sign autographs for the fans lined up behind the ropes along the red carpet, and I take a moment to glance back to where I last saw Darius and his fancy little whore. They're no longer standing there, so I nonchalantly scan the area, but they're nowhere in sight. I squint, forcing myself not to frown in annoyance, when I suddenly feel the fine hairs on the back of my neck prickling again.

I freeze in place, sensing his presence behind me, afraid to turn around for fear of what seeing him up close and personal will do to me. He's standing so close I feel the heat of his body through the thin fabric of my black satin dress, and I shift back slightly until I'm barely touching him with my shoulder and my ass, and he leans into me.

Did he just sniff me?

He growls low in his chest, quietly enough I'm sure I'm the only one who notices, and my breath catches at the same time my heart stutters in my chest. I inhale slowly through my nose, catching the familiar scent of him beneath the expensive cologne he's wearing at the same time his finger grazes my ass cheek and strokes up to the skin at my lower back. I grind my teeth together, trapping the gasping moan that threatens to erupt, my focus shifting suddenly to Peter, who's waiting patiently for me to take the hand he's holding out to me.

I smile at him, grabbing his hand like the lifeline it is, allowing him to pull me close until we're pressed tightly, chest to chest. His hand skims down my back, and my gaze jumps to his face to find he's not focused on me at all, but on a spot behind me. He strokes his fingers from the small of my back down along my ass cheek, the reverse of how Darius touched me a few moments ago, and he smiles haughtily like he wants other people to know how much he enjoys putting on a show.

I hear a much louder growl behind me, and I tense, pushing at Peter's chest, but he doesn't release me. Instead, he moves his hand from my ass to the back of my neck and presses his mouth against my lips with such force my mouth opens automatically. And then he puts on a proper show, not giving one fuck as the crowd cheers wildly. After a few moments, he releases me, a self-satisfied grin on his face as he once again looks behind me. I turn around to peek, but Darius is gone, and I'm unsure if I'm relieved or disappointed.

Rattled, I follow Peter into the theater, and we eventually find our seats. Lilith is next to me, and beside her is a man I've never seen before. He's not as good-looking as Peter; however, he appears similar in his features. Lilith stands as I move to take my seat beside her, and she catches my hands in hers and leans closer like she's going to give me an air kiss, but instead, she whispers, "Good job."

I lean closer to her and whisper back, "What do you mean? I feel like this was a mistake."

She gives a small laugh. "Oh, no. It was perfect. You should've seen the look on his fucking face."

I'm genuinely surprised. I suppose I was so taken aback by the entire encounter I lost track of what was happening around me. Since Tony and Matt were the ones out there, keeping a close watch on his actions and reactions, they would certainly know what his outward reaction was.

I can't help but smile a little smugly as Peter comes over and gestures for me to sit beside him. I do, and when he reaches for my hand, I give it over willingly.

And then, for the rest of the night, I give an Oscar-worthy performance of a woman in love with her man.

Chapter Three

Toni

WE DIDN'T HAVE TO wait long to find out what Dare thought about my little date with Peter.

I figured it would take him a time or two before it would've pushed him over the edge, but Tony and Matt were sure this one time was all it was going to take. And they were right.

What Dare wasn't expecting when he broke into our Parisian apartment was that my new friend, Hans, would be waiting for him. Hans is a retired black ops specialist turned muscle for hire, and since he knows a thing or two about the Beast, he was all too happy to pull one over on him. The look of shock on Dare's face when Hans grabbed him from behind was poetic, and I think it was that two-second delay that prevented him from being able to escape.

All it took was a well-positioned take-down move and a solid rear-naked chokehold, and that fucker was down for the count. And

I made sure the last thing he saw before he lost consciousness was my smiling face. It was glorious.

Now, here I am in my bedroom, watching him being strapped down like an offering from the gods, and I can't help but chuckle to myself. The fact we so easily turned the tables on Darius Hughes is fucking amusing. I didn't expect him to be out for so long, but Tony said Hans had given him a little nip of something to keep him out longer; otherwise, there's no way they'd be able to restrain him. It must have been a decent nip, considering it's been twenty minutes, but that's fine. I can wait.

I glance at my watch again and then decide I have time to head back to the kitchen to grab some water. The fucker will probably be thirsty when he wakes up, so I may as well prepare.

My journey there or back is uneventful, so it doesn't take very long, but I'm startled when I return to the bedroom and find the bed empty.

"Motherfucker," I sputter as I spin to leave the room. I go to raise the alarm, but I'm a few moments too late, and his hard body presses against my back, his firm hand covering my mouth.

Excitement pitter-patters in my chest, but I ignore it and bite down hard on his palm. Dare curses, his hand falling from my mouth, and I bring my foot up and quickly stomp down hard on his instep. He flinches in surprise, his arm loosening on me enough for me to break free.

I don't have anywhere to go because he's standing in the doorway. I rush to the far side of the room and dive for the bedside table, where I have a gun stored in the drawer. Dare slams into me from behind, one of his hands hitting the drawer shut before I can get my hand inside. He yanks me back, and we both go down hard onto the floor, where we roll around, both of us grappling for the upper hand.

Dare is fucking huge. At a glance, you wouldn't realize what a big guy he is, but when you're wrestling with him on the floor, vying for dominance, you'll know you're out-matched rather quickly. I get in as many pot shots as I can, going for his eyes, a punch to the throat, then another to the kidney, but before I know it, I find myself pressed face down into the rug, his heavy breath in my ear as he growls, "That's right, baby girl. I know you like it rough."

I attempt to squirm beneath him, but it's no use. The pressure of his body presses down even harder until I'm having difficulty breathing, so I snap my head up sharply, catching him on the cheek. He curses, then laughs as I snarl, "Get the fuck off me, you asshole."

Adjusting his whole body over me, he presses one of his hands on the back of my head to keep my face firmly against the floor. Then his teeth are on my neck, and along my jaw, right where it meets my ear. He bites down hard, then says, "Why would I do that? Not when I have you right where I want you."

I try to yank my face away, but I can't move. I grit my teeth, almost choking on my rage as I spit out, "You don't get to just have me anymore, Dare. You treacherous fucking snake."

His face hardens into lines of fury. His hand on my head suddenly tightens in my hair, pulling my head back sharply so he can look directly into my eyes as he snarls, "I'm a treacherous fucking snake? What about you? Do you think you can parade around town with another fucking man's hands on you and get away with it?"

Before I can come up with a response, he suddenly removes himself from me, and I'm yanked up off the ground. He hustles me backward until my back is up against the wall. I attempt to get a couple of cheap shots in, but he snags my wrists with his hands and pins them over my head. He pushes his body into mine, pressing firmly against me from chest to hips. He has me completely boxed in; the tension vibrating off of him.

I wait until he leans closer, then try to head-butt him again, but he flinches out of the way. He shifts his grip to hold both my wrists in one hand and moves his free hand to my throat, squeezing with enough force to keep me immobile. I whisper, "What are you doing?"

He leans in and runs his nose over my cheek, then pulls back and looks into my eyes. "I'm going to remind you who you belong to, minx."

I'm annoyed that my insides clench at his words, so I glare at him and retort, "I don't belong to anyone."

He chuckles, and the sound washes over me, causing a shiver to roll down my back at the sinister undertones. He squeezes my neck a little tighter as he says, "Like fuck you don't. It seems, in my brief absence, you've lost sight of how things are between us. And I'm going to fucking remind you, so you never forget again."

I try to yank my hands free and bring my knee up in the hopes I can catch him off-guard, but once again, it doesn't work, and he leans in closer. He seems bigger to me now. He was always a fit man, but he looks bulkier than before. So, I ask, "What the fuck, Dare? Have you been working out?"

He gives me that same dark chuckle, pressing himself even closer so I feel the hard ridge of his cock against my stomach. He leans his head down until he's painting a fiery trail down my neck and ear as he responds, "Oh, yes. I had a lot of time for recreation while in prison."

I frown and pull my head back a bit to look him in the face. "Prison? What do you mean, prison?"

Dare's shoulders rise in a slight shrug. "Do you think I've spent the last few months living in the lap of luxury, fucking movie stars, and drinking champagne? Not a care in the world?"

I snort. "Well, from the brief glimpse I've gotten, that is exactly how it would appear."

His hand releases my neck, stroking down the front of my body as he eases back a bit. His fingers graze down over my breasts, floating across my stomach until he's covering my pussy, his fingers flexing against me. He lifts his head, his gaze meeting mine as he says, "Things aren't always as they appear, Antoinette. You, of all people, should know that by now."

He presses his finger against my clit, and I choke back the moan bubbling up inside me. It's everything I can do not to spread my legs wider for him, to give in entirely and beg him to remind me who I belong to. But there's still that part of me that questions, that requires answers in order to submit.

I squeeze my legs shut, trapping his hand between them, and he smiles at me, tilting his head as he says, "You want to do the work for me? Ride my hand until you come apart, moaning my name?"

I give him a bland look. "Not fucking likely. Get off me."

He bares his teeth at me. "No."

I pull violently against his hold on my hands. "What do you mean, no?"

Dare gives me an amused look, the humor twinkling in his golden eyes infuriating me even further. I struggle against his hold, but that only brings him in closer, and he leans his head down so he's once again giving me that dark chuckle against my ear.

That motherfucker.

He releases my hands. "Go ahead. Fight me, baby girl. You know I love it when you struggle against me, and I have to persuade you to give in."

I let my hands rest on his shoulders for a moment, then reach up and grab him by the hair, yanking hard. He flinches a bit but doesn't stop me when I lean forward and bite onto his neck, sinking my teeth in. He laughs again, his hand delving into my hair and yanking me off him before he says, "Now, now, Antoinette. I won't let you go bleeding me out or anything."

He yanks my head further back and lowers his mouth to my neck, biting down, sucking hard, then licking gently before pulling back and gazing down at his handiwork. I'm sure he left the biggest hickey I've ever known, so I pull my hand back and crack my palm against his cheek. "Why the fuck did you do that, asshole?"

This time, he laughs outright and says, "Oh, this is part of the process of me reminding you of who you belong to. I'm gonna put my mark on you everywhere I can find."

I push against his shoulders and bring my leg up, slamming my knee into his gut. He doesn't budge and instead grabs my leg and pulls it up and around him, so now I feel his hard dick pressing right against my pussy. He chuckles again and leans down to the other side of my neck, giving small little pushes of his hips against me.

A quiet moan escapes, and his breath hitches. "That's right, baby girl. I know you don't wanna like it, but you fucking love it. I bet if I put my fingers in your pussy, I'll find you dripping wet for me. Your body wants me to rail you so fucking hard. Just admit it. Tell me you want it."

I shake my head in denial as my hips instinctively press against him. I hate that I want him. When he pulls my head back and gently puts his mouth against mine, I bite down sharply on his bottom lip until I taste blood. He winces and pulls back, then I retort, "Don't be fucking nice to me. Do you think I'm going to give you any part of me? You're going to have to fucking take it if you want it."

His golden eyes bore into mine, flames burning in them as he growls, "Oh, fucking right, I'll take it. I'll fucking take it over and over and over again, and there's not one fucking thing you can do to stop me."

I bare my teeth at him and snarl, "Then shut the fuck up, and get on with it."

He growls deep in his chest. With his jaw clenching, he yanks me away from the wall with such force my teeth crack together. He half-drags, half-carries me across the room, and the next thing I know, I'm bent over the bed, and he's securing my wrists behind my back with what I assume is his tie.

I attempt to sit up, but he forces me back down with the weight of his upper body. He leans over me, his face right next to mine where it's pressed against the comforter, and purrs, his words clinging to me like a hot caress. "I'm going to get the fuck on with it just as soon as you tell me what I need to know."

I snort indelicately. "Oh, my fucking Christ. You and your fucking talking."

He growls again, abruptly removing his weight from me as he moves behind me and yanks at my yoga pants. The cool air hits my ass as he pulls them down my thighs. I try to sit up again, but he pushes me back down. Craning my head around, I ask, "What the fuck are you doing?"

He gives me a smug look. "Not fucking talking. Isn't that what you wanted?"

I glare at him, not trusting this situation one bit. There's no way Darius Hughes would switch gears that quickly unless he was up to something, and I doubt he's going to fuck me without getting what he wants first.

I feel the stinging pain on my ass before I even realize he has moved.

The fucker spanked my ass.

I thrash on the bed, but he leans back over me, and I can't get the leverage I need to force him off. I stop fighting against him and lay there, out of breath, cursing the very day I met him, and he says, "You ready to talk to me, baby girl?"

I snap my mouth shut and shake my head. What's he going to do? Keep spanking my ass until I crack? Not a fucking chance.

The next spank is significantly more powerful, and I barely hold back a gasp as fire spreads over my ass cheek. Then he immediately does the same to the other cheek, and I'm a strange mix of apprehension and turned on.

He asks no more questions, instead continuing to punish my rear end until both cheeks are blazing with heat, and I'm clenching my thighs together to prevent me from humping the mattress. I haven't so much as made a peep, but I'm relatively certain he knows exactly what he's doing to me.

Then I hear it. The clink of his belt as he unfastens it and then the whir of it being pulled from the belt loops. Surely, he won't hit me with his belt. Right?

Fuck.

Chapter Four

Toni

I WAKE WITH A start. Disoriented, I blink against the dim light, confused when I glance around and see sunlight peeking around the curtain where it's not quite closed. I shake my head, trying to clear it, but everything feels fuzzy.

Rolling over onto my back, my eyes widen at the pain in my backside, a shining ache that zaps my brain into focus.

Darius.

That motherfucker.

I roll onto my front and slowly maneuver myself to the edge of the bed so I can stand. I take a moment to collect myself before forcing my legs to bear my full weight. It's a good five minutes before I feel confident enough to take a step, and I slowly make my way into the bathroom, where I squint at my reflection in the mirror.

I'm a hot mess. My hair stands up in all different directions, likely from his hands and my sweat. What little mascara I have left is in streaks under my eyes, only disturbed by the tear tracks running along my cheeks. There are bite marks and hickeys all over my person. There is no way I have enough makeup to cover all this.

I huff and roll my eyes, and when I turn, I get a twinge in my ass cheeks that has me spinning in slow motion so I can get a glimpse of the damage my pleasures cost me.

"Motherfucker," I mutter to myself.

My ass is covered in tiny bruises, welts, and what looks suspiciously like a complete set of upper and lower teeth. I try to peer a little closer, but the angle isn't right, so I give up and make my way over to the shower. I reach for the door when I see a Post-it stuck to it.

Yours.

I peel the note off the door, bringing it closer to get a better look. It appears as if he pressed a bloody fingertip to it, his way of signing it in blood. My lips twist, and I can't stop the flutter in my chest at the implication.

Moving the note to the counter, I go about getting myself as ready as I can for the day. Luckily, it's supposed to be on the cool side, so I can cover up most of this mess with some form of clothing. I'm relieved he left me mostly blemish-free from the neck up; there are a few spots on my neck I'll have to cover, and I'm honestly surprised it's only that given his overtly possessive overture of the previous evening.

The initial assumption that we had him right where we wanted him after our little show on the red carpet was incredibly short-sighted. We all figured once we got his attention, he would feel inclined to make some sort of declaration, but I don't think anyone ever considered that he would literally wage war on my person.

Bruises, welts, and love marks were not at all how I saw him responding, though I'm not complaining. But if the man wasn't as serious about his aftercare as he is about making a point using physical punishment, I'd be an entirely different hot mess right now.

When he first removed his belt, I had some mixed feelings: excitement, fear, apprehension. A deep vibrating arousal. And at first, I wasn't entirely sure what he was going to do with it.

He started giving me the option of either accepting that he's the only man who will ever touch me again, or I'd be asking for a few lashings. I may have chosen the lashings with my continued silence. Maybe that's because I have faith that he would never hurt me unnecessarily.

Not that a few of them didn't hurt; when he set out to get my attention, that's precisely what he fucking did. But after a while, I was so hot and bothered that I was begging him to let me come. Frankly, I would've agreed to anything by the end.

When he was done with the belt, he shifted me so my knees were on the bed with me still face down and left my hands tied behind my back, so I couldn't hold myself up at all. I was laying there, like a limp ragdoll, at his mercy for him to do what he wanted.

It was fucking glorious. I lost track of how many times he edged me with his mouth and fingers, leaving me waiting for him to push his huge fucking dick inside me, but he never did.

My pussy clenches at the thought, and from the small twinge of discomfort this causes, I have to believe it was probably a good thing he didn't. If he had, he most likely would've broken me right in half, and I would've been limping for days.

I make my way back into the bedroom and spot another note stuck to the door when I go to open it. This one only has one word on it, *mine,* and the same bloody fucking fingerprint. This time, I roll my eyes, but I can't help but smile like the besotted fucking fool I am. I should be angry that he was here and never actually gave me any answers, but part of me is a bit relieved because once I have those answers, I'll have to decide where those answers leave us.

Tony doesn't believe I truly understand the whole undercover dynamic Dare may be living at this point. I understand it, but that doesn't mean I have to like it. If he was having to fuck other women to maintain some cover story to protect me, is that still cheating? Are we even together enough for it to be called cheating? And if we are, at what point does your cover story become an extension of another lie? It's not like he's the police or anything. He's a fucking criminal doing criminal work with other criminals.

I leave the note on the back of the door and make my way down the hall to the kitchen. I stifle a yawn as I walk over to the fancy coffee machine and grimace. "How come there's no Mr. Coffee in this place? I want a regular cup of coffee."

Tony laughs as he walks over and shoves me out of the way. "Let me help you. You look like you had a long, hard night."

Sitting on the stool at the counter, I watch Tony pressing all these shiny buttons, until finally, he's placing the smallest cup of coffee I've ever seen in front of me. He smiles at me, so I pick up the tiny cup and take a little sip, swallowing my moan of pleasure as the richness of the hot liquid hits my tongue.

Setting the cup down; I clear my throat. "So, which one of you rigged Dare's restraints so that he could get out of them?"

Silence meets my question. I glance around at everyone in the room, trying to decide which one is the guilty party. I don't believe it's Lilith, because I'm certain she's entirely on my side. Of course, that doesn't mean she wouldn't work against me if she felt it was in my best interest, so I suppose I should leave her on the list of possibilities. At the top of the list is Tony, but at a glance, he looks genuinely perplexed. And Matt looks tired. That only leaves one other person.

"Where is Hans?"

Matt and Lilith shrug as Tony responds, "I think he may be outside. You need to see him?"

I nod, and he pulls his phone out, probably sending a quick message, and within a few moments, we hear a door open and close, then the heavy footfalls of a large man walking down the hallway.

Tony must've told him I wanted to see him because he comes right over to me and stops in front of me. "Antoinette?" He's looking me in the eye with cool detachment, but I see the tiny twitch in the corner of his mouth. That fucker.

I tilt my head at him as I ask, "Hans, who do you work for?"

He glances briefly at Tony before bringing his eyes back to mine. "I work for Darius Hughes."

I laugh and shake my head, then laugh and laugh and laugh until all three of them are staring at me wide-eyed. "Of course you do. Everyone works for Darius fucking Hughes."

I look over at Tony and ask, "Did you know about this? When we set up this whole little trap Dare plan, did you know the big guy was going to make it easy for him to flip the script?"

Tony gives me a sheepish look. "I actually didn't. Though in hindsight, not considering it was stupid on my part."

I shake my head, rubbing a hand over my face as I catch my breath. I bring my attention back to Hans. "You didn't drug him at all, did you?"

He shakes his head, giving me a bored look. "We have a protocol for every scenario that you could ever dream up. That way, if we're ever put into a position where we can prevent harm from coming to him or where we can give him a leg-up, the options are simple."

I raise my brows, crossing my arms over my chest. "Explain."

Hans glances at Tony, and I jump to my feet, getting right in his face as I snarl, "Do not fucking look at him. I'm the one asking the questions here, and you'd better give me all your attention, or else I may decide to get stabby with you."

Lilith laughs behind me. "Ooh. I do love stabby Toni."

Hans glances at her, then brings his focus back to me. "I'm not at liberty to discuss this with you."

I nod. "Then get the fuck out."

Hans frowns at me but doesn't move. So, I take a step toward him, poking my finger into his chest. "You can leave now. If you're going to keep secrets and do his bidding, then you're not welcome here. We don't need you. Get out."

He shakes his head. "I cannot do that."

I frown. "What do you mean, you cannot do that? Turn around, walk out the door and go tell that fucking prick we all said to go right to hell."

He gives me another bland look and then takes out his phone and types out a message. He pauses, staring down at the screen for a few moments before putting it back into his pocket. "I'll be staying here with you."

Then he turns around and books it back the way he came, the door slamming shut behind him.

I turn to Tony, my blood pressure rising with every step I take toward him, when my phone rings from the counter. Considering anyone who would call me on that number is sitting in the room with me, I give my phone a suspicious look, then check the ID.

Unknown.

I grit my teeth as I hit accept, putting the call on speakerphone, but I don't say anything. "Hans stays," comes out of the speaker, then silence as the call ends.

I squint at the black screen, instantly seeing red at the nerve of this fucking prick. Reaching over, I grab a utility knife from the block on the counter, then rush down the hallway and out the same door Hans exited from. Lilith and Matt are right on my heels, their words telling me to cool it and to think about what I'm doing, but I ignore them, my murderous gaze on the only treacherous fuckface I can get my hands on right now.

Hans turns and sees me coming a few seconds too late to fully stop the trajectory of the knife. I thrust toward his side, but he knocks my swing enough where the blade glances off his ribs instead of piercing between them as I intended. He grunts, jumping away from me as I attempt to parry closer, and then he maneuvers around to the other side of the vehicle he was standing next to when I started my attack.

I'm screaming mad. Adrenaline courses through my body, making me feel twitchy, and my grip on the knife handle tightens. "Get the fuck out of here! Go back and tell Darius fucking Hughes that if he wants to overlord over me, he better come here and fucking do it himself! If I see you here again, I will slit your throat in your sleep!"

I don't wait for an answer. I whirl around and start walking back toward our apartment. Matt, Tony, and Lilith are all staring at me, so I snarl, "What?"

"Nothing," they all say in unison.

They fall into step behind me as I enter the apartment, and we all end up back in the kitchen. I grab my phone and see it's already lit up with missed calls and text messages, so I pick it up and drop it into the pitcher of orange juice that's on the counter.

I turn to Matt. "Get me a new phone, please. A secure one this time." Then I turn to Lilith. "Call Mickey. Tell him to send some men. The mean, loyal kind, if that even exists anymore."

Lilith is nodding at me enthusiastically, and I see the slightly maniacal twinkle in her eyes. "Oh, they definitely exist. That is not a problem."

I'm tired of feeling like I'm being led around by the nose by overbearing men who don't have the courtesy to explain the situation to me. I'm sure part of it is that they don't fully know what the situation is, but even admitting that would be something. Instead, they continue to handle me with kid gloves and treat me like a fragile plaything they're afraid will break.

It's about time they learned I am no fragile plaything.

Matt has told me several times that the amount of information he could pull on me is sparse. Born off the map and raised off it, too. I didn't even exist in the system until I was an adult working at the accounting firm. It makes me wonder if I even have a legitimate degree or if I've been winging it this entire time.

"Nettie." Tony's voice is quiet as he walks over to stand in front of me. "What are you doing?"

I raise my gaze to meet his. "Taking my fucking life back."

He nods. "Okay. Tell me what you need."

"I need you to decide," I say calmly. "Are you with me, or are you with Darius Hughes?"

Tony frowns. "I'm with you. Whether you like Dare's methods, we are all with you. Sure, he's a meddlesome, infuriating, overbearing, fucking dickhead, shitbag, but even with whatever fucked-up shit he's got himself into right now, he's also still with you."

I place my hands on my hips as I reply, "None of that really matters right now. He's off doing whatever undercover bullshit he feels he needs to do with no conversations or consideration for the other people involved. So, he can go do his stupid shit and we're gonna come up with our own plan. Try to understand what's going on. I will not continue to live like this. It's time to find the bad guys and eliminate them, and then we can all get on with our lives. I refuse to live in the dark any longer."

Tony smiles, then laughs. "Shit, Nettie. It sounds to me like you're ready to fuck around and find out."

I roll my eyes at him and snort. "Don't you ever get sick of that line?"

He frowns. "Sick of it? No fucking way. It's like my tagline. If I was a video game character, it would be on a halo over my head everywhere I went."

"You're an idiot." Tony and Matt both laugh, and I find the sound reassuring. I look over at Lilith, and she's staring at me with a faraway look in her eyes. "What is it, Lils?"

She smiles, tilting her head at me as she replies, "Welcome back, sis. Welcome back."

Chapter Five

Dare

THAT FUCKING BITCH.

Just when I think we've come to some kind of understanding, Antoinette goes completely off the rails and fucks up my well-thought-out plans. I get it; she's probably a little sick and tired of not being privy to the intricate details of these plans, but the fact she cannot get it through her stubborn head that not knowing the details is in her best interest infuriates me to no end.

Sometimes, I feel like I need to drop a flowchart to explain how, in our world, not knowing things is always better. The need-to-know basis is concrete, as the more you know, the bigger the target you have on your back. And the more her memories return, the larger that target will get.

I know little about Antoinette's past. Matt told me from the start he could not find much information on her, which was automatically a huge red flag. And my tendency to hold my cards close to my chest, even with my closest friends, was probably a mistake. If I had known this information before becoming close to her, I would've either stayed the fuck away from her or chained her in my basement and made her tell me what I wanted to know.

By the time I knew there was an issue, I had stupidly dragged my feet in getting the details, and the next thing I knew, she didn't even know who she was. A few times, Tony questioned whether her amnesia was real, that maybe she was playing an extra-long game. Her doctor believed no one could fake this level of memory loss for this length of time. I was also relatively certain that it would be impossible for anyone to maintain this level of undercover work without slipping out of that character for that long.

I get that she's upset—rightfully so, even. But the fact there's nothing I can do about any of it right now is enough to make me want to fuck shit up. I want to go over there and shake her until her teeth rattle. And now, I can't even get her on her phone, which means she likely dumped it. The fact I also can't get any of those other fucking cunts on their phones has me toeing the line on Crazytown.

Those motherfuckers.

I get it with Lilith. She doesn't give two shits about me. She's solidly on Antoinette's side, and that will never change. She would slit my throat with minimal provocation, and I don't doubt she could pull it off if she wanted to. Actually, the only thing keeping me alive could be Antoinette telling her she's not allowed to kill me.

Then there's Tony and Matt. It seems my boys have gone to the other side. I mean, I get it. This is a long game in every sense of the term, and each one of us must do what must be done, whether or not we like it. And let's not forget they have explicit orders from me to stay with her at all costs, so it's not like I can really be mad that they're doing what I told them to do.

Toni is pissed that I went to see her, and instead of providing any information, I played games and then vanished. Sure, she enjoyed the experience, and I did what I could to make sure she recovered well, but when she went to the trouble of setting me up to be taken, that was not at all the result she was looking for. I fully expected her to retaliate, but I did not see her attempting to slice and dice my man, Hans.

If I could've explained any part of what was going on, I would've done my best to do so. But the fact of the matter is, I don't know a lot. We've been fucking around out here for weeks, trying to get someone, anyone, to try something, and so far, all we've earned for our troubles is a bunch of dead ends and Toni deciding to join the fucking limelight. I spend most of my time worried I'm being followed while hoping I'm being followed because I'd rather be bound to a chair in another disgusting warehouse where I might get some answers than continue to stand here with my dick out.

The only reason I managed to sneak out to see Antoinette is because Carolina helped me. It turns out she's a very skilled actress. She acts like we're too enamored with each other to leave the house outside of work engagements, and I sneak in and out as needed. Easy peasy—no fuss, no muss.

Until Antoinette went fucking insane, anyway.

I realize Hans is still standing there, waiting for me to give him further instructions. I look him up and down and ask, "Are you going to live?"

He scowls at me, crossing his arms over his chest as he replies, "Are you being serious? I'm fine. If it had been anyone else, I would have broken their neck. But it was Antoinette, so I did not."

My blood pressure rises at the very thought of him touching her. She stabbed him, and from the looks of it, she intended to inflict some serious harm on him. Seems my baby girl has toughened up over the last few months. I laugh. "It was a near-miss there, wasn't it?"

His scowl deepens. "If she had been quieter about it, I might not be standing in front of you right now."

I chuckle again. "Yeah, sounds like she was in quite a lather. Sorry about that. I never in a million years would've thought she'd attack you. Seems there's a lot about her I don't know since I've been gone."

He tilts his head at me. "She has definitely changed. The last few months have been rough on her, and she had to toughen up. If she keeps going down that line, not very many people are going to fuck with her."

I raise my brows. "Interesting. Do you think this has to do with her getting more of her memories back or more from the situations she's been in?"

Hans presses his lips together for a moment and then responds, "Perhaps a bit of both. She's getting memories at a more rapid rate, but they seem to come in random order, so nothing relevant from when she was younger."

I inhale deeply through my nose and then release a long breath out of my mouth. "So, she has remembered nothing from before she was taken?"

He shakes his head. "Most of her newest memories are from the time you worked together before that happened, but mostly it's feelings and snippets of interactions with you. Occasionally, she appears as if she's grasping at something, but nothing ever comes of it. She gets pissed, though." He shrugs, then raises his brows at me. "So, do you want me to go back in there or what?"

"No, she'll definitely cut you up if you show up there again. Why don't you take a week to recuperate and then head back home? Anything changes, I'll let you know."

Hans doesn't argue. He gives me a nod, then turns around and disappears out the door. I don't doubt that he would've gone back in if I told him to, regardless of how many times she might try to stab him. It doesn't sound very smart, but he's quite an intelligent guy, which is why I've had him on Antionette. He would protect her and listen effectively.

It seems to me Antoinette may not need protection for much longer. Not that she won't always have protection, but I wonder how much longer before she notices the other people that are tailing her. Matt and Tony definitely know about it, so I guess it depends on if they decide to let her know. Lilith might tell her, but I don't think she'll say anything because she's as protective of Antoinette as I am. I wouldn't be surprised if she has her own men on her, too.

I leave my office and make my way down the hall into the kitchen to grab a bottle of mineral water out of the fridge before walking into the sitting area where Carolina is relaxing on the sofa. I sprawl in the chair across from her, and I must look a sight because she raises her brows at me and grins. "Having a rough day?"

I narrow my eyes. "Do you think?"

She laughs, springing up in her seat and bringing her feet underneath her as she asks enthusiastically, "What happened? I saw Hans coming and going, and he did not look too happy."

I sigh, taking a long drink of my icy-cold mineral water before explaining. "Yes. Let's say he and Antoinette had a difference in opinion."

She gasps, her eyes widening. "Antoinette made him bleed?"

"You don't have to sound so excited about it." I say exasperatedly.

She raises her shoulder dismissively. "Well, you've always made her sound so docile. You know I love it when a kitten finds her claws."

I laugh at the idea of Antoinette ever being referred to as a kitten.

I don't believe she's ever had a docile bone in her body, even in the time she didn't remember who she was. If amnesia Antoinette is any indication, the real Antoinette is going to be a real pain in the ass.

"It appears she has found her claws. I tried to tell her how it was going to be, and she decided she was going to show me I'm no longer calling the shots for her."

Carolina grimaces and then relaxes back into her seat in quiet contemplation. After a few moments, she responds, "Then what does that mean for your plans for her? If she's going to fight you on everything now, then how can you even proceed?"

I place my mineral water on the table beside me and rub my hands over my face before letting them drop into my lap tiredly. "I honestly don't know. It's not like I can get close enough to her to tell her anything, and I'm not even sure what the hell to tell her at this point. I'm mostly in the dark, you're mostly in the dark, everyone's working in the fucking dark here. And I know with her, there's no way in hell I'll be able to have a super quick conversation because she's going to be a full-on hellcat the moment she sets eyes on me. We'll end up caught before I can even get a word in."

Carolina frowns and tilts her head at me. "Are you sure about that? I know I'm an outsider here, but it seems to me if she has flipped the script that drastically, then maybe her response will be a bit more cautious. She's smart; she must know something big is at stake here, even if she doesn't know exactly what."

I nod. "This is true. I don't really know what's going through her head, but it seems safe to say she may be a bit more cautious. I still don't think I can chance it in public, though. And I'm not getting an opportunity to sneak in again anytime soon."

"I could do it."

"No way. I don't think it's a good idea for you to get any more mixed up in this than you already are. As of right now, no one knows that you're even privy to who she is to me, and it's probably best to keep it that way."

She rolls her eyes and scoffs. "Oh, fuck off, Darius. You know nothing about the circumstances of my involvement in this situation, so save your sanctimonious preaching for people who need your protection. The odds I'll ever get out of this tangled web in one piece is nil, so for once in my life, I'd like to pick the path that I'm going to be on. I said I'll do it, and I'll fucking do it."

I scowl at her again. What is with these women lately? Every time I turn around, one of them is busting my balls. I likely deserve it, but maybe I'd like a bit of a break now and then. Maybe I'd like somebody to call me and pretend they give a shit about my opinion.

"I still don't think it's a good idea. Obviously, we don't have a lot of other options, and this is likely our best one, but I still feel it's a mistake. I get you feel you're already in over your head with all this bullshit, but we never really know which path leads us deeper into the shit storm until it's too late."

She nods, but I can tell from the look in her eye that she will not change her mind. I sigh, allowing myself to sink back further into my seat, resting my head back as I say, "Fine, we'll do it your way. Honestly, I can't say that my way has worked out very well lately, so maybe you're right. Maybe I need to sit back and let someone else drive the bus."

Carolina cackles. "Surely you mean the crazy train. The crazy train right through to Crazytown."

I can't help but laugh in response. She's not wrong. And perhaps, in some strange way, Antoinette is right to cut me out of the equation.

Maybe it's time to divide and conquer.

Chapter Six

Toni

THERE'S SOMETHING TO BE said for autonomy over one's choices.

My decision to cut the cord on Dare's overbearing bullshit was impulsive and fueled by rage, but I don't regret it one bit. I'm sure he's fuming. He's maybe even smashed some shit up, but I'm so done with anyone trying to lead me around by the nose. I may not remember much about my past, but I'm certain that some part of me was raised to stand on my own two feet, fight my own battles, and either come out victorious or die.

Of course, now I'm not convinced having Lilith continue to withhold the details of my existence is the right choice. I can't help but wonder if having her lay it all out on the line for me would trigger something in my brain that would have it all come rushing back to me. I have to ask her more questions when I have that weird sense of something being within my grasp, hoping it will nudge it into reality.

It doesn't help that some memories that seem clear to me were planted by Darius when he was helping me adjust to having no memories. Being able to differentiate between what someone put there intentionally and what is reality is excruciating, and sometimes, it feels impossible. As if the taxing effort is pointless and that maybe it's all for nothing.

This also leads me to the eternal question: does it matter who I was before?

Lilith is of the mind that it doesn't matter at all. That once you reach your ends of being, you let it rest and continue in your current form without regard for your previous self. She believes we're both better off forgetting about the past and going about our business with a clean slate. Most of the time, I'm inclined to believe her, but then some random thing will pop up and reignite a burning question in my mind.

For example: why the fuck would I give Darius a watch, never mind one with a tracking device in it? Sure, we had a dalliance, and it seemed like it would grow into something serious, but why would I feel inclined to track him? It seems to me like gifting a tracking device disguised as a trinket would be more something he would do to me.

I asked everyone this question, and they all shrugged. I believe Tony and Matt are genuine in their response; however, Lilith seems a little more suspicious. So I occasionally bring it up, to see if I can get her to slip up. Like right now, I'm sitting here, staring at her, waiting for her to elaborate. She's staring at me with a look I can't quite place. Guilt? Annoyance? Bafflement? All three?

Finally, she sighs and rolls her eyes. "Toni, would you let it go already? The only answers I have to that question are irrelevant and pure speculation. And also, it would only lead to a bigger conversation about our family and upbringing, and I still believe it's pointless. For all I know, you decided you wanted to track Darius because you were a super jealous person, and you didn't trust him. Or maybe you were going to use it to play practical jokes on him. I seriously do not know. But if you really want to break this down and go over every scenario that it could be, then I'll get a whiteboard and dry-erase markers, and we'll get right the fuck into it."

I frown and cross my arms over my chest defensively. "I'm sorry, Lils, but being unable to make heads or tails out of anything is frustrating. I know you say it doesn't matter, but part of me is concerned that it does. Obviously, we were raised apart for many reasons, and sometimes, not knowing these reasons is fucking hard."

She nods. "I won't pretend to know how it feels; all I can do is focus on what a relief it is to me that you don't know everything. For me, the feelings that would arise from the fleeting unnecessary knowledge aren't worth it. If they come back to you over time, then so be it. But I will not force unnecessary baggage on you. Most of the people involved are dead and buried, and any memory having to do with them should remain dead and buried."

I take a deep breath and nod in agreement. I know she's right. None of it matters. "You're right. It's not like we don't have enough going on already."

"Speaking of having enough going on already, we have a lead we should check up on. We need to do a little shopping this afternoon and see what comes our way."

I grimace. "Shopping? Really? I hate shopping."

Lilith rises, walking over to me and pulling me onto my feet. She gives me a little push toward the door and says, "Too fucking bad. We're going."

We bicker about this shopping excursion all the way out of the apartment and continue our verbal sparring in the town car until we're dropped off near the Franklin D. Roosevelt Metro on Champs-Élysées. It's these moments that make me think less about the past. Regardless of what happened in the time span I can't remember, I'm eternally grateful to have Lilith in my life now. It's in these moments I feel less inclined to want to learn about the past because I worry my memories will taint my relationship with her.

We explore the designer shops and then make our way through the boutique stores along the 8th arrondissement, taking our time to enjoy the ambiance of Paris and the breathtaking architecture. All-in-all, it's rather enjoyable, since it's not like we've had any time to be sisters, to dick around and joke like ordinary people.

We're leaving one upscale boutique after trying on the ugliest dress ever created when Lilith gets a call. She answers but says nothing, listening for a moment before ending the call and pocketing her phone. "There's a cafe up a ways from here we need to go to. Follow me."

It seems our good time is over, and it's back to business. I follow behind her as nonchalantly as I can muster, given the fact the unknown makes my heart pound. "Do you know who we're meeting?"

She shakes her head. "I'm not even entirely sure what it's about. Honestly, I would probably ignore it entirely if I wasn't out of options. Which totally feels like an amateur move, but here we are."

I snicker, slinging one of my arms over her shoulder as I lean in and tease, "Uh oh. Is my old lady sister losing her edge?"

She glares at me and shoves me off her. "Not fucking likely. But sometimes, when things aren't going your way, you're forced to try something a little different."

I laugh as we make our way into a café. It's dim inside, but there's a table off in the corner that's empty. We head in that direction, and each take a seat. As we wait for a server to come over, I glance around the small area, taking in the décor and Parisian atmosphere. I let my gaze settle on the other patrons, one by one, until suddenly, I do a double-take on the woman sitting at the table across from us.

What the fuck?

Lilith glances at me questioningly, and I kick her under the table, silently telling her to follow my glance. She scowls at me, her gaze bouncing around the room as inconspicuously as one could muster in such a small space. Then she hisses at me, "What the fuck, Toni? Stop kicking me."

As I sit there silently arguing with her to be quiet, I glance up to see that woman staring at me from her seat. Then she winks, and the next thing I know, Carolina Tennent has risen from her seat and is standing next to our table, a humorous glint in her eyes as she says, "All I can say is he definitely didn't exaggerate about you two."

We both frown and, in unison, question, "Who?"

She laughs, and her already beautiful features heighten, and I kind of want to smash her face in. "Oh, I think you two know who I'm referring to."

Lilith cocks her head at her. "So, you're saying he talks about us?"

Carolina makes a face. "Incessantly. Frankly, it's kind of annoying." I make some random choking noise, and she looks at me and grins. "Especially you, Antoinette. Sometimes, I can't decide whether he wants to kill or keep you. Kudos on stabbing Hans, though. That was a delight."

"He told you I stabbed Hans?"

She nods, sitting down in the empty chair without invitation. "Oh, yes. It was quite comical, really. He was not expecting that."

I glance at Lilith and she gives me a slight shrug, her eyes wide. I motion for her to do something, and finally, she looks at Carolina and says, "We're actually meeting someone here, so piss off back to your table."

Carolina gives Lilith a sympathetic look. "Oh, I know. That would be me."

"You? What the fuck do you want?"

Carolina raises an elegant brow as she says sarcastically, "Maybe I want to hang with the girls."

Lilith gives me a murderous look, and I grimace, reaching a hand out to rest on her arm as I say to Carolina, "Cut the shit. Tell us what you want, and then get the fuck out of here, or I'm not gonna be responsible for Lilith slashing your pretty face."

Carolina doesn't even flinch; instead, she laughs. I know she's an actress, and from what I understand, a talented one. But I'm surprised she doesn't seem at all concerned for her own safety, especially if Dare has been telling her about us. He may not know what I'm all about, but he sure as fuck knows Lilith is a little crazy.

Lilith picks up a little teaspoon and examines it a bit too closely for comfort. Carolina's eyes widen as she watches the spoon inspection, but then she asks in a severe tone, "Could you really kill someone with that thing?"

This makes Lilith frown, and she gives her a curious look as she responds, "Well, of course. But I don't need a weapon either way."

Carolina rests her elbows on the table and leans over, her chin resting in her hands as she says, almost dreamily, "That is fascinating."

"Is she for fucking real?" Lilith looks at me, then glances back at Carolina like she's an alien specimen or something equally horrific.

I raise my hands, helplessly. I'm not sure what the baseline for weird is, but this seems way above average weird, even for us. I snap my fingers right in front of Carolina's face, and she sits up, her hands settling in her lap.

"What do you want?"

Carolina's cheerful expression shifts, her brow furrowing and the corners of her lips turning down as she grits her teeth. She inhales through her nose slowly before opening her mouth to respond. "I'm here for several reasons. The first one being Dare–"

I interrupt. "Do not fucking talk to me about him."

She glares at me, leaning her upper body forward a bit, so she's looking me right in the eye as she says, "I will fucking talk to you about him. I'll fucking talk to you about him, and you're gonna fucking listen. What you choose to do with the information I give you is entirely up to you, but I came here to say something, and I'm gonna fucking say it."

Lilith laughs, and my focus shifts to her as I raise my eyebrows at her. "Really?"

"I enjoy the fact she's got a little spice."

"Are you saying that I should listen to her?"

She nods and shrugs at the same time. "May as well. She came all this way, and I have to assume her coming here was not without risk. So, for that, hear her out."

I glare at her, then turn back to Carolina and give her a nod to continue. She gives Lilith a tight smile and straightens in her chair, her hands now gripped together on top of the table, the tension in her features noticeable as I reply, "I'll listen. That's the only promise I'm going to make."

She nods. "Thank you. I already know the information I'm going to give you won't be enough. I know you're looking for the minute details, but all I can say is *we* don't even have those. Darius has only shared as much information as I need to have in order to help him, and most of it is about you and his relationship with you. I know you're pissed at him. I'm sure you have every reason and right to be pissed at him. But any form of dictatorial lording over that you feel he is doing is only because he's really at odds on how to protect you from afar."

I interject, "Maybe he should spend less time trying to protect me and more time trying to figure out what the fuck is going on, so we can permanently eliminate the problem."

She laughs humorlessly. "That may be so, but frankly, he's still trying to figure out where you fit into this puzzle because the fact they took him and lost him but still left you alone makes little sense. He didn't explain to me why it made little sense. Some of what I'm saying is what I gathered from his ramblings when he thinks I'm not listening—"

Lilith interrupts her, "How exactly are you involved in all this?"

Carolina grimaces. "Well, I'm an actress born into a criminal family. Technically, Darius hired me to get himself more public exposure in the hopes it would draw out the real bad guys. Of course, so far, all it did was draw you out of America, and now Darius is paranoid that you've set yourself up for your own downfall. If he had his way, he'd ship you straight back to America and lock you in a tower for all of eternity." Carolina laughs again, sighing as she continues, "I want to assure you nothing has ever happened between us. Short of the odd touch and chaste kiss for cameras, nothing untoward has ever happened. That man is so wrapped up in you, I don't think he even sees other women at all. It's quite comical, really."

Heat rushes over me at her words, and I avert my gaze, staring at the wall over her shoulder. I grit my teeth in horror as I feel the oddly familiar sting of tears behind my eyes. I don't know if I ever truly considered the lengths he would go to complete a job, but it's a great relief to know this wasn't one of them. Not that I would want the guy to fall on his own sword to avoid sticking his dick into someone else, but it is what it is.

Lilith rests her hand on my arm and gives me a little squeeze. "See, Toni. You still got the man completely pussy whipped."

Carolina giggles as I glare at Lilith. "Oh my god, Lils. Stop."

Lilith cackles, and Carolina joins her in being entertained by my discomfort. I look between them, then reach over and pick up a butter knife, pointing it at them. "Don't think I won't fucking stab you in public."

They laugh even louder, and I shake my head in disgust, a small smile playing on my lips as I watch the two of them commiserating so easily. I don't want to like this woman, but I respect she went out of her way, likely putting herself in danger, to come here and reassure me that my not-boyfriend hasn't been fucking her. And I can't say that Darius is wrong in thinking I may have put myself in direct danger by coming over here in search of him. This theory is one we briefly considered, but we decided it was a chance we'd have to take because we had nothing else to go on.

I wait for the two of them to get control of themselves before turning to Carolina and asking, "Do you have any idea who took Darius?"

She shakes her head, "No, he hasn't said too much about it, though I heard him muttering something about an Agatha at some point."

Lilith gasps, and when I look over at her, she's sitting there wide-eyed. I glare at her and snap, "What is it, Lils?"

Lilith grimaces. "It's nothing."

I narrow my eyes at her blatant attempt at deflection and lean in close to her, saying through my gritted teeth, "Don't fucking lie to me. Who the fuck is Agatha?"

The look on Lilith's face can only be described as petulant. Her eyes are everywhere but on me, and she's twitchy, her knee bouncing nervously. Finally, she sighs. "I believe she is referring to Agatha," she pauses, then continues with a resigned expression. "Agatha Ferro. Our sister."

I gape at her. "Our sister? What fucking sister?"

She shrugs. "I don't really talk about her."

I pound my fist down on the table and whisper-shout, "Well, you're going to fucking start now."

Lilith glances at Carolina and then back at me. "Can't this wait?"

I shake my head, my arms crossing over my chest defensively. "Not a chance. You may as well get it all out now so Carolina can relay it back to that douchebag Darius firsthand."

"Fine. I'll tell you the little I know, but it's not much. I honestly thought she was dead."

"Kind of like you thought I might be dead?"

Lilith shakes her head, giving me a dirty look. "No. I barely even knew Agatha. Most of what I know about her is hearsay and what I overheard from others. There wouldn't have been much point mentioning her to you before since you didn't really know her, either. I wasn't even sure if you knew about her, given you were separated so young."

"What do you mean 'separated'? We lived together at one point?"

She snorts. "Yes, as small children. But not long enough where you'd remember any of it."

I must have an odd expression because Lilith continues, "Toni, things are different in our world. It doesn't matter if we're considered an asset, collateral damage, or a weakness. You never keep all your eggs in the same basket. A lot of the men in power have their children scattered all over the world to keep them safe until they're old enough to learn how to defend themselves. As soon as we're born, we're kept off the map."

I frown. "So they didn't separate us immediately?"

She shakes her head. "No. I was quite young when you were born, so exactly what happened isn't clear to me. I woke up one morning, and you and Agatha were gone."

Lilith looks away, and I see she's struggling a bit to tell the story. I'm surprised. I rarely see Lilith show any type of emotion that resembles sadness. Carolina breaks in. "Well, if they're siblings, then it would be obvious to Darius that they're related?"

"I haven't seen Agatha since she was a child, but the resemblance would be undeniable. I imagine at a glance, he probably shit his pants, thinking he had been poetically double-crossed."

That Dare may have felt double-crossed by me even for an instant makes me feel equal parts elation and sadness. I'll always get a bit of joy from causing him pain, but deep down, I would never want him to feel betrayed by me. This doesn't stop the small smirk of satisfaction that crosses my face and the little snort of laughter that escapes. "I bet for a few moments there, he must have been feeling scorched earth with no one to direct it at. I'm surprised he didn't have a stroke."

We laugh for a few moments, but then Lilith sobers. "If Agatha is involved, that could mean anything. I know next to nothing about her, and I bet finding out anything of interest about her will be nearly impossible since she's been off the grid since childhood. He must've sent her far away to keep her under wraps like this."

Carolina's eyes widen a bit as she asks, "So there's no way to tell if she's friend or foe?"

Lilith shrugs. "I'm leaning heavily on foe. But there's really no way to tell."

Carolina snickers. At my questioning look, she explains, "I was just thinking I now understand Dare's fuck-around-and-find-out mentality. Seems that's the only way you can get to the bottom of anything in this mess. If you fuck around long enough, you're bound to find out something. Like how big of a target do you have to put on your back before something pops up? And then we hope that whoever pops up doesn't have a good enough sight on it, or else you're gonna be fucking dead. If they even waited."

Lilith leans closer to her and says, "I think it's about time you explain your involvement in a little more detail. For all we know, you're on the other side. Whatever fucking side that is."

Carolina looks uncomfortable as she leans back in her chair, meeting Lilith's stony gaze without flinching. "There isn't a lot to tell. I'm doing someone's bidding to keep other people alive."

"What people and why?"

"What does it matter? You know how it is in our world. Women have been carrying the weight of family obligation on their shoulders for generations. We get handed out and tossed around like whores, collateral damage, or spies. We spend our entire lives working a job from the inside, sometimes not even fully understanding the role we're playing until it gets us killed. Or worse." She pauses, her jaw clenching as she stares out into the distance vacantly before shifting her focus back to Lilith. "Frankly, I don't give a fuck about much, but how easily children are abused and tossed aside is disgusting. I would literally live in the pits of hell for the rest of my days if it would save any of them even one moment of the agony this life can bring to them."

She's right.

Even for all I don't remember about this life she speaks of, I've learned enough in the short time being privy to it to know women are entirely dispensable. Even in the rare situation where a father dotes on his daughters, they will be strewn about like cannon fodder.

Sure, some of these women come back, but rarely do they return unscathed. Mostly, they come back as pieces of their former selves, only to have those pieces remolded and thrown back into the next job. It pisses me off.

Lilith growls, and I see the maniacal light burning in her eyes as she says, "You're right. You're so fucking right, and I'm so fucking sick of it. So, what are we gonna do about it?"

Carolina shrugs with a startled look on her face as she asks quietly, "What the fuck can we do about it?"

Lilith looks at me, and then we all look at each other for a few moments.

Then I smile, a zing of electricity zipping up my spine as I reply, "Looks like it's our turn to fuck around and find out."

Chapter Seven

Toni

Tony and Matt are pissed.

When we return from our shopping excursion, I give them a brief rundown on how we want to proceed. That we could easily move forward without them puts a serious twist in their panties, but in the end, they decide they want to stick around. Lilith made it clear they're expected to stay firmly on our side of the fence, and if we find out they're playing both sides, they will be permanently eliminated. They both glance at me like they expect me to interfere; however, I remain quiet and unflinching in my support of Lilith.

The fact of the matter is, we've wasted too much time being divided on what our key priority is. Looking for Darius, protecting me, and searching for answers. Well, we know where Dare is now, and I no longer need protecting. That leaves one primary goal. Figuring out which questions are most imperative and getting them answered.

Our first line of business is figuring out exactly who Agatha is and then determining whether she's a friend or foe. Lilith insists she's a foe, but I can't help but be curious about what her motivations are, given most of our family is dead. If all she wants is power, she can have it. Frankly, Lilith and I are both sick and tired of the constant push and pull of this life, so if she wants to come in and lord over the underworld, she can take it.

Meanwhile, the extra muscle Lilith requested from Mickey arrived in short order, and I'm a little impressed. Lilith says she's known most of them for her entire adult life, and she's correct that you cannot buy loyalty. I was even more surprised to find a few women on the crew. At first, I thought they were spouses or partners of the men, but this assumption was quickly corrected, and they all laughed in my face.

Even knowing firsthand how tough women can be, I'm still susceptible to the typical stereotypes that women carry. As if all they're good for is arm candy and decoration. I'm quite certain any of these women is highly capable of mass murder—stilettos or not.

I gave them strict instructions that if Tony made a pass at them; they were free to stop him in whatever way they saw fit. Of course, I gave this instruction in front of him, which earned me a solid glare.

Whatever, he can fuck off.

Matt wasn't very successful in finding information on Agatha, which means we must be a bit more resourceful in how we gain the information we need. Since all of us are sick of sitting back and waiting for people to come to us, we decide to figure out a way to get to her first. It is difficult to track down a ghost, but not entirely impossible.

And that's how I find myself hunkered down in an abandoned building across from another old, abandoned building, freezing my ass off, all for the slim chance someone of interest may walk by. So far, this whole staying out of sight and staying out of trouble thing is boring.

Carolina has had her own issues keeping Darius off her back since he made it clear he doesn't, for one second, believe I took the information she gave me and did nothing. She finally told him he could think whatever he wanted, but she would say nothing to him about it, so he might as well save it for someone he could control. Apparently, that didn't go over very well, but I'm happy to report that Carolina gives no fucks.

It was through Carolina we got this tip that Darius was going to be meeting a contact at some point tonight. We were given a few locations for said meeting, requiring us to be spread across the city, hoping one of us would be in the right place at the right time. We know the odds are not in our favor and we're likely wasting our time, but lately all we have is time, so we do what we can.

I'm not sure how long I've been sitting here, but it's fucking cold. My toes are going numb, and I'm pressing my hands into my armpits, trying to warm them up. I'm muttering to myself about how stupid this entire plan is when movement in the distance catches my attention. I lean closer, trying to get a better look and make out the silhouette of a large-ish person walking toward the other vacant building. Digging out my night-vision binoculars, I zero in on the shadowy figure, suppressing my urge to crow in delight when I make out the distinctive features of one Darius Hughes.

I search through my pile of burner phones until I find the one I'm looking for, then send a message off to the group, letting them know I'm tonight's lucky winner. I ping them my location to remind them of where I am and then turn my attention back to Dare.

I watch him disappear into the warehouse, then I carefully exit this building and creep through the shadows to a vantage point where I can see the doorway he disappeared through. A few minutes go by, then a car pulls up, and I press myself tight against the building as a woman exits from the rear of the vehicle. She follows the same path into the warehouse as Dare, and I briefly contemplate making a move before she can enter the building.

If the vehicle she arrived in had driven off, I likely would have taken my chances, but all the unknowns make it too risky, so I sit back and watch her disappear into the warehouse.

I send another message, letting them know there are now two people in the building and a vehicle with an unknown number of occupants parked on the curb. I sneak around the outside of the building and make my way toward the back in search of another entrance.

The total area appears to be deserted: an oddity given these types of lots typically attract the homeless. I come to a door and try the handle, finding it's unlocked. This is slightly suspicious, but having no other option, I ease the door open and squeeze my way in, shutting it silently behind me.

I enter a small office area that's barely illuminated by the light coming through the window. I walk to the doorway and peer around the corner into the hallway. It's pitch-black, and I wince at the thought of having to go out there. I consider using the night-vision goggles I have in my bag, but reconsider, given the likelihood of someone flipping on a light and blinding me to a target.

I slowly edge my way through the doorway out into the darkness, then painstakingly tiptoe down the dark hallway, listening intently for any kind of sound that would lead me toward Darius. As my eyes adjust to the blackness, I make out faint shapes, and after a few moments of moving at a crawl, I come to a dead-end. Figuring I missed a right-hand turn somewhere, I switch to the other side of the hallway, then backtrack the way I came until I run into a break in the wall. I pause, listening intently, then hang a left down the hallway, but I still hear nothing other than the hum of some type of ventilation system.

A bang resounds around me, stopping me dead in my tracks, and I tilt my head, attempting to focus my hearing on the direction the noise came from. I continue down the hall slowly, then pick up my pace a bit as I hear the faint murmuring of voices in the distance. I follow the sound of the voices as they become louder, and I make out a dim light up ahead as I get closer. Getting low, I creep in the shadows until I'm right at the doorway and peek around the corner before ducking back into the shadows again.

I can't make out what they're saying in their hushed tones, but neither appears to be happy to be speaking to the other. There's silence for a few minutes, and I chance another peek, doing a double-take when I see those two fuckers embracing in what appears to be a rather passionate lip-lock.

My blood boils in my veins, and even though I hear the voice of reason in the back of my head telling me not to be fucking stupid, I pull my gun and release the safety. Darius has his back to me, and from the way they're focused on each other, I'd be surprised if they even knew I was there. And if they catch sight of me, it's going to be too fucking late.

I briefly consider getting close enough to kill them both with the same bullet, but then I remember what a vindictive bitch I am and how I wouldn't want anyone to get off the hook too easily for being a two-timing motherfucker.

I sidle up right beside them, raising my gun and pressing the barrel firmly against her temple.

"Don't move."

They both freeze, their bodies shifting apart slightly, and Darius curses under his breath. I look at him and then back at the woman still standing in his embrace. It's almost like looking in a mirror, but the more I stare at her, the easier it is for me to make out our subtle differences. But at a glance, she looks like me, and it's disconcerting.

Dare's voice breaks through my reverie. "What the fuck, Agatha?"

She gives me a closed-lip smile, and it's all I can do to stop myself from bashing her face in with the butt of my gun. "Well, I told you if she was in the building, I'd get her to show herself without too much effort. And that's exactly what I did."

Darius carefully extricates himself from her grasp, wiping at his mouth with a grimace. "I think it would've been fine if you'd yelled out that you knew she was there and she should come out."

She laughs, her eyes meeting mine as she says, "Yes, but this was much more fun."

I reach out and grab her by her hair, yanking her closer to me as I grit out, "Not as fun as me shooting you in the face."

I hear the telltale clicking of guns being cocked around me, and she laughs. "Not this time. You're surrounded, so you may as well give up."

I bare my teeth at her and snarl, "In the words of Wyatt Earp, they may get me in a rush, but not before I turn your head into a canoe."

She glances at my face and then at the gun I have pointed at her head. "What's with the hand cannon, sis? There are much less conspicuous weapons that do the job just as well."

"What can I say? I like big guns. Right, Dare?"

I look at Dare to find him staring at my gun. His eyes meet mine, concern on his features as he says, "Put the gun down, Antoinette. No one's gonna shoot anyone tonight."

Agatha and I both give him a dirty look and say in unison, "We're not?"

He makes an exasperated sound, his hands coming up to his hips as he tilts his head back and stares up at the ceiling, muttering to himself. I meet Agatha's gaze as I ask, "Is he okay?"

She shrugs. "Hard to say, really. He seems to talk to himself a lot—"

Darius interrupts us, walking over and yanking the gun from my hand. I yelp and glare at him as he says, "What the fuck, Antoinette? Why are you carrying a gun at all, never mind this giant fucking cannon?"

I try to snag the gun back, but he holds it out of my reach. Finally, I give him a jab in the solar plexus, earning a grunt in response. "Give it back to me. I promise I won't shoot her. Yet."

Darius eyes me suspiciously, then looks over at Agatha, who gives him a nod. I'm annoyed he's seeking direction from that bitch, but then I remember the sounds of the guns all around me, and it makes more sense. He's making sure I won't get shot for carrying it.

He holds my gun out to me, but when I grab for it, he pulls it out of my reach, grabbing my wrist and tugging me closer. "Where's your holster?"

I glare at him and pull one side of my jacket open, showing him the holster. He steps in close to me until I feel the heat of his body, and his eyes burn into mine as he slowly, firmly slides the gun into the leather, a small shiver running down my spine. Suddenly, my mouth is dry, my breath catching in my lungs, and I find I can't look away as he leans into me. I lick my lips, my hands gripping onto his suit coat, and I sway into him, waiting for him to move closer to me before saying, "You guys are fucking disgusting. Next time, get a goddamn room instead of making me want to puke."

He gives me a dirty look, then glares at Agatha. "There's nothing going on between us to need a room. She's a fucking pain in the ass, kind of like you sometimes."

I'm jealous; I admit it. All of my burning questions are being overridden by my juvenile urge to beat the whore down for touching my man, and I'm exceedingly annoyed with myself for getting so off-track that I can't even focus on the actual issues at hand. Her earlier comments, paired with his current response, feel legitimate, but that doesn't remove the initial sting of the scene that played out before me; it doesn't take away the bitter taste of betrayal still coating my tongue.

I step back from Darius, and my urge to shoot Agatha in the face amps up again at the self-satisfied look on her face. That meddlesome fucking bitch. "What are you even doing here?" I ask.

Dare goes to reply, but Agatha interrupts, "We needed to speak to you, and this seemed to be the best way."

"You're saying that you tricked Carolina into sending all of us out in the wind without a clue because that was the easiest way for you to speak to me? How did you even know that I would be in the right place at the right time? It could be Lilith standing here right now, in which case, I don't think it would've worked out well for either of you."

Dare smiles. "Have you forgotten already how easy it is for me to keep tabs on you?"

I take a moment, but it finally dawns on me how he always finds me.

The tracker.

I growl, suddenly struggling to control my urge to shoot him in an area that will hurt him but not kill him. He's giving me a smug look, so I sneer, "Well, I guess I know what I'll be digging out of me later."

The smirk falls from his face, and he frowns. "Please don't do that. I promise I'll try to only use it when there's truly an emergency, but don't remove it."

I stare into his unblinking eyes for a moment, that stubborn side of me kicking and screaming for me to get a knife and cut it out of me on the spot. He knows I'm on edge, likely seeing the obstinance in my demeanor, my urge to prove I don't need anyone keeping tabs on me, overriding the good sense that even Lilith would agree with.

Finally, I give a curt nod, muttering to myself in annoyance. I know he's right, and that Lilith would also agree with this makes me more inclined to accept that the tracking device is there for my safety. But it still frustrates me that everyone can keep tabs on me while I still live mainly in the dark.

I step further away from him, turning my back on the two of them as I calm myself down. The initial rush of adrenaline is fizzling out, and I'm left with this flat, dark feeling. I hate feeling powerless, incapable of handling what's being thrown at me, and unable to maneuver these intense feelings that continuously rush over me without warning.

Dare walks up behind me, his hands resting on my shoulders, his warm breath against my ear as he leans into me. I force myself not to lean back against him, and he chuckles against my ear, the sound triggering a shiver to run down my spine. I grit my teeth, feeling the answering smile playing along my lips.

That bastard.

I clear my throat, shaking him off me, and then turning to face him. "Tell me again, what are you two doing out here?"

He puts his hands in his pockets, leveling me with a serious look. "Waiting for you."

I raise my eyebrows at him and snort. "And sucking face was required?"

He smiles. "As you already heard, Agatha figured that was the easiest way to get you to show yourself. Otherwise, we figured you were going to wait it out until you could get her alone and then try to snatch her."

I incline my head at him because that's accurate. If I had to choose between getting my hands on either of them, I would've waited around to grab her. "Seems to me like we have a lot to talk about."

"Yes, we certainly do. But not now."

I glance around, finally noticing Agatha has left the room, and I feel my blood pressure rise again. "Where the fuck did she go? I have questions for her."

Dare inclines his head toward the exit, showing that she left the building. "Her job was done for now, so she's waiting outside until I'm ready. I don't have a lot of time, so I'll give you as much of an explanation as I can."

"So what? You're consorting with the enemy now?"

"Agatha isn't the enemy, Toni. We're trying to work together to locate and eliminate the real enemy."

I frown at him, shaking my head in disbelief. "How can she not be the enemy when she bought you, then vanished out of the country for months?"

"This is where things get complicated."

"How complicated can it be? She purchased you, put you on a plane, and flew you to another country. She then kept you hidden for months, and from what you said, at some point, you were in prison."

He gives me a patient look, and I'm overwhelmed with an urge to wipe the condescending look off his face. He's silent for a moment, obviously considering his words before he finally speaks. "At a glance, that's exactly how it would seem, but that's not what happened. Someone else purchased me from Dickwad. Agatha executed an epic double-cross, which resulted in me going directly to her instead of to the person who purchased me. Unfortunately, somewhere between where I first met Agatha and our second rendezvous point, we were ambushed, and both of us were taken. That's how I ended up in prison. That's how we both ended up caged."

I gape at him and ask, "Well, how the fuck did you get out of it?"

"With a lot of planning and a lot of luck. Agatha has a small crew, but they've been with her for a very long time. So, when things went to shit, they did what they had to do to locate her and get her back.

I'm the lucky fucker who got to tag along at her insistence because, frankly, they would've left me there."

"How the hell did they even find her? She could've been anywhere. That's insane."

He laughs. "Apparently, we're not the only ones who understand the value of a well-placed tracking device."

My mouth drops open in shock. Suddenly tired, I walk over to the chair in the middle of the room and sit down, leaning back and crossing my arms over my chest. "A fucking tracker. Who would've thought micro-chipping ourselves like animals would be so useful? What amazes me is how this isn't standard procedure at this point."

He nods. "Seems humans are far more serious about locating their lost pets than their lost humans. And apparently, there's this whole thing about ethics, whatever the fuck that is."

I chuckle, then catch myself and stop. I clear my throat, narrowing my eyes at him. "That doesn't explain who is behind any of this. Do you know anything about the man who bought you from Dickwad? Or the person who took you after Agatha diverted your delivery? Are they the same person? None of this makes sense."

"Well, we know who took us and kept us prisoner, but so far, we know nothing about who bought me. The few leads we've had have led us nowhere, and since I can't find Dickwad, I have made no progress there."

"He's dead."

Dare frowns at me. "Dead? What do you mean, he's fucking dead?"

I shrug my shoulders as I reply, "He wouldn't talk, so we tried to make him talk, and evidently, his heart couldn't take it. It was quite anti-climactic, if you ask me."

Darius groans, his hands coming out of his pocket as he paces back and forth a few times. I can tell from his demeanor that he's pissed off, but there's nothing I can do about the guy having a weak heart. "We didn't mean to kill him; we barely even touched him when he keeled over."

Dare curses under his breath and stops pacing. He stands there, staring at me with his hands on his hips. "That's fucking great. Are you sure he was dead?"

"Well, I didn't request an autopsy, but he appeared rather deceased."

"This is no time for jokes, Toni. There are a lot of ways for crafty old men to fake their own death in plain sight. So, unless you cut off his head and set him on fire, you can never be sure he's truly dead."

I frown, trying to think back to the time when we had Dickwad in our clutches. The information-extracting business was new to me, so I wasn't there when it came time to dispose of his corpse. "I could ask. But I have a hard time believing they would not have ensured he was dead."

"Find out. If that motherfucker isn't verified as being deceased, we need to double down on our efforts to find him. And anyone even remotely connected to him."

I take out my phone and type out a message to Lilith as I respond, "As far as I know, Lilith made sure he and anyone even remotely connected to him were eradicated from the earth, permanently. You know how she gets. You can't talk to her."

Dare rubs his hand over his face tiredly. "Oh, yes. I know. The wrath of Lilith Ferro echoes throughout the halls of the underworld. What's funny is I've heard a few people say that her sister is even worse, and I get the impression they're not talking about Agatha, so that's a little confusing for me unless you've been up to some evil deeds I'm not privy to."

My nose wrinkles, my lip curling in distaste. "I would find that hard to believe, though I still don't remember a lot. I like to think some of the violence I've witnessed in the last few months would've triggered some kind of memory if that was truly my life." My phone lights up in my hand, and I read the incoming text from Lilith. "Dickwad is deceased. Like shark bait deceased."

He frowns again, his lips pressing together in annoyance for a moment before he says, "Well, there goes another lead to the truth." He sighs deeply and stuffs his hands into the pockets of his slacks as his eyes meet mine. "So, what have you remembered about your old life?"

"Not a lot. Most of my memories have been about you. About us. I'm not even sure if they're true, but I suppose that conversation will have to wait for another time."

The corner of his mouth lifts slightly, his eyes softening as he removes his hands from his pockets and walks over to where I'm sitting in the chair. He stops in front of me, squatting down and grasping my hand gently in one of his and raising it to his lips. He presses a soft kiss on the inside of my wrist and then another to my palm, and I bite the inside of my cheek to keep myself from outwardly reacting, to giving in too quickly.

The intensity of his gaze sends a tiny tremor through my body, and he shifts, one of his knees resting on the floor as he leans in even closer to me. His other hand comes up, his fingers stroking the skin of my throat before skimming behind my head, his fingers delving into the hair at the nape of my neck. He tightens his hand into a fist, twisting until the pull on my hair borders on pain, and my mouth falls open on a gasp, forcing my body closer to him until his face is mere inches from mine.

His eyes search mine, and I'm not sure exactly what he's looking for, but he seems to find it as he smiles at me. "There's my good girl."

I push closer to him, his words igniting a deep throb between my legs, making me feel desperate. Something about the cadence of his words, the gleam in his eyes, and the feeling of his hand fisted in my hair makes me feel a sense of belonging. Almost as if I've been here before, and I want to sink into it and allow myself his haven, even if I can't understand where this feeling is coming from.

I skim my nose up his neck, placing a kiss on his pulse point before biting down hard enough to sting. He flinches but doesn't pull away, so I bite down again, my tongue coming out to taste him as I pull him so close he almost falls over.

That deep ache in my chest attempts to override the throbbing in my pussy, and I feel the familiar sting of tears behind my eyes. I try to blink them away; the fact I've developed such an intense attachment to this man after spending more time away from him than with him is making me crazy. He must sense my unease because he releases my hair and wraps his arms around me, pulling me into his body. His head drops closer to me, his face against my neck, and he whispers, "It's okay. I've got you."

Emotion rolls over me like a tidal wave, and I can't stop it, can't push it down or force it away. "I don't know what the fuck I'm doing anymore."

He squeezes me tighter—so tight it feels like he's trying to keep pieces of me from floating away or trying to fuse the already broken pieces back together again. "All we can ever do is the best we can with what we have. Nothing is perfect. No one is perfect. But we continue to do our best, anyway."

I can't stop the burning behind my eyes, so I half-heartedly attempt to break free. He adjusts his hold on me, shushing me a bit, and I feel his lips press softly against my neck, then my ear. I allow myself to relax into him, giving myself permission to let it all go, to feel every fucking cut, every bruise, every deep puncture wound in my psyche that remains a huge, gaping hole in my being. My first tears are silent, so I ask, "What if my best isn't good enough?"

At first, he's quiet, his arms around me so tight he almost steals my breath, and then his voice is rough with emotion as it cuts through the silence. "You're enough. You'll always be enough."

I sob, clutching at him as the negative energy that's been festering inside me crashes over me. All the anger and sadness, months of uncertainty and pain, it all kaleidoscopes behind my eyes like a slow-motion picture, and it tears me up, ripping me to shreds. I sob again painfully, my words a broken whisper, "What if I'm not strong enough?"

A humorless laugh breaks free from him, and somehow, he pulls me even closer, holds me even tighter. He repeats over and over, "You are. You are."

So, I let him take me. I lean into him and allow him to hold me up. And then I cry.

Chapter Eight

Dare

I wait until Lilith comes to get Toni before leaving.

I was aware from the information I'd gotten from everyone that, somehow, Toni had managed to not have any kind of breakdown over the past few months. Regardless of what triggered it in the warehouse, I'm relieved it happened, and I'm glad I was there to absorb at least a tiny fragment of what she's feeling.

Everyone deals with trauma differently; there's no right or wrong way to work through it. Even before all of this, we tried getting her therapy, but there wasn't any way we could make that happen without setting off some red flags. And it's rather difficult to provide therapy for memories that don't exist for that person.

Since her memories are coming back now, they're bound to adversely affect her, whether she wants to admit it. Lilith will talk to her about the need for psychotherapy, but I wouldn't be surprised if she outright refused. There's also the option of hypnotherapy to help unlock what's still being repressed, but the last time that was mentioned, she was adamant that she didn't want to do it. She trusted her brain to keep what she couldn't handle out of her reach, and that was the end of the discussion.

It's moments like these where I feel I should just lay it all out on the line. I should tell her everything I know and see if that information turns the key on the lock in her brain. I know there are a lot of things she would be better off not remembering; however, not at the expense of forgetting the important pieces.

Me.

Once she's secure with Lilith, I head back down the street where Agatha is waiting for me. I get into the passenger seat of the car, and she looks at me expectantly, a worried expression on her face as she asks, "Everything okay?"

I take a deep breath and nod. "It will be."

She remains quiet as she pulls away from the curb. She drives for a few moments and then she reaches over and pats me on the leg, and I narrow my eyes at her in confusion. "Why are you touching me?"

She shrugs. "Honestly, you look like you could use a hug, but that's too far for me."

"I'm fine. I wish I could do more for her, but I know she's in excellent hands."

She glances at me, unconvinced. "If you say so."

I realize we've never had the chance to have a proper conversation about anything other than how we think we might get ourselves out of the shitstorm we've been in. It's proving impossible to get ourselves out of something we don't understand, especially when we're still not sure who's fueling the fire.

I turn toward her. "Do you know anything about Lilith?"

She shakes her head. "Not really. I was raised away from her and didn't even know anything about her until recently. I wasn't aware I had any siblings until my so-called father brought it up to me that if I wanted an opportunity to be at the top of a bigger organization, I could take it for myself. And since, according to him, my much older sister, Lilith, had already eliminated most of the competition, it probably wouldn't be difficult. But then, the more information I gathered about her revealed she would not be easy to overturn at all. And then there's the fact I didn't even know if I wanted to be at the top of the food chain because it kind of seems like the shittiest job ever. I was hesitant to get involved."

I give her a knowing look. "So, you took me as a ploy to potentially take over The Dead?"

She laughs. "No. I took you to be annoying. And not to be annoying to only Lilith, but also to be annoying to whatever fucking asshole thought they were gonna buy you and do whatever they pleased with you. I couldn't have that. But then my twatface father had to interfere, trying to teach me a lesson by locking us up in hell for a couple of months. I wish I could've had the pleasure of stabbing that fucker in the face myself, but I know in those types of situations, you never let the bad guy breathe for a moment longer than he needs to. I don't care what information you think they might have; eliminate them before they find an opening to overpower you."

I nod. "Abso-fucking-lutely. We see it all the time: someone wants to gloat, and the next thing you know, they're fucking dead."

She snorts, nodding her head with me. "Fucking right. Never let the enemy speak."

I pause for a moment, thinking over the events of the past few months. We're still not sure who bought me, most likely intending to torture and murder me, and since I now know everybody involved in that entire event is dead, that leaves us back to square one. I've had to smoke out ghosts before, but this one seems to be a little smarter than the rest.

There must be some reason they've remained anonymous for so long. I turn back to Agatha, saying, "This person has to be directly related to the infrastructure of The Dead. Some unknown link, an unknown entity—something. Some skeletons in the closet that somehow stayed a secret for this long. Someone with not only an agenda but also a big grudge. They're also smart enough to know that once we have a face, the odds of them pulling off any kind of coup goes down significantly. It's much harder for us to defeat the faceless enemy."

She nods, shrugging her shoulders as she maneuvers the car through a spot of late-night traffic. "I'm the last person who would know anything like that. I was sent away to another country as a child, and they did not mention it to me at all until recently. I was raised to believe my family was my family, and our reach was limited to the city we lived in. I'm not even sure if my father brought up my biological family because he wanted me to take that power for myself or him. I have no fucking idea. I suppose hindsight being what it is, asking him these questions now would be ideal. But c'est la vie."

I chuckle, thinking about our rescue from prison and how her men leveled every enemy without pause. It was quite magnificent and definitely the way to handle those types of situations when the enemy's intentions are unclear and too much talking will only get you killed. They asked no questions and killed anyone and everyone who posed a threat, getting us out of there without nary a scratch on any of them.

It wasn't until we were well away from there that her man told her he had shot her father in the face for daring to double-cross her. She blinked in shock but didn't seem too upset by the turn of events, so I assumed no love was lost between them. "Did you love your father?"

She jacks the brakes, the force of the car coming to a stop, locking my seatbelt as I'm thrown forward toward the dash. She twists in her seat until she's looking directly into my eyes and says quietly, "My father was a vile waste of a human being, and his being dead is a tremendous relief to me and everyone who ever had the displeasure of knowing him. My only regret was not being able to end his miserable life by my hand, slowly and painfully."

I can't stop the bark of laughter that falls from my mouth, and she narrows her eyes at me and asks, "What's so funny?"

I laugh even harder as I explain. "All of you sisters are the fucking same. Blood-thirsty and deadly. It's shocking, given the fact you weren't even raised together."

She scoffs. "Yeah, well, we were all raised with the same ill intentions, so you get what you get."

"What does that mean?"

She gives me an impatient look, then continues. "I don't know a lot about you, Darius, and frankly, I don't fucking care. But one thing you need to understand about the women in my world, in our world, is that we're kept for the sole purpose of men getting ahead. They are disposable, replaceable, and very few people mourn them when they're gone. The only way you can get ahead is to set yourself up a path to freedom with no one being the wiser, and even then, the odds of survival are close to nil."

"And this is what you were doing when you made the plan to steal me from whoever bought me from Dickwad? Paving your way to freedom?"

She shakes her head. "No, that was a stupid flex that almost got us both killed. A total man move, really. And I knew better, but did it anyway because I was an impulsive asshole."

I laugh, inclining my head at her as I reply, "An impulsive asshole move I will always be grateful for. If you hadn't done that, I would most likely be dead, or worse, wishing I was dead."

She sighs, nodding in agreement. "Most likely, yes. And we're fortunate we're not both dead, given how close my men were to not being able to get us out. They took an enormous risk coming for me, and I took an even bigger risk insisting you come with us."

"Why did you, then? Why didn't you wash your hands of me and leave me behind? It certainly would've been the easier option."

"Easier option at that moment, maybe. But the long-term repercussions wouldn't have been worth it."

I frown at her in confusion. "Long-term repercussions?"

She looks at me like I'm a moron but then says, "Yeah, Toni never would've forgiven me if I'd let you die. I'd have spent the rest of my days looking over my shoulder, waiting for her to seek retribution for the death of her one true love."

"Now, you're being dramatic."

"No way, man, that crazy bitch loves your dumb ass, that much I am certain of.".

I sigh and look away. "If you say so."

Her fist connecting with my arm draws my attention back to her, and she meets my eyes and asks, "Has she never told you, then?"

I shake my head in response but say nothing. It's not like there have been many chances for heartfelt declarations since I let how I felt slip to her so many months ago. And the constant state of high stress and endless unknowns hasn't allowed for anything more than crisis mode, so it's not surprising that she hasn't felt the overwhelming urge to profess her undying love for me.

Agatha's laughter brings me out of my thoughts, and I turn back to her. "What's so funny?"

"You are. You lovesick fool."

I scowl at her, clearing my throat and straightening in my seat. "Shut the fuck up."

She cackles, "Oh my god, you are!"

My scowl deepens as I grumble at her. "See what I mean? You sisters are all the fucking same."

She smiles at me, and for a moment, I see a much younger Lilith beaming back at me. They all look so much alike that it's disconcerting, and I'm reminded that they're all fucking crazy in their own way. I shake my head at her. "Just drive the car, asshole."

She doesn't say anything else as she puts the car in gear, and we continue our journey.

Laughing all the way.

Chapter Nine

Toni

I SURVIVED MY BREAKDOWN. It amazes me how hollow you feel after
a good emotional purge. Not that I recall having very many of them,
but this feels oddly familiar, so I figure I must have lived through at
least one in the past. Which gives me a one hundred percent survival
rate so far.

It takes me quite a while to get my bearings, get a firm grip on
myself, and tether my frayed emotions back down into the darkness
I keep reserved for them. Part of me feels like this is normal, even if I
don't understand how I keep myself together so well most of the time.

Lilith stays with me for the duration, moving from one spot in our
apartment to another as I shift through a never-ending carousel of
emotions that I can barely put into coherent words. It's almost like
I'm sifting through the stages of grief in a flip book, and everyone
around me must be getting whiplash from the experience. But Lilith

doesn't flinch; she remains an unwavering force by my side, absorbing my sadness, pain, and anger and coming back with whatever response I need in that moment.

Eventually, I exhaust myself into an uneasy sleep, and when I wake up a few hours later, she's curled up beside me, fast asleep. I was sleeping facing her, so I turn to roll off the other side of the bed only to run into the sleeping form of Tony. I frown and sit up, looking around the room to see Matt sprawled in the chair in the corner. He grins at me and whispers, "Well, good afternoon."

I scowl at him and ask, "What are you both doing in here?"

He looks at me like I'm an idiot but responds, "Making sure you're okay. Shit, making sure we're all okay."

I frown, flopping back on the bed as I mutter, "Is anyone ever truly okay?"

He moves closer to me, and then his hand is on my foot, so I sit back up and look at him. He holds his hands out to me, and I grab them and allow him to pull me up from the bed, leaving the two sleeping beauties to their own devices. We leave my bedroom, and I pause at the guest bathroom in the hallway, using the facilities and freshening up by splashing cold water on my face. I look like shit, but I feel a lot better. Lighter.

I make my way out into the main living area, relieved to see Matt has taken it upon himself to prepare some food. I don't remember the last time I had a proper meal, and my stomach growls in protest. "What's on the menu? What can I do?"

Matt gives me a look, then laughs as he tosses me some vegetables. "You can cut those up and stay out of my way."

I frown. "I can do more than cut up vegetables."

Matt shakes his head and squints at me. "No, you're not. You've proven you pick up a lot of new tricks easily, but you have also proven that cooking is not one of them."

I glare at him. Then silently accept he is correct and pick up the mushrooms and start cleaning and slicing them accordingly. It feels good to do something as mundane as cutting up some vegetables. Matt sets a drink in front of me, and I nod my thanks, happy to sit in silence for a few moments.

I don't even mind the moisture that gathers in the corners of my eyes in response to him asking me if I'd like some music. I nod, afraid to speak for fear he'll recognize I'm still a bit of an emotional fucking nutcase, but then I chuckle to myself because it's not like he doesn't already know that.

He puts on my favorite alt-rock playlist, and as the music lifts my spirits, I finally ask, "You're making chicken marsala, right? Please tell me you're making marsala."

He laughs, nodding his head. "Of course, I'm making your favorite. You can even choose if we're going to have pasta or potatoes."

My eyes widen in excitement, and my mouth salivates. "I don't know if I can decide. Why do I have to choose? I think I've earned all the carbs at this point."

He nods and places a bag of potatoes and a package of fresh pasta on the counter as he says, "That's exactly what I thought you'd say, so I came prepared. That also works nicely for my other plan for the evening, so prepare yourself to feast."

I'm not about to argue about any plan that ends with me consuming a giant pile of carbohydrates, but I must ask. "What other plan is it you speak of?"

Matt stops what he's doing and goes over to the fridge, opening the door and showing me the variety of alcoholic drinks he purchased for us. "We are going to get shit-faced and pretend we have no problems in the world."

I laugh. I laugh, and I laugh, and that tiny vibration of joy that shoots up my spine immediately triggers the waterworks, but at least this time, they're more happy tears than stabbing-agony tears. Regardless of what happens over the next few days, weeks, or months, at least I'm surrounded by a few people who give a fuck.

Tony's voice breaks through our moment as he strides into the room. "What the fuck, Matt? What did you say to her? Why is she crying?"

I laugh even harder, almost choking on my laughter, as Tony walks over and punches Matt's arm. Matt yelps, then punches him back as he explains, "She's not crying-crying. She's cry-laughing. There's a big difference, you fucklicker."

Tony frowns at him, seemingly unconvinced. He walks over to me, bending down in front of me and looking me straight in the face as he asks, "You okay, Nettie? Do I need to maim him?"

I shake my head, wiping the tears on my cheeks with the back of my hand as I attempt to get control of myself. I hiccup, which sets off another torrent of giggles, and now Matt and Tony are staring at me like I'm crazy. That thought makes me laugh even harder.

Lilith breaks through my laughing fit as she rushes into the room, the sounds of my broken laughing hiccups likely cueing her to a problem out here. She shoves Tony to the side, sending him sprawling, and takes his position bent over in front of me, looking me straight in the face. "Are you okay, Toni?"

Suddenly, Lilith disappears, Tony having knocked her feet out from under her, sending her crashing to the floor in a heap. He pounces on her, and they spend a few seconds grappling before Lilith takes control and puts him in a submission hold, using her legs around his upper body. "Tap out, asshole."

Tony shakes his head, obviously enjoying this position more than he should be from the smile on his face. She growls, squeezing him more tightly, and his face reddens, but he doesn't tap out. She looks up at me, and I shrug, my laughter finally abating as they distract me with their antics.

Lilith eases her grip on him, and Tony doesn't waste any time flipping their positions, attempting to grapple for a submission hold of his own. They're in a no-holds battle for domination, so I move to the other side of the kitchen island, continuing my dinner prep duties.

Matt shakes his head at them, bumping me with his elbow and giving me a questioning look when my eyes meet his. I shrug my shoulders, sending him a small smile, which he returns as he picks up my drink and hands it to me. He grabs his own drink, holding it up as he says, "What shall we cheers to first?"

I squint, cocking my head at him as I contemplate my options. Then I smile. "To giving no fucks."

He smiles back at me. "Yes. To giving no fucks for the next twelve hours."

"Hey, wait for us!" Tony and Lilith pop up beside us, completely disheveled and panting. Tony grabs two drinks from the fridge, opens them, and hands one to Lilith.

Tony raises a hand, interrupting our cheers. "And we're sure that getting blitzed and giving no fucks for twelve hours will not bite us in the ass?"

Matt winces, glancing at Lilith as he says, "Yes. It's fine."

Lilith narrows her eyes at him. "What did you do, Matt?"

He sighs. "I may have made one itty bitty call to ensure we are indeed safe to let loose and give no fucks for a brief amount of time."

Which means he notified Dare.

Lilith pokes him in the chest, then shoves the same finger into his face, and he leans away from her slightly as she says, "You're on thin ice. But I'll let it slide...this time."

Tony laughs. "Yeah, because she wants to get fucked up, too."

Lilith rolls her eyes, but doesn't disagree. None of us are big drinkers, but this seems like a good time to forget about the shitstorm we've been living for the last few months and attempt to have a good time. Even if we'll likely regret it in the morning.

No one says anything for a few moments, and we glance around at each other, taking in the moment of relief we get from knowing we can relax and let our guard down without worrying someone is going to sneak in on our blind side and attempt to eliminate us.

Then we raise our drinks between us.

"To giving no fucks."

Dare

When Matt called me about the impromptu house party he wanted to have, I was less than impressed. But then he explained how upset Toni was when she returned to the apartment with Lilith and how he felt a few moments of giving no fucks would benefit her. So, I caved.

I set up extra security around their apartment and put a few men in the building across the street to keep an eye out for possible suspicious activity. Carolina and I set up camp at a hotel nearby, and even though I doubt she really wanted to hang out with me, she was being a good sport as my cover story. Having her with me made it easier to explain being seen at a random hotel.

It's after midnight when Matt sends me a video on my burner phone, and I open it to see Toni, obviously feeling no pain, standing on the coffee table. I chuckle, shaking my head at her antics. Carolina gives me a questioning look, so I hand the phone over, and she smiles, also shaking her head at the cackling coming from the video. She hands my phone back to me, her eyebrows raised as she looks at me. "Maybe you should go over there?"

My eyebrows furrow in response. "What for?"

"Someone's going to need to put her to bed," she says with a laugh. "I doubt she's going to go willingly if she's having a good time."

"True. But eventually, she'll have no choice, and she'll crash."

Carolina frowns. "What if she crashes emotionally before she crashes physically? There won't be anyone there to help her out of it since it seems like everyone will be crashing before too long."

I groan. She's right in her assumption that Toni may have an emotional crash before a physical one. And since everyone appears to be three sheets to the wind, it's unlikely anyone there will be much help if it comes down to it. So, I rise from my seat, grabbing my coat and room keycard as I shove my feet into my shoes. "I'll be back."

She smiles at me knowingly. "Take your time."

I roll my eyes but say nothing as I leave our room and make my way out of the hotel. It's a short walk to Toni's place, but I hurry along anyway, worried she may already feel the depressant effect of the booze she's been drinking all night.

I check in with my security detail, letting them know I'll be entering the apartment, then let myself in, stopping to listen for movement before making my way further into the living area.

Tony is passed out on the sofa, snoring softly, and I begrudgingly stop myself from fucking with him like I used to back when we were young and dumb—well, younger and dumber. Matt is laid out on the smaller sofa, his arms and legs hanging over the edges, and I stop to take a picture of how stupid he looks before scanning the room for Lilith and Antoinette.

Lilith is curled up in the armchair, her knees tucked up under her chin, her arms wrapped around herself, and I pick up a throw blanket, settling it over her gently. She looks so much younger in her sleep, the normal tension I see etched on her face nonexistent. My chest tightens as I feel a pang of something that feels a lot like regret for the young woman she might have been if not born into such a life as the one she knows.

Shaking off the uncharacteristic feelings, I turn around, concerned I don't see Toni anywhere. Turning to leave the room, I notice a soft glow coming from behind the chair, so I peer over Lilith and see Toni sitting on the floor, her back to the chair; her gaze focused on a video playing on her phone.

The video is blurry, so I walk around the chair, whispering her name so I don't startle her too much. She starts a bit, but then her features brighten when her eyes connect with mine. "You're here," she whispers, her voice and expression dreamy as she reaches her hand out to me. I take her hand, but rather than sitting down beside her, I use my grip to urge her to her feet. She stands unsteadily, so I scoop her up, and she giggles, her head coming to rest on my shoulder, and I see she's still watching the video on her phone as I walk down the hall and into her bedroom.

I set her on her feet, and she wobbles a bit, but then gets her feet stable underneath her. Antoinette reaches out and yanks the comforter down, then scurries up on the bed, grabbing all the pillows and piling them up against the headboard. She turns back to me, and I raise a brow at her in question as she reaches her hand out to me, beckoning me to join her.

Tsking at me, she then sighs. "Come on. You get to be my headboard." Her words are slightly slurred, but she sounds happy and fucking adorable, and I groan inwardly, silently praying for strength as I get a vision of her innocently using me as her own private jungle gym in her drunkenness. I can do this. No problem.

She moves out of the way, and I sit on the bed, then scoot up and settle myself against the pillows as she instructed. I make room for her between my splayed legs and hold my arms out as she watches me, obviously pleased with herself. She pauses and shakes her head. "Off with the shirt."

I drop my arms, frowning as I ask, "Why?"

She looks at me like I'm stupid. "For skin-to-skin contact, duh. The absolute best kind of bonding experiences require skin-to-skin contact."

My frown deepens. "Isn't that for babies?"

She glares at me, then scoffs. "It's not just for babies!" she exclaims, quickly pulling her dress over her head as she continues, "Skin-to-skin contact is beneficial for everyone." There goes her bra. "It increases oxytocin levels and boosts serotonin and dopamine levels, which lowers stress levels."

She's standing in front of me, wearing nothing more than a scrap of material she likes to call underwear, and I barely manage to avert my eyes, swallowing my groan of frustration as her tits taunt me with their hard peaks. I am being punished for being a duplicitous motherfucker for most of my life.

I quickly pull my shirt over my head and throw it on the floor, raising my hands and indicating for her to join me. There's no way she's going to miss my hard dick poking her in the back, but I try my best to make it less obvious as she settles against me. She pulls the comforter up over her naked body as she gets comfortable, and I sigh with relief that at least I won't have to continue to pretend I'm not distracted by her bare form lying prone against me.

She sighs, pressing her upper body back against me firmly as she gets her phone out and starts watching the video again. I peer closer, my breath catching in my throat as I recognize the people on the screen.

Us.

Us before.

Us before all the bullshit, back when things were still new.

"Where did you get that?"

She smiles softly, not taking her eyes off the screen as she replies, "I found it buried in my cloud. It was labeled 'my ends of being'." She pauses the video and looks up at me before continuing. "Do you know what that means?"

My breath catches in my throat, and I clench my jaw, biting the inside of my cheek sharply as I think over my response. Then I say carefully, "I think it had something to do with you leaving your old self behind." I pause, hoping she'll accept this vague bit of information and move on, but she raises a brow at me expectantly, so I continue, "We met under somewhat odd circumstances. I won't go into detail, but let's say we weren't supposed to end up together, and there were some people who wouldn't take too kindly to the idea. It's like a fork in the road where you must decide if you're going to continue down the path as your current self in your current existence or if you're going to take the new, unfamiliar path and leave everything behind for this new version of yourself."

She snort-laughs a bit incredulously, then says, "So, you're saying you were my new, unfamiliar path?"

I smile, pulling her closer as I reply, "Not exactly. More like I was on the path as you walked by, and when I held my hand out for you, you made the choice to take it."

Her brow furrows, but she's quiet as she smiles and nods, and then goes back to watching the video, oblivious to the tornado of emotions swirling inside me. I swallow the lump in my throat and look away from the video for a few moments, needing to get enough control over myself to go on without her noticing the quiver in my voice. She giggles, glowing with pleasure as she listens to the old me telling her I'm going to eat her pussy until she begs me to stop. I groan, and she turns her head toward me, her eyes questioning as she asks, "Do you remember this?"

Now unable to speak, I nod, relieved when she doesn't press me to say anything more. In her silence, I work to collect myself, pushing the wash of memories down where they can't physically touch me. I grind my teeth together again to do so, and I almost bite a hole through my cheek as the force of it all attempts to overwhelm me.

Focusing on the bitter taste of iron in my mouth, I turn my focus back to the video still playing in front of her. She doesn't feel the agony of the past, doesn't have any recollection of what went on before or after—she's completely enraptured by the dirty fairy tale that's playing on a loop in her hands. I won't ruin it for her—not yet.

I wrap my arms around her, pulling her back tighter against me, pressing my face into her neck and inhaling her scent as deeply into my lungs as I can before slowly exhaling. She giggles, my breath against her neck tickling her, and she turns her face toward me and licks my cheek like a dog.

I yank my face away from her, then wipe my cheek against the side of her head as she laughs and then goes back to her video. She sighs, snuggling herself back into me, and I let her sink into me, let her warmth and scent surround me, lulling me into a deep sense of contentment, short-lived as it may be.

"I love you."

My heart stutters in my chest, and my breath jams up in my lungs as her softly whispered words break through the silence. Every memory I've ever had seems to kaleidoscope in my mind. Every sporadic moment of contentment, every brief interlude of peace, and I can't say for sure if anyone has ever said those words to me before.

Pressing my face into her neck again, my eyes squeeze shut against the burning behind them as I tighten my arms around her even more. I'm squeezing her so tightly against me she struggles a bit, her arms pushing against mine, and my urge to take her breath, to take her heartbeat and keep it for my own for all eternity, overwhelms me.

Easing my grip on her, I inhale a stuttering breath as the chaos inside me releases its stranglehold on me. Inhaling again, I feel the demons abate, the claw marks permanently etched on my being, leaving a burning path in their wake. After a third breath I open my eyes, the throb of her heartbeat beneath the skin of her neck like a beacon of hope to the dormant parts of me I forgot ever existed.

"I love you," I whisper back, my lips against her ear, nipping at her earlobe and then pressing a soft kiss on her neck.

She sighs, relaxing back against me once more, and we lay there in silence, watching the couple on the screen continue to live their dirty little fairy tale.

And for now, it's enough.

Chapter Ten

Dare

I SHOULD GO.

I lost track of the number of times we watched that video. She didn't ask me questions and made no more comments as she lay there with a small smile on her face until she finally fell asleep.

I'm not sure how long I've been lying here, wrapped around her sleeping form. I should have left ages ago. I should have removed myself from her bed and gone about my business back to the hotel, but here I am, daylight now creeping in through the curtains. I should get up and go right now. I should carefully shift her from my arms and quietly leave the apartment and focus on sorting out this never-ending clusterfuck. But I can't bring myself to do it.

I don't want her to wake up without me. I don't want her to wake up in a fog and wonder if I was ever even here. I squeeze my arms around her tighter, disturbing her a bit as she squirms against me, muttering sleepily but without waking.

Since she fell asleep, she's been slowly sliding further and further down my body. I sigh, accepting that I can't stay here much longer. I scoot down, shifting my body as I slowly and carefully roll her until she's lying on her stomach beside me. Gently positioning her arms, she gives a small yawn, then snuggles down into the mattress as she continues to sleep.

My cock hardens in my pants at the sight of her nude body beside me. She's still wearing her underwear, the black lace covering her ass a poor excuse for an undergarment—not that I'm complaining.

Slowly, I slide her underwear down over her hips, and she shifts her body slightly, allowing me to slide the scrap of lace down her legs. I toss them on the floor, and she shivers, so I stand up and remove the rest of my clothing, then climb over her, straddling her legs and pressing my torso against her back.

If she wants some skin-to-skin contact, then I'm going to fucking give her some. I press my dick against her ass, and she pushes back against me slightly. Pressing closer, I settle more of my weight on top of her.

I had forgotten how much smaller she is than me. Or maybe I forgot that I'm on the larger side, even more so from the time I spent locked up with nothing more to do than pump iron and fight for my life. And while Antoinette is not a petite woman, she appears so when she's lying beneath me.

I bring my hand up, balancing the bulk of my weight on one arm as I smooth her hair back from her face and off her neck. Bracing myself on my forearms, I lean closer and press my face against her pulse point, gently scraping my teeth along the delicate skin there. I trace a path down to where her neck meets her shoulder, earning a soft moan in response.

Pulling back, I look at her face, but she's still asleep, or at least more asleep than awake at this point. I go back to nibbling on her neck and her shoulder, one side and the other. I shift down and lick along the back of her neck, anywhere I can reach without having to take my cock off her ass.

I shift my hips back until the tip of my dick is pressing between her legs, and I feel how wet she is. Pushing myself into her slightly, I pull back, only to thrust in a bit more until just the tip of my dick is penetrating her wet cunt. I grit my teeth, my eyes closing as I push down my urge to shove my dick all the way inside her and rut into her like the fucking animal I am.

If this was something we had ever spoken of, I would do it. But given her history, and the many unknowns surrounding it, I restrain myself. She needs to know what I'm doing. I want her to be fully aware of how I own her, mind and body.

I remain motionless, my cock still inside her as I brush my lips along her shoulder and up her neck. "Toni. Toooniii," I sing song into her ear. "It's time to wake up."

She doesn't so much as flinch, so I push my dick in another inch, my teeth sinking into her neck aggressively, my tongue coming out and massaging each bite mark as I struggle to hold myself in check.

I hear the hitch of her breath, then feel her ass moving, forcing me deeper with each rotation of her hips. "That's right, baby girl. That's right. Take what you want."

She's more awake than asleep now, and her hands come up, gripping my wrists where they're braced by her head. She pushes her hips back with more force, shoving herself back on my cock, her wet pussy sliding back as she purrs beneath me. Then, she gasps, "Matt."

I freeze.

What the fuck?

I raise my upper body off her and peer down at her face. Her eyes are closed, but her lips twitch a few times, and then she smiles, immediately breaking out into giggles.

Apparently, my naughty little minx thinks she's fucking funny.

Which means she's looking to get punished.

I growl deep in my chest. "You little fucking bitch. That how you wanna play it?"

I move one of my hands to the hair at the base of her skull, squeezing the strands in my fist and yanking her head back. She continues to laugh, so I adjust myself over her, my other hand grabbing her throat as I pull my cock out until I'm nudging against her cunt.

She stops laughing, choking on a moan as I grit out, "It seems like you need a reminder of who's fucking you."

I press my hips forward, pushing my cock all the way inside her as I pull her back against me, using my hands still gripping her by the hair and the front of her neck. I lick up the side of her face, then bite down on her earlobe, and when she tries to flinch away, I tighten my hands and growl, "My little minx wants to fuck around? You wanna find out, huh?"

She has a bratty twinkle in her eyes, the twitch in the corners of her mouth as she releases a breath, part giggle, part moan. I chuckle against her ear, feeling the beast rattle in my chest as I slide my tongue down her pulse point and bite down, sucking the delicate skin into my mouth until she moans loudly.

I release her without warning, using my hands to press my upper body away from her. I pump my hips, slamming my cock into her sharply, once, twice, watching the in and out slide of my dick in her wet pussy as I work to restrain my urge to fuck her into the mattress.

I move away from her, reaching my arm down under her hips and pulling her up onto her knees. I grab her arms, yanking them behind her back and crisscrossing her wrists. "Don't fucking move. If you move, I'll stop."

She stops trying to speak and lays there face down on the bed, panting. I see her shifting her weight from knee to knee, blatantly wagging her ass at me, so I reach out and give one cheek a good slap. She yelps, so I do the same to the other side, then take both of her ass cheeks in my hands and massage them as I bend down and run the flat of my tongue from her clit to her entrance.

I stab my tongue inside her pussy a few times, then trace my tongue up over her ass cheek, licking and biting one side, then the other, before slowly trailing a line with my tongue to her back hole. As soon as she realizes what I'm doing, she tenses, her arms shifting away from her back.

I slap her ass again, my lips brushing against her reddened skin. "I won't tell you again. Don't fucking move or I'll stop. And I don't mean I'll stop licking your tight little asshole. I mean, I'll stop all of it, and I'll leave you here, wet, quivering, and needy, with no chance for the release you're aching for."

She curses sharply and before she can talk anymore shit, I interrupt her, "And keep your fucking mouth shut. The only words that should come out of your mouth right now are my name and all forms of begging and pleading."

She presses her lips together, then pushes her face into the mattress and mutters incoherently. She fixes her arms, crossing them behind her back and sinking her torso lower until she's presenting herself to me at an even better angle.

I waste no more time talking; I start right back at the beginning, massaging her clit with the flat of my tongue. I cock my head to the side, fluttering the tip of my tongue against her clit until her breath catches, and I feel the tension coiling in her. I move up once again, penetrating her pussy with my tongue and fucking her rapidly as my fingers massage her clit. Her breath catches again, then she sobs, and I shift, my mouth taking the same path across both her ass cheeks until I'm hovering over her back hole again.

I rim the outside with the point of my tongue, adjusting my stance behind her so my knees are wider and pressing two fingers into her pussy while my other hand massages her clit. I add a third finger to her cunt, pushing my tongue into her ass, using my lips and teeth to tease and torture as she pushes back against me.

A growl vibrates up from my chest, the pitch and volume of her moans increasing with each stroke against her clit, the push of my fingers in her cunt. She quivers beneath me, so I speed up the movement of my mouth on her asshole, reveling in the sounds she's making as the tension builds higher and higher. I have half a mind to edge her. To fuck both her holes and circle her clit right up to where she's about to fall and then stop.

My beast purrs at the thought of having her curse, scream, and thrash at the pleasurable pain of being denied, but I push that idea back. Instead, I twist my fingers in her pussy, ignoring the odd, painful tension in my hands and my arms, the awkward cramping in my neck and back from being hunched over.

Her hips buck, her earlier inhibitions forgotten as she pushes herself back against me. She's moaning, begging, and pleading for me not to stop, to make her come, and I pick up my intensity until I feel her quivering beneath me. I feel the pleasure unraveling, feel both holes twitching around my fingers and tongue as she sobs her release into the mattress, cursing glorious words of affirmation.

And my name.

My fucking name.

I straighten, removing my now-drenched hand from her pussy. I let my saliva pool in my mouth for a few moments, then open my mouth to dribble it into my already wet hand. I rub the mixture of my saliva and her arousal on my cock, my other hand gripping her hip as I line myself up and slowly push the tip inside. She gasps and moans, attempting to push herself back forcefully, so I bring my other hand up to grip her hip to steady her. "You want my dick, baby girl? Want me to fuck you so hard and so deep you'll be feeling me for days?"

I don't wait for her to respond, my grip on her hips tightening, my fingertips digging in as I shove the full length of my cock inside her in one sharp thrust. She sobs incoherently, her face still pressed into the mattress, her hands still crossed behind her back, and I pause, reveling in the feeling of her hot, wet pussy quivering around me.

Slowly, I pull back, sliding halfway out before immediately pushing back inside. I keep this up, setting a steady rhythm, and I quickly feel the thread of heat igniting at the base of my spine, the heaviness in my balls slapping against her clit.

I thrust all the way inside her, then stop, continuing to press my hips forward in little pulses that grind myself against her. I remove one of my hands from her hip, pushing her crossed arms down. "Touch yourself. Rub that needy little clit for me."

She quickly moves one of her arms by her head, bracing herself on one hand as the other disappears beneath her to rub her clit. I feel her fingertips brushing my balls with each stroke, and then she reaches further, and I feel her hand on my balls, stroking and then squeezing. I choke on my breath, then growl, "Unless you want this to be over prematurely, I suggest you don't do that."

She mutters incoherently, so I brace myself on my hands and lean over her. She turns her face toward me, and I nuzzle her cheek, then nip at her jaw by her ear. "What do you want, baby girl? Tell me."

She's panting, her hips squirming for friction when I remain motionless inside her. "I wanna see your face. I wanna look at you while you fuck me."

I chuckle, my lips and tongue sucking her neck. "Whatever my girl wants."

I push myself up and sit back, resting my hands on my thighs as I watch her relax on her front for a few moments before she rolls onto her back. She spreads her legs, watching me with a self-satisfied smirk on her face. "This is what I want."

I smile, my hands grabbing her by her thighs and pulling her down the bed toward me. "This is what you want? For me to lie on top of you and give you a nice, lazy missionary fuck?"

She laughs, raising her hands and pulling my upper body down on top of her. "I don't know about lazy, but definitely yes to a nice missionary fuck."

I put most of my weight on my forearms on either side of her, then slowly slide my dick back into her pussy. She clenches around me, and my own incoherent sex noises fall into her neck as I squeeze my eyes shut from the intense feeling of pleasure.

Her arms snake beneath mine, her nails digging into my back as her heels come up and press against my ass. She bucks her hips, fucking me from below, and I curse, attempting to push my upper body away from her, but her hands grip my back, stopping me. She pulls me down closer, rubbing her tits against my chest, her legs tightening around my hips, with her lips and breath against my ear. "Stay like this. Stay close to me."

I spread my knees wide, lowering my hips to sink into her fully, pushing my dick into her until my pelvis is rubbing against her clit. She moans, her legs sliding down until her ankles are hooked around my thighs. Her breath is on my neck, and I feel her teeth and tongue amidst her panting breath.

I continue to rock my body into her, and I feel her inner walls intermittently clenching, then releasing. Her panting moans escalate into broken sobs, the tension in her body coiling tighter with every press of my pelvis against her clit.

I pull my hips back a fraction, then press back inside until her breath catches and her back arches, her head falling back. I force my upper body up, and her hands slide down my back until she's gripping my ass, trying to pull me deeper.

I set a steady rhythm of small pushes, giving just enough friction to drive me mad. My head falls forward, and I lick a line from her neck up to her mouth. I take her lips, eating her moans and her curses. I tangle my tongue with hers, and when I try to pull back, she follows me.

She wraps her arms around my neck, once again pulling me down on top of her, so I slide my hands beneath her, grabbing her ass and lifting her up into my slow grinding thrusts. She gasps with the change of position, her sobbing pleasure vibrating against my tongue as we continue to devour each other.

Part of me wants to pull away; the rational and calculated side of me wants to flip her back over and push her face down and fuck her into the mattress like an animal. But that's not the beast talking.

No, the beast in my chest, is purring and reveling in the deep intimacy thrumming between us, getting off on the intense vibrations of delight knowing that we're two people so intertwined in each other that the only force that will ever separate us is death.

I try to tear my mouth from hers, but once more, she squeezes me tighter. I feel her heels digging into my calves, eliciting a loud moan from my lips. She swallows it down, and I feel my body sinking impossibly closer with her arms and legs wrapped around me fully.

I rotate my hips, pushing my dick deeply inside her, my pelvis grinding against her rhythmically. Her pussy clenches, the tension in her body building, the desperation in her moaning pants against my mouth reaching a fever pitch.

I don't bother curbing the curses building up as my release pulsates in my balls, electricity tingling in my pelvis and along the base of my spine, and I grind my teeth. Her head falls back, her eyes squeezed shut, and I grunt out, "Look at me, Toni."

Her eyes flutter open, her face twisting with pleasure as she chokes out, "Oh, fuck, Darius. Fuck, that's good. Don't stop. Don't stop. I'm gonna come. Fuck. Fuck."

I increase my pace a fraction but continue the grinding press against her clit. She clings to me, and I feel my orgasm barreling down on me, and I know I can't stop it. I press my face into her neck, biting down sharply, then licking and sucking as I mutter, "That's right, baby girl. Come all over this dick. Be a good girl and come for me."

Her breath catches on a sob as she rises against me, clutching me to her and pushing me away at the same time. "Fuck. Oh, fuck. Do it. Come inside me. Give your good girl what she deserves."

She breaks apart beneath me, her cunt clenching and spasming as her body shakes. She curses, moans, and sobs, pushing me over the edge, and I slam into her, pushing in as deeply as possible as my cock pulses. I pull my hips back, slamming back into her once, twice, in quick succession as I empty my balls into her clutching depths.

I'm grunting like an animal, practically frothing through my teeth as I bite down right where her shoulder and neck meet. I suck at my bite mark, then lick a line up her neck lazily, my hands releasing their grip on her ass and moving up alongside her shoulders, removing some of my weight off her.

We're both panting, our skin clinging from the sweat on our bodies, and I press my hips into her, enjoying the slide of our mixed release as a shiver runs through her. She laughs breathlessly, her hands slowly relaxing and sliding down my shoulders as she melts into the bed beneath me. I raise my head and look down at her, chuckling softly at her half-closed eyes and smiling lips.

I try to pull back, but her legs tighten, keeping my dick firmly inside her as she asks, "Is it always like that?"

I lower my head back down until my eyes meet hers. "Is what always like that?"

She gives a small shrug, her brows furrowing. "Us. Intensity. Electricity."

I want to lie to her. I want to sugarcoat the whole thing and give her the rose-colored glasses view I'm sure she wants to hear right now. But I won't. Instead, I round out the sharp, ugly edges enough to appease her without lying fully. "Short answer: yes. But let's call it tumultuous. A bit touch and go. But deep down, hindsight being what it is, there was always this connection. This electric intensity."

She swallows, and I think she's going to say something further, but she gives me a tight smile and a small nod.

She knows.

Deep down—down in the far recesses of her psyche—we live there. Amidst the darkness and the light, blood-red is smeared, and between it all, there's the truth.

She relaxes her legs, and I pull back. I take a moment to appreciate the mess I made of her pretty little pussy, snapping a mental picture of my cum oozing from within her.

Finally, I force myself to leave her bed and venture into the ensuite bathroom to clean myself up. I grab a washcloth and run it under the stream of warm water, squeezing out the excess before heading back into the bedroom with it. I climb back on the bed to clean her up, but she stops me, taking the warm cloth from my hands. I look at her questioningly, and she smiles. "I know you need to leave. It's okay. I'm okay."

I'm not.

I'm not remotely fucking okay.

But I can't really argue with her because she's right. Leaving here in broad daylight is a stupid fucking move. I grab my phone and text Agatha for help in getting me out of here unseen. Carolina would have sent her an update last night, given the fact she was likely expecting this to happen. Because she knows if anything's gonna make me a fucking moron, it's this woman—and my dick.

She immediately texts me back, letting me know it'll be ten minutes in the underground parking garage. I pick up my clothes that are strewn around the floor and quickly dress while watching her, still sprawled on her back with a cooling washcloth on her stomach.

One corner of my lip curves up lazily, unable to suppress the self-satisfaction bubbling up inside me at the knowledge that she's in no hurry to wipe my seed from her body. I kneel on the bed between her legs, using three fingers to scoop up my cum dripping from her and slowly pushing it back inside. "Don't wanna waste that, little minx. I gave that to you. It's yours."

She moans her approval, her back arching slightly as she gives me a devilish look. I glance at the clock by the bedside, then growl as I pull my fingers from her, cleaning them off in my mouth as I stand up and move up the bed, bending close to place a soft kiss on her smiling lips. She kisses me back lingeringly. "That'll have to hold us over for a while."

She smiles. "I know. It's okay. We're okay."

I stare into her eyes, bright with life and emotion, and my breath catches in my throat. But are we?

I turn to leave, and her voice behind me stops me. I turn back to her, and she's rushing off the bed and heading over to a small suitcase that's placed on a chair. She grabs something from inside it and then walks over to me, holding her hand out to me.

My eyes widen as I take in the object she's holding out to me. "How did you get this?"

It's my watch.

The watch that was taken from me months ago when I was first getting on that plane.

She shrugs, shaking her head. "Long story. Take it. Try not to lose it this time."

I bark out a laugh, taking the watch from her hand and putting it back on my wrist where it belongs.

I pull her into me, holding as tightly as I can as I breathe air in, breathe us in.

I pull back, our eyes meeting one last time, before I release her.

Then I turn and walk out the door.

Chapter Eleven

Toni

I WATCH DARIUS WALK out the door with a heavy weight on my chest. I force myself to take a deep breath, grimacing at the increasingly familiar sting of tears behind my eyes.

I give myself a sharp pinch on my thigh. "Snap out of it, Toni. You have shit to do; there's no time for all these fucking feelings."

I feel a tickling trickle between my legs and grimace. Now that sexy time has passed, the sticky wetness coating my inner thighs isn't so hot.

I get up, walk to the bathroom, and turn on the shower before facing the mirror. I inspect myself. Once again, I look a mess.

I cock my head, raising my eyebrows at my reflection, noting the various hickeys and love bites across my person. I stick my tongue out at myself, then go about getting ready for the day.

Eventually, I make my way out to the main living area and head to the kitchen. I see Tony and Matt sitting in the breakfast bar, drinking coffee.

About halfway across the living room, I stop in my tracks and look around. There are two men tied to chairs in the middle of the room.

I look over at Matt and Tony, who now notice my presence, and I raise my brows at them questioningly. They both give me innocent grins, and I roll my eyes. "For fuck sake, guys. You can't tie people up in our living room."

Tony frowns, raising a hand toward the men currently tied up in the living room. "Apparently, we can."

I frown, then walk over and give him a friendly punch on the arm. "What are they doing here?"

Matt speaks up. "I caught them lurking around the property."

"Well, maybe they live here?" I'm not sure how many apartments are in this building since it's enormous, but each unit also appears to be large. The parking garage spans the entire bottom floor, but they use it for public parking as well, so it's difficult to gauge how many people have access to the main building.

Tony shakes his head. "Nope. I went down and hung back long enough to hear them talking. They were waiting around to grab Darius."

My eyes widen, and I catch myself gaping at him dumbly before I snap my mouth shut. I look over at the two men, who appear to be regular-looking folks. Apparently, I've seen too many movies, and I think all the goons should look like goons. I turn back to the guys and ask, "What have they told you so far?"

They both shrug, then Matt answers, "Nothing yet. We haven't asked them anything."

"How long have they been tied up there?"

Matt glances at his watch. "Few hours, I guess. It's best to let them be extremely uncomfortable for a bit before bothering to question them. Especially since I don't want to get blood on the carpet."

Tony eyes the living room floor critically. "That's definitely a rug, and likely an expensive one at that."

Matt gives Tony a bland look as he replies, "Carpet. Rug. Who gives a fuck?"

"Pretty sure the insurance adjuster would." Tony deadpans.

Matt glares at him, then picks up his cup of coffee and sips it loudly.

I roll my eyes at the two of them. "You two are fucking children, I swear. How you guys have lived this long, doing the work you do, is amazing."

Tony grins at me. "I guess we're plain old lucky."

I go over and grab myself a cup of coffee or espresso or whatever the fuck this pitch-black nectar is, then turn and lean against the counter. "So, are we gonna do this here or take them somewhere else?"

Tony sighs, obviously put out by the situation. "I considered here, but it's not exactly soundproofed, so unless we can get information without them screaming bloody murder, we may have to go somewhere else."

I squint at the two men, then turn to Tony. "Well, if you move them to the tub, that will at least help with the mess."

They both raise their brows and look at each other before looking back at me. Matt speaks first. "Well, well, Toni. It seems you're really thinking outside of the box here."

"What can I say? I'm feeling brilliant today." I give them a smile and waggle my eyebrows at them.

There's a ruckus behind me and turn to find Lilith standing over one man, who is now tied to a chair that's on its side. Blood pours from his nose, and Matt says from behind me, "So much for no blood on the carpet."

Tony laughs. "I don't think Lilith gives any fucks about the rug."

Lilith gives him an annoyed look over her shoulder, then she turns back to the bleeding man. "I think this fucker will squeal like the pig he is without too much trouble."

The man's eyes widen, and I see the fear in them as he stares up at her. She kneels in front of him, pulling some kind of leather pouch from the inside pocket of her jacket. She holds it out to him and says something so quietly I can't quite make out what it is. His eyes widen further, and he shakes his head, then says loudly, "No, Lilith. Not that."

I walk over toward them, stopping by the man's head so I can see what Lilith is doing. Lilith bares her teeth at him and runs her tongue over her upper teeth before chomping them at him, and he flinches. She stands up, removing brass knuckles from her right hand as she spits out, "That's what I thought."

Lilith puts the brass knuckles and leather pouch back into the pocket of her jacket and then turns to Tony and Matt. "There shouldn't be any more blood necessary. This fucking dipshit will talk. If he doesn't, I'll make him."

Tony and Matt go into the living room and work together to stand the chair upright. Tony turns back to Lilith and says, "You may want to get some stain remover for that mess on the carpet."

Lilith narrows her eyes at him and flips him the bird. He laughs in response, then turns back to the man.

Lilith makes her way into the kitchen, and I follow her. She's making herself a cup of coffee and then stands there with her back against the counter. "Can I help you with something?"

"What did you threaten to do to him?"

"Nothing. There isn't anything you could do to that man physically to make him give a shit. But unlucky for him, I know all his weak spots."

I frown, then shift over so I'm standing beside her, leaning against the counter, watching Matt and Tony do their work. "So, you know him? And what's his weak spot?"

"Yeah, I know him through Jimmy. Most people have a weak spot. It may be difficult to figure out what these weaknesses are, but with enough foresight and dedication, it always comes to light. It's dumb luck that I know that guy has a family hidden away. If you want to get to someone, you go to the things they leave hidden to find out where it hurts the most."

I glance over at her, taking in her blank face before asking, "And you would hurt his family?"

She doesn't hesitate. "Yes. I will destroy anyone and everyone if it means protecting my family."

I'm not surprised by her answer. I get it. Lilith has lived this life since birth. While she doesn't believe that blood is thicker than water, for the few people she considers her family, she will literally do anything for them. But don't mistake this for a free pass to be a piece of shit for life.

Lilith turns around, setting her coffee cup on the counter before turning to me and looking me right in the face. "There's a lot of collateral damage in our world, Toni. A lot of innocent people murdered for the sake of greed and power. That man considers himself to be collateral damage. He knows, either way, he's dead. He figures the safest way for his family to live is to speak to us. He has a choice: he can roll the dice and assume that whoever he is working for doesn't know about his family, wouldn't exact retribution on his family, or he can divulge their whereabouts and request protection for them from me. It's most likely he will choose the latter."

"So, he will die to protect them, and they will have to learn to live without him. And knowing that he died to protect them?"

She nods. "Better to live knowing that someone put their life on the line for yours than for the whole lot to be rotting at the bottom of the ocean."

Lilith gives me a strange look, her blue eyes almost vacant as she says quietly, "You'd be surprised at the lengths one might go to protect someone they love. The terrible things they'd do. The deep sacrifices they'd make. The idea that someone would literally lie down and die if only to give that other person one moment of peace. Some people say love is a weakness, but I don't see it that way. Truly, that deep crazed connection to someone else–there's strength in that. It fortifies your mind and steels your spine. It provides such a peaceful clarity in the mind. Other people might call that insanity, but I call that love."

I swallow painfully past the sudden lump in my throat. The stinging behind my eyes is back, and I blink rapidly as I step in closer to her. I suddenly have this overwhelming need to speak, so I grab her by her shoulders, forcing her attention on me. "I love you. I would lie down and die at your feet if I thought it would bring you a moment of peace."

Her jaw clenches, and her breath catches. Her blue gaze is that of an ocean as she stares at me, unblinking. Then she jerks me closer, wrapping her arms tightly around my shoulders, her face pressed into my neck. She whispers, "I know, baby. I know."

She squeezes me once more, taking a deep breath before she pulls back. She blinks away the tears I see swimming in her eyes, and I attempt to do the same, though less successfully. I swipe my lower eyelids with my fingertips, then clear my throat. "That's all you have to say?"

She smirks at me. "Ditto."

I glare at her, reaching out and giving her a little push on her shoulder. "What, you're Patrick Swayze now?"

"Now you know who Patrick Swayze is?"

I raise my brows, my hands coming up to rest on my hips. "Of course. *To Wong Fu. Ghost. Next of motherfucking Kin.*"

She laughs. "Do you remember these as a memory?"

"No. Way back when I was bunking with the boys, we did a Patrick Swayze marathon." I sigh, then smile. "That man sure could dance."

Lilith smiles, nodding her head in agreement. "I bet that man could do a lot of things." She inhales deeply, releasing the breath as the tension in her shoulders eases. "Sounds like I missed some good movie nights. Maybe we'll do that next time instead of a get-shitfaced night, because I kind of feel like shit."

"Same. I guess I needed a reminder of why I don't drink. Back to the flavored mineral water for me."

She nods in agreement, the grimace on her face indicative of the sour stomach she must have. I move to walk around her, but her hand on my arm stops me, so I turn back and meet her eyes. She whispers, "I love you, Toni. Always remember that."

I give her a bright smile, my hand coming up and squeezing hers. "I know, baby. I know."

Then I turn, sparing a passing glance at the group of men still deep in a conversation in our living room as I head down the hall to my room.

It's time to prepare.

Chapter Twelve

Dare

SHOCKINGLY, AGATHA IS RUNNING a few minutes behind. I wait for a few moments, then a text comes through from her, saying she's parked on the other side of the parking garage.

I walk over that way until I see her taillights, where she pulled into a spot on the far end. I pause, pretending to check my phone as I assess the current situation.

There's no way Agatha would be so stupid as to pull all the way into a parking garage and then park nose-first, but that's her car. And the texts are coming from her number.

I send a text to Matt and Tony, which delivers immediately. I wait a few moments, hoping to see a read receipt on that fucker, to no avail.

I continue unhurriedly, sighing deeply as I resign myself to whatever shit show is currently in play. Considering I'm going in completely blind, and I have some concerns about the state of Agatha, I figure I may as well just roll with it. I crack my neck, then straighten my shoulders, lengthening my stride as I toss both phones away as nonchalantly as possible.

I walk over to the passenger door and fling it open, then fall into the seat without a glance at the driver. The first thing I notice, other than the silence, is the smell. I know that smell, and it's not Agatha's intentionally annoying perfume.

I turn my head, my eyes clashing with the eyes of one Carolina Tennent. I frown, opening my mouth to say something, but she gives a tiny shake of her head.

I feel the tension radiating off her. She swallows, her hands on the steering wheel white-knuckled as she stares straight ahead like she's waiting for something. I go to say something and then close my mouth again.

What can I even say at this point?

That's when I feel it. The presence behind me and then the cold metal of a gun barrel pressed behind my ear.

"Well, isn't this a nice little plot twist." I murmur good-naturedly.

Carolina whimpers but says nothing. I turn my head to look at her, then attempt to turn my head further to get a glimpse of whoever is behind me. Instead, I'm met with the impact of the biting steel of the gun barrel as it connects sharply with my cheek.

I flinch, then straighten. The gun disappears, and a black cord drops over me, quickly tightening around my neck, yanking me back in the seat. My heart rate spikes, and I have just enough time to pull in a deep breath before the cord squeezes my throat.

I try to reach back with my left hand but come up with nothing but air, so I drop my hands in my lap and wait to see what's going to happen. I hear Carolina crying and yelling beside me, and I wish I had enough air to tell her to shut the fuck up.

The most important part of air deprivation is pushing aside the deep inclination to panic. It's difficult to know if this is a scare tactic or an attempt to kill me. And there's also the option that they're trying to incapacitate me for a short time to restrain me. Which is incredibly fucking stupid, considering if they asked, I'd likely go with them without a fight.

After about three minutes, I let my head drop in front of me, making sure my entire body goes limp. I figure he'll probably wait another minute or two before releasing the tension on my neck, but, shockingly, he barely waits thirty seconds before loosening the cord.

He reaches over and gives my shoulder a shove, and I allow myself to fall forward onto the dash. Caroline is crying even harder, and thank fuck, he's finally telling her to shut the fuck up.

There's rustling in the back, then the rear door opens and closes. As soon as the door bangs shut, I reach out, pushing the lock button on all the doors.

Just as suddenly, Carolina stops crying.

I sit up, quickly expelling what's left of my breath and inhaling slowly as she sits there, frozen in my gaze. I hear the man outside the car shouting at her to open the door, unlock it, and let him in. She sits there, her watery eyes a mixture of relieved triumph, and that's really all the answer I need on what's going on with her in this situation.

I warn her, "If you touch that lock, I will snap your neck."

She swallows and gives me a small shrug. "That may actually be a blessing at this point."

I narrow my eyes, mulling over my options. Considering I don't know the status of Agatha, I can't kill the two of them outright and go about my day.

A loud thump on the window draws my attention outside. That fucking asshole is trying to kick the window in. I flip him the bird through the blacked-out window, then turn back to Carolina. "Do you know where Agatha is?"

She nods. "They have her. I'm not sure exactly where they brought her, but she was alive last I knew."

"I was hoping you were going to say she was in the trunk, so that complicates things. I'm going to assume the gentleman out there acting a fool is not the person I need to be concerned with?"

"No, he's entirely expendable. I was pleased they sent the fucking yahoo to grab you, though, for a second there, I was concerned."

"You go out there and tell that dumb fuck to back off. I'll go willingly."

She nods, reaching over and manually unlocking her door, quickly stepping outside. As soon as her door closes behind her, I relock it.

Carolina walks around the back of the car, and I adjust the mirror so I see what they're doing. She says a few words to him, and he gets in her face, shouting. She doesn't flinch or cower. She stands there with this blank look on her face, and it's almost as if she wants to roll her eyes and is barely refraining from doing so.

Carolina says a few words in response to whatever he's shouting at her, and his face reddens. He reaches a hand out and grabs her by the hair, his other hand coming up to slap her hard across the face.

What the actual fuck?

I unlock the door and exit the vehicle. It only takes me a few strides to come up behind him and grab him by the scruff of the neck, roughly squeezing. He releases her instantly, his knees buckling as I dig my fingers into the pressure point on his shoulder. My free hand comes up to the front of his throat, so I'm holding him up by the neck, and I lean my head in close to him. "Now, that will be enough of that."

Carolina straightens, her hand coming up to her cheek and running along the corner of her lip where it's bleeding. I growl deep in my chest, the beast rattling to be freed, and I squeeze his throat harder as his hands come up and claw at me. "We don't hit women. We don't abuse those weaker than us."

My eyes meet Carolina's as I ask, "How expendable is this fucking asshole?"

She shrugs. "Entirely. He knocked around Agatha, too, muttering something about her being a fucking crazy bitch or something. Totally uncalled for, given the fact she was already incapacitated."

The growl deepens in my chest; the rattling reverberating throughout my whole body as she gives me a pointed look, so I squeeze harder. I dig my fingers deeper into his pressure point until he's entirely incapable of standing on his own feet, and then I fucking squeeze.

I bend over, looking him right in the face, wanting him to look me in the eye as I squeeze even harder. He gurgles, his clawing hands becoming weaker as I lean even closer. I want to make sure that I'm the last fucking thing he sees as his life drains from his body.

I bare my teeth, my voice like gravel as I whisper, "Die."

After a few moments, his hands drop, his eyes no longer fixed on me, and I inhale the last bit of life that whispers from his body. My heart pounds in my chest, the rattling vibration overwhelming my senses with the comforting feeling of unhinged euphoria.

I continue holding him up by his neck, looking over at Carolina. "Open the trunk."

Carolina rushes around, popping the trunk and opening it for me. I not so gently toss him in, then slam the trunk closed. I lean over, resting my forearms on the back of the car as I peer at Carolina, giving myself a few moments to allow the haze to clear from my senses.

After a bit, I straighten, motioning for her to get in the driver's seat as I make my way around to the passenger door. "I assume you know where you're going."

She says nothing as she gets behind the wheel and closes the door quietly behind her. I fall into the passenger seat; the door slamming behind me, then I stare at her expectantly. She starts the car, and her throat moves as she swallows. "I suppose you have a lot of questions?"

"Not really."

Carolina glances at me warily, her hands tightening on the steering wheel as she backs the car out of the space. She maneuvers us toward the garage exit, stopping when we reach the street. She looks over at me. "What now, then?"

"You need to take me to whoever has Agatha."

She nods, then puts the car into park, popping the trunk as she exits and walks toward the back. She disappears, then the car moves where she's rummaging around the dead guy. She closes the trunk with a thud, and she's back in the car, handing a phone to me. "Text Vincent."

I open the text app, quickly typing out a message to Vincent letting him know the mission was complete and we're awaiting further instructions. Only a few moments go by before a reply comes in, and I read off the address to Carolina, who pulls out onto the street without a word.

I watch her silently. Her hands are flexing on the steering wheel. The tension rolling off her is palpable as she clenches and unclenches her jaw. Finally, I ask, "Can I ask you one question?"

She glances at me, raising her brows. "You can ask me any fucking thing you want to, Darius. I'll tell you anything you want to know."

"I only need to know one thing."

"Anything."

"Who did they take?"

She flinches, a pained expression crossing her features as she replies, "My daughter."

I nod, turning to look out the side window. I always figured Carolina was straddling some kind of line between sides. While I felt she was genuine in most of our interactions, you can always tell when someone's holding back. I tend not to pry because everyone has their secrets. Even now, knowing her intentions conflict with my own, I still don't.

It's likely that, regardless of our individual secrets, one or both of us is going to end up dead at the end of this. I'll be protecting Toni, and she'll be protecting her daughter, and all we can do is sit back and hope at the end of it all, they will at least be safe.

It doesn't take long before we pull into the parking lot of yet another warehouse. This one appears relatively new, especially compared to the last few we've been in. Regardless, I'm still entirely fucking sick of warehouses, and if I get the chance to revamp my operation, there will be no more warehouse-like structures.

Carolina weirdly parks in the corner of the parking lot, and I look at her questioningly. She gives another small shrug. "No cameras over here."

"How would you know that?" I ask, frowning.

"I handled the security in most of their locations. They seem to not remember it most of the time, which so far is benefiting me."

I chuckle, shaking my head. "I'll tell you what. If we make it through this shit alive, you and I are going to sit down for a long talk with an enormous bottle of whiskey."

"Deal," she replies with a tentative smile.

For all I know, I'll meet my maker with a bullet to the back of my head from her own hand. But for some odd reason, I'm willing to chance it.

We both exit the vehicle, and I follow her around to the door on the far side of the building. She digs into her pocket, pulling out a small object wrapped in what looks like a bloody handkerchief. She unwraps it, revealing what appears to be a severed finger.

"What the fuck Carolina?" I say with a grimace. "You seriously went back there and cut off that fucker's finger? And then you put it in your pocket?"

She grins at me. "Did you think you're the only one with tricks up your sleeve? Your ego is huge—huge."

I shake my head, muttering to myself, "It's true. I'm fucking surrounded by crazy-ass women."

She does a little jig with her shoulders as she presses the finger against the reader, and the light turns green. She opens the door, wrapping the finger back up with the handkerchief and placing it back in her pocket. "In case I need it later."

I grimace again. "Just don't let it go through the laundry."

Her face twists in distaste. "That's gross. Why do you have to be gross?"

I give her a smile as we make our way through the door and into a hallway. "I'm gross? You have a severed finger in your pocket. I think that takes the cake on gross."

"You know very well that in this business, we do whatever we must—gross or not."

I nod, falling silent as we quietly make our way into the building. She makes her way down the hallway, obviously knowing where she's going, but to me, it feels like the long way.

She puts her hand up, stopping me as she peers around the corner, then motions for me to look around her. I step close to her, then lean over so I can get a look at the other room. Agatha is tied to a chair, but there's no one else in my line of sight. Unfortunately, that doesn't mean there's no one on the far side where I can't see them.

Carolina indicates for me to wait, then she squares her shoulders and walks into the room like she owns the place. She walks right up to Agatha, who's snarling behind the gag in her mouth, but when Carolina leans down and whispers into her ear, she settles slightly. Agatha's eyes shoot daggers at Carolina as she straightens and asks loudly, "Where the fuck is everyone, bitch?"

Agatha narrows her eyes at her, cursing threats behind her gag, which makes Carolina laugh as she looks around the room, then glances back at me. Turning her attention back to Agatha, she says, "I guess I better go find them. The fucking incompetence of these idiots."

She heads off in the opposite direction, and I slowly make my way into the room. I glance around the room as I ease nearer to Agatha, and once I verify that there is indeed no one there, I hurry to her side. I quickly remove the gag from her mouth, then move behind her and work on releasing her hands. We work together to untie her ankles from the chair, and she stands up slowly, stretching her muscles as she moves toward the hallway where I came from. I reach out, grabbing her elbow, and she turns to me. "What? We need to get the fuck out of here, Dare."

"We can't leave Carolina here."

Agatha scoffs, glaring at me. "Fuck her. If I see her again, I'll kill her."

I shake my head. "She's doing whatever she has to do, Agatha. It's not personal."

She yanks her arm from my grip and snarls, "Don't tell me it's not fucking personal. Because of her, I got my ass kicked. Because of her, I got to hang out tied to a chair for hours. Because of her, everyone's locations are compromised."

"That may be true, but also, because of her, I'm here getting you out of here. She didn't have to bring me here."

She gives me a murderous look. "For all you know, she brought you here because that was part of her orders. To get you to come here willingly so we can then end up with our throats spliced open."

"They have her daughter, Agatha. She's only protecting her, kind of like how we're protecting Toni."

"I don't fucking care. And you shouldn't care either."

She's right. I shouldn't care. As soon as I verified Carolina had brought me to the right location, I should've snapped her neck. I'm not even sure why I didn't since it's not like I have any genuine affection for her. Deep down, I don't really give a fuck about her at all, so my hesitancy to eliminate her is quite out of character.

"Regardless, I'm not leaving her here. So, you can scurry off if you like, and I'll meet up with you later."

She screams silently behind her clenched teeth, her hands balling into fists, which she raises in front of her and shakes. She inhales sharply through her nose before expelling the breath loudly out of her mouth. "Fine. I'll help you. But if this backfires, like I figure it will, I'm going to kill you myself."

"Deal. Let's go."

We head in the direction in which Carolina disappeared, pausing every few feet to listen. It's eerily quiet so far, and since there aren't any places to make turns, we continue straight down until we reach the end of the hallway, where it opens into another spacious room.

I hear the faint sound of voices, but then the voices suddenly get louder. Someone is shouting, and then there's the sound of what can only be a fist hitting flesh.

I tense up, and it's only Agatha squeezing my arm that stops me from rushing in. I look over at her, and she glares at me. "Don't be a fucking moron."

I nod, and she leans closer, whispering, "I know who I'm looking for, so I'll go first."

I nod again, stepping back and allowing her to pass.

I watch her take a few steps into the room, and then I follow.

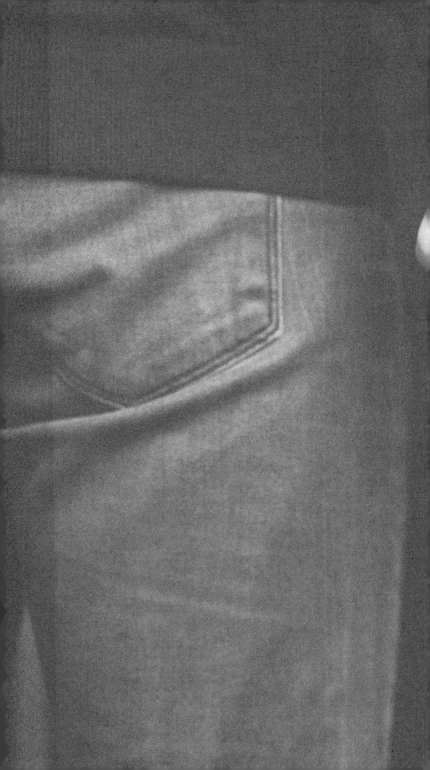

Chapter Thirteen

Toni

I'M JUST COMING BACK out of my room when I hear Tony and Matt cursing a blue streak. They're racing around the living space, shouting obscenities, shaking their phones, and accusing each other of being the worst dipshits ever born.

Lilith is standing in the kitchen, watching them with disinterest, so I walk over to her, taking a position beside her as they carry on like fools. "What are they going on about?"

She shrugs. "I don't know. I'm waiting for them to shut the fuck up and explain the issue to the rest of the class."

I nod, standing back and watching them dart around the room aimlessly. Finally, Matt races over to us, setting a tablet on the counter and tapping away like a madman. "Fuck. Fuck!"

Tony hurries into the room, another tablet in his hands. He sets his tablet beside Matt's, then peers over at his screen, grimacing at whatever he sees there. "This is fucking bad. How could you let this happen?"

Matt glares at him. "Me? What about you? You got the same fucking message I did!"

Tony glares back. "So, fucking what? You're the one in charge of coms. You should've been all over that shit!"

Lilith and I glance at each other, then Lilith speaks up. "What the fuck is the problem now?"

Tony and Matt look at her with matching guilty expressions, but they don't say anything.

I wait a moment, then step closer, pushing Matt out of the way and snagging the tablet that's on the counter. It's open to text messages, and I slowly read the message stating the mission has been compromised and help is needed.

The message was sent over an hour ago.

From Darius.

Which means he must have sent it from the parking garage while he was waiting for Agatha.

I turn my gaze to Matt, who can barely meet my eyes. "Where is he now?"

Matt swallows, his jaw clenching before he replies. "Both his phones show he's still in the parking garage."

I turn to Tony, my heart in my throat as I ask, "And was he there?"

He shakes his head, reaching into his pocket and pulling two phones out, which he sets on the counter next to the tablet. "I found these, but he's nowhere to be found. He must have ditched them when we didn't immediately reply."

A look of shame crosses his features for a moment, but then he takes a deep breath, and it passes. "We're already tapping into the cameras in the garage. We don't have GPS on Agatha's car, but we know the make and model, so we'll attempt to trace it once we know which direction it was headed when it left here."

I nod, my heart pounding in my chest as I let the reality of Dare's disappearance sink into my bones. I laugh, and all three of them give me a look, which makes me laugh even harder. Finally, Lilith asks, "What the fuck could be funny right now?"

I attempt to stifle my laughter but mostly fail. So, I choke out, "Dare got himself kidnapped again. Like, how is that even possible? It's completely preposterous."

Lilith stares at me, not saying anything. But I see the glint of humor in her eyes and the twitching of her lips as she forces herself to remain silent. "You have a point. It is entirely ridiculous, and I will happily heckle him about it once we get him back."

Tony and Matt nod in agreement, and I swallow back the rest of my laughter before it turns into complete hysteria. Because even though I see the humor in the situation, I'm still terrified we won't get him back.

Matt and Tony are both tapping away on their tablets and now they're also on the phone, barking orders about camera angles and locations. I take it all in for a few moments, then interrupt their information-gathering mission. "That's all entirely unnecessary."

All three of them once again look at me like I'm a crazy person. Tony speaks first. "What the fuck are you on about? How else are we going to find him? Crystal ball?"

I glare at him, pulling my phone out of my back pocket and tapping a few buttons before turning it around to show them the screen.

And the little green dot that's blinking a merry jig.

Matt's eyes widen, and he snatches the phone from my hands. "How? What? Holy fuck, how is this possible?"

Tony snatches the phone from Matt's hands, holding the screen inches from his face so I can see the blinking green dot reflected in his eyes. "This is Dare? Are you sure?"

I nod. "Of course, I'm sure. Unless he managed to lose his fucking watch again, not even an hour after I gave it back to him."

Matt grabs me by my biceps, swinging me closer to him so he can look me in the eye. "You gave him back the watch? Just this morning?"

I nod again, and he yanks me into him, wrapping his arms around me and lifting me off the ground. "Oh, you wonderful, crazy fucking genius."

Tony comes up behind me, wrapping his arms around me so I'm sandwiched between them. I glance around until my eyes meet Lilith's. "A little help here, Lils."

She smiles at me, walking over and completing the group hug.

I squirm, but it's no use. I'm a prisoner.

I give them a few moments to enjoy their sigh of relief, then shake them off. I step back, putting some space between us in case they decide to get touchy-feely again.

Matt turns his focus back to my phone, tapping away on his tablet and then handing my phone back to me. "Shockingly, he's at a warehouse on the other side of the city. A very nice warehouse, but still a warehouse."

"Of course he is." I huff, rolling my eyes.

I look around, noting the absence of the two goons in the living room. "Where'd our guests go off to?"

Tony gives me a bland look. "Disposed of."

I scowl. "Well, did you learn anything from them or what?"

He nods, but remains, so I look to Lilith. "Lilith?"

She yawns and blinks at me, so I yell, "Would someone please tell me what the fuck you learned from our unwanted guests?"

Lilith winces, raising a hand up as she says, "Okay, okay. Jesus, keep your voice down. I'll tell you."

I glare at her, crossing my arms over my chest as I wait for her to continue. She glares back at me, mirrors my stance, then walks over to stand beside me. "We're dealing with some guy named Vincent who apparently runs an underground operation that deals mostly in skin trade but also dabbles in arms and drugs. There are limited details about this Vincent outside of the specific jobs those two had been sent on, mostly being watching Darius, and searching for you. It seems their orders were to snatch Darius and/or outright kill you, but there was a bit of discrepancy on the kill you part. So, I guess we're lucky the other people took Darius because the alternative wouldn't have been ideal."

"Who is Vincent? And what did I ever do to him?"

Lilith shrugs, pulling out her phone and holding it out to me. "Maybe you recognize him?"

On the screen is a blurry photo of a youngish man staring un-smilingly at the camera. I take her phone from her, squinting down at the picture in confusion. He seems oddly familiar, but no distinct recognition jumps out at me, so finally, I hand it back to her. "No idea."

Lilith puts her phone back into her pocket, then rubs her hands over her face briskly. She looks over at Matt and Tony. "We ready to do this shit?"

They both nod, gathering their things and heading off toward the exit to the parking garage as Tony says, "We'll meet you there. We need to make a stop first, so don't do anything stupid."

Lilith goes to follow them, then stops, turning back toward me as I stand there. "You coming to rescue your man or what?"

She holds her hand out to me.

I take it.

And off we go.

Chapter Fourteen

Dare

I'M NOT SURE WHAT I thought I was walking into, but I'm almost certain this wasn't it.

The first thing I see is Carolina being held up by her hair and some idiot motherfucker slapping the shit out of her.

My blood boils, and Agatha punches me in the sternum to get my attention. I glare at her, and she scowls back. "Keep it together, asshole."

I give her a curt nod, shaking the fog from my brain and refocusing my attention on our surroundings. There are only a few other people in the room, which means there are likely a lot more lurking in the shadows, waiting for a reason to show themselves.

I assume the idiot motherfucker slapping Carolina around is the Vincent who sent the yahoo out to pick me up. He's tall, maybe a few years younger than me. He also looks oddly familiar, a feeling I'm never comfortable with.

Always know your enemies.

I turn back to Agatha. "Shall we make an appearance?"

She nods. "May as well."

I steadily step forward, my voice ringing out through the room. "Put the lady down, dipshit."

Agatha groans beside me, jabbing her elbow into my side as she hisses, "For fuck sake, Dare. Ever heard of subtlety?"

"I gave up on subtlety a long time ago," I say with a shrug.

She shakes her head at me, then walks further into the room, stopping when she's a few yards from the idiot motherfucker still holding onto a now-bleeding Carolina. "Let her go, Vincent. She did exactly what you asked her to do."

His expression remains impassive, but he uses his grip on her hair to shake her, and she whimpers in pain, her hands gripping his wrist to ease the pull on her scalp. His voice is void of emotion as he replies, "Don't tell me how to manage my fucking wife."

I barely keep the surprise off my face, but Agatha turns and gives me a look. I frown at her. "Hey, you're the one who hired her to act as my beloved, not me."

Her frown deepens, but she doesn't reply as she turns back to Vincent and crosses her arms over her chest. "Let her go. You got what you wanted: we're both here. Tell us what the fuck you want so we can all go home."

He releases his grip on Carolina, letting her fall to the ground in a heap. He motions to one of his men beside him. "Get her the fuck out of here and don't let her out of your sight."

The man nods, bending over and lifting her off the ground with more care than I would have expected. Vincent isn't paying any attention to either of them. His focus is now directly on me. "Darius

Hughes, you slippery fucking twatbag."

I incline my head at him but remain silent. I'm too furious to say anything productive, anyway.

His gaze shifts to Agatha, his eyes full of rage. "And you, dear sister."

Now, I do frown. "Sister? Agatha, what is he talking about?"

She glances back at me. "I have no idea, Dare. Why don't you ask him?"

"I'd really rather not."

She sighs in exasperation, then turns back to Vincent. "Where would you ever get the idea that we're siblings? I don't know of a fourth sibling, never mind a brother."

He snorts, walking closer as he explains. "Well, you likely don't know shit being raised halfway around the world by that snake, Angelo. He only ever had his own aspirations in mind when he agreed to take you on. Keeping you away from your true family was only the beginning of his deception."

She yawns. "You're not telling me anything I don't already know. Get to the fucking point."

He glares at her, coming to a stop in front of her. "I'm the baby who died in childbirth when you were a toddler. I wasn't dead; I was taken and hidden away until the time was right to push buttons on the entire operation. Then your stupid fucking sister went and got herself tied up with that fucking twatbag and ruined all my plans."

He points at me like he wants to stab me in the heart for getting with his sister. But this means he's been lurking around far longer than the last six months.

I step closer to him, leaning in so I'm in his personal space. "And when exactly did you find out I was tied up with Toni?"

He gives me a humorless smile. "When is not important. But that bitch ruined my plans more than once, and retribution is at hand."

My entire body tenses at his words and I restrain my urge to reach out and choke the life out of him at the mere inference that he means to harm Toni.

Agatha gives me a pointed look, and I ease back, putting some space between us before I give in to my urge to end him for good. It's important that we make sure he's the one at the top before eliminating him. Because if he's not, he may be the only link to the person attempting to destroy us.

Agatha gives him a patiently annoyed look. "You're going to have to be more specific, Vince. Toni has fucked up a lot of plans for many people, but I don't see anyone else wasting incredible amounts of time and money attempting to hunt her down. So that means you either have a much bigger axe to grind, or you're just a dumb motherfucker. Please tell, which is more accurate?"

Vincent's jaw clenches, and he steps closer to Agatha, raising his hand as if he's going to strike her. I step forward, grabbing his wrist and yanking it back down. "I wouldn't do that if I were you."

He turns his furious eyes on me, his lip curling in disdain. "Or what? You're going to step in and protect her?"

"Hardly," I say with a snort. "Believe me when I say Agatha can protect herself perfectly fine with no help from anyone."

He frowns, but his arm relaxes enough that I finally release my iron grip on his wrist. He steps back a bit, his gaze suddenly shifting behind me, and his face blooms into a huge smile. "Well, well, well. Isn't this a pleasant surprise?"

I groan, and Agatha curses beside me. "Toni, turn around and leave right now."

Toni glares at her. "Not without Darius."

Agatha rolls her eyes, groaning in frustration. "What is with you two and your distinct lack of self-preservation?"

I open my mouth to respond, but Vincent interrupts. "Now, now. Let's not scare our beloved sister away just yet. We have so much to talk about."

I glance behind me, the look of shock and horror on Toni's face clear as she remains frozen in place. Lilith is a few feet from her, a wary expression on her face as she takes in the scene before her.

I look back at Toni, and she appears to be zoned out, staring at Vincent as if he's a ghost.

This can't be good.

Toni

My fucking brother.

How is it even possible that I have an adult brother I never knew about?

I look at Lilith, who's shaking her head at me, her hands coming out in front of her as she shrugs helplessly. "I had no idea, Toni. I was always told the baby died. He must have taken him and sent him away like he did all of you."

I take a shaky breath, attempting to clear my head of the riot currently taking place in my brain. There's a stabbing pain, like a lightning bolt up my spine, and then white-hot heat settles behind my eyes and at the base of my skull.

He's running his mouth again about his lovely sisters and how nice it is to finally be in the same room together, like a family. His words and the look of maniacal rage on his face don't match at all, and the more he speaks about siblings, family, trust, and loyalty, the more I keep thinking about Lilith and her shortlist of rules for engaging with an enemy.

One of the first rules Lilith taught me was to never go into a dangerous situation and let the enemy speak.

Once you get your sights on them, once you have confirmation of who they are, you never give them time to speak. Because the time an enemy takes to speak is more opportunity for them to turn the tables on you.

That's all that's in the back of my head as I'm staring at this fucker, watching his lips move, yet I'm unable to make him stop.

I'm not a good enough shot to hit him from this angle. Lilith might be, but she's on the wrong side of the room. Tony and Matt still aren't here, and I keep praying with every itty-bitty ounce of me that may believe in a god that one of them will drop from the ceiling and shut that motherfucker up. Still, for now, his mouth keeps moving, acidic words falling from his lips and polluting the air, cutting us all down with their poison.

I'm not even entirely sure what he's saying through the roaring in my ears, but tiny zaps of electricity keep shooting up my spine every time he brings up my mother. No, not just my mother...

No, our mother.

Lilith.

I shift my focus to Agatha, the look of shock on her face the only sign that I heard him correctly.

Lilith is our mother.

That's what he said. There's an odd look of surprise on his face, but it isn't until the conversation shifts again that those little bolts of electricity turn into what feels like a hot iron rod shoved into the back of my skull.

My breath catches, and I double over as my stomach flips. I can't quite grasp what his words mean: double-cross, duplicitous, liar.

I am a double-crossing, duplicitous liar.

Me.

I frown, a whimper falling from my lips, uncontrolled and uninhibited.

I glance at Lilith, who has a pained-yet-furious expression on her face. I see her fingers twitching, and I'm certain she's wishing she had a sure way to get him to shut the fuck up.

I can't catch my breath.

I glance over as Darius's voice breaks through my panic, and I hear him telling me to breathe.

Breathe.

Breathe.

Breathe.

I finally manage to take a painful inhalation of air, then quickly exhale on a sob. But the fucker's lips are still moving.

Never let the enemy speak.

I still don't have a shot.

His lips are moving again, but so are Agatha's and Dare's—all this chattering of voices swirls around me, and I choke down the bile rising in my throat.

Lilith.

My mother.

Me.

The enemy.

I'm the enemy.

In my head, I hear myself screaming. I hear my denials, my refusal to believe any of this is true.

But the look on Lilith's face doesn't lie.

My *mother* doesn't lie.

I watch her face, my voice a broken whisper, "Why? How?"

She shakes her head, her eyes never leaving that fucker, and I glance over and see his lips are still moving.

Never let the enemy speak.

The roaring in my ears increases, that hot iron rod digging further into my psyche. I bend over and dry heave, then I hear a tussle on the other side of the room.

I glance up and see Agatha being dragged away. She's fighting the two men attempting to overpower her, but more join in, eliminating her efforts to get free.

Never let the enemy speak.

I see that fucker has shifted my vantage point on one side, giving me a bigger opening in which to make him stop talking.

Darius is speaking to him, and then they're exchanging infuriated words, with their faces reddening in rage, spittle flying, and curses booming. Two men come out and pull Darius back, keeping him from putting his hands on that fucker who's still talking. Darius struggles, and more men come out to restrain him, rendering him immobile—a chained beast.

Slowly, I stand, my hand pulling out the pistol I keep hidden on my ankle, gripping it firmly as I rise to my full height.

Breathe.

Just breathe.

That fucker is laughing. I don't know what he's saying, but the look on Dare's face is nothing less than murderous, and he struggles even harder. I see Lilith out of the corner of my eye as she slowly eases closer to me, and it appears as if the group of men on the other side of the room have yet to notice she's there.

I don't want to believe any of the words that have fallen from his treacherous mouth, but there's no missing the pained fire in Lilith's eyes as she continues to edge closer to me. Beneath the rage, beneath the murderous glint in her eyes—there's sadness.

That fucker laughs again, raising the gun in his hand and pointing it at me as his words suddenly become clear. "And now you can watch the fucking bitch die."

Never let the enemy speak.

I don't have time to think. I raise my gun with my steady hand at the same time he raises his, and I squeeze the trigger, mentally bracing myself for the blast and the kick.

Click.

I pull the hammer back again and pull the trigger. Click.

His eyes light up as he points his gun at me, throwing his head back and laughing, the pure glee behind it making my skin crawl as his lips move again.

Agatha is shouting from one side, and Darius is shouting from the other, both struggling against the groups of men holding them back and still, that fucker's lips are moving.

Never let the enemy speak.

I growl deep in my chest, the vibrations tickling the hot iron rod that continues to stir my brain, and I scream, "Shut up!"

I pull back the hammer and squeeze the trigger in quick succession. Click. Click. Click.

Boom.

My unfortunately timed game of Russian roulette has my last squeeze of the trigger letting loose like a cannon, and now that fucker is not talking. He's frowning.

His eyes narrow, and he's still pointing his gun at me, and I give no fucks as I see the blood blooming on his white shirt. I'm sure the smile on my face can only be described as a self-satisfied, evil grin, and as those warm tingles shoot up my spine into the back of my skull, I laugh.

But then all hell breaks loose.

For a moment, I'm frozen, unable to move, but then the next thing I know, I'm knocked to the side as bullets rain down. Everyone's shouting, screaming, and cursing, the metallic smell of gun smoke, fear, and rage swirling in the air.

The wind is knocked out of me from the force of being knocked down onto the concrete floor. Pain rips through my side, and a heaviness drapes over my body, so I lay there for a few moments, eyes closed, in a daze.

Slowly, the fog in my brain dissipates, as does the screaming, shouting, and cursing, until finally, all I hear is the whir of a fan, the rumble of a train, and water dripping.

My side aches relentlessly, and the weight on top of me takes what's left of my pained breath. I peel my eyes open, and I stare up at the shadowed ceilings. The lights blink at me. The fans turning in a slow rotation, almost mocking me.

I slowly raise my head, grimacing as my abs contract and a new pain slices through me. I look down and see the weight holding me down is Lilith sprawled over me, so I give her a little shake. "For fuck sake, Lilith. Get off me."

She doesn't move immediately, so I wiggle around until she slides to the floor beside me. "Lilith?"

I look down at myself, covered in blood. I know I'm hurt, but I also know this isn't all mine. My heart stops in my chest, my breath suddenly stuck in my throat. "No, no, no, no, no."

I sit up, scooting closer to her and rolling her onto her back to look at her face. Her eyes are closed, and she's so pale I can see her veins through her skin. I place my ear against her chest, releasing the breath I was holding as I make out her heartbeat, faint but steady.

I shift again, getting up on my knees to take inventory of her injuries. It doesn't take me long to find the two holes in her chest, and

I watch in horror as they push out blood with every beat of her heart. My stomach drops, the bile rises again, and I push away from her and pull off my coat, bunching it up and pressing it against her wounds. Then I yell, "Lilith! Lilith!"

Her eyelids flutter, her face twisting as her eyes slowly open and meet mine. My eyes stare back at me. Her eyes. My eyes.

She gives me a small smile, then coughs, a bit of blood spraying out as she does so, and I whisper, "No. Don't do this, Lilith."

She swallows, clearing her throat as she whispers back, "It's okay, Toni. Everything's going to be okay. You'll see."

I shake my head at her, leaning my weight onto her to put more pressure on her chest. "I don't know where the fuck you think you are, but this doesn't feel okay. Don't you fucking die on me."

She laughs softly, then winces. One of her hands settles over mine that's pushing on her chest, and her other hand reaches up, moving the hair from my face, then cupping my cheek. She's looking at me softly, a small smile on her lips. "I wish things had been different. I wish you'd known your entire life how much I love you. I wish I'd had the option to dote on you, to nurse you, to show you deep affection as a mother should. All I can do now is hope you understand how I always did as much as I could to protect you, to show you in any way I could just how much I love you."

A sob gets stuck in my throat, and I shove down the agony, swallowing painfully. "I guess you'll have to make it up to me now, won't you? You know me. I'll never believe it unless you show me."

She smiles and laughs, and I hear her breathing, the odd wheezing gurgle that punctuates each exhalation. I choke back a sob, whisper-shouting, "Don't you die on me. God fucking damnit, don't you dare die on me."

Her grip on my hand eases a bit, her hand on my cheek slowly falling to rest on my forearm. She has a vacantly dreamy expression, and I lean closer to her as she whispers, "I wish I had time to show you, but I don't think we have the time. Everything you need to know, you can get from Micky. He's going to need you, too. He's going to be so pissed I went off and got myself killed."

I choke on a bitter laugh, tears streaming down my face as her grip on my hand gets more and more lax. "No, no, no. Don't do it. Don't fucking die. I'm not ready. Don't go. Please. Please."

"It's okay, love. It doesn't hurt."

I sob, the pain in my chest unbearable as I watch the life slowly seep from her eyes. I shake her a few times, the tears coming so freely now I can barely make out her face in front of me. But she doesn't move. Her hand simply falls from mine, and she's gone.

"No, no, no. Please, no. I need you. You can't leave me. Please, Lilith. Please. Please. Please."

My upper body falls on top of her, my cheek pressing against hers as pain slices through me. I sob, curse, beg, and plead. She remains motionless beneath me. Cold. Unyielding.

I'm still sobbing when Tony and Matt show up, and then I turn my agony onto them, screaming and cursing at them for not being there to stop this. I scream and swear until I'm a limp, broken mess, still clutching her to me.

Tony grabs onto me, wrapping his arms around me tightly, his voice broken yet calm in my ear as he tells me I need to let her go. I struggle against him, the agony intensifying as I fight for him to let me go.

Matt's yelling, but I can't make out his words, and then Tony's hands are on me, and he's going on about the blood as he pokes and prods me. The pain in my side sharpens, and he pulls his shirt off, folding it and pressing it against my torso. He removes his belt, wrapping it around me, securing the shirt when he pulls the leather so tightly I feel it dig into my flesh, and for a moment, it takes my breath.

But then he wraps himself around me fully, using his leverage to shift us both away, and I cry and fight harder, sobbing as Matt scoops Lilith up and walks away with her.

Tony shifts behind me, his face against my neck. I vaguely make out what he whispers in my ear, and I hear the pain in his voice as he tries to tell me everything will be alright.

But it won't be alright.

And I'm still screaming when darkness takes me.

Chapter Fifteen

Dare

THERE'S AN ANNOYING CLICKING.

It takes me a few moments to realize my eyes are open in a room so pitch black that I can't see anything surrounding me. I groan, trying to sit up before scrapping the idea and lying back in my prone position.

I hear my name whispered from somewhere in the room, and I freeze, holding my breath as I listen for the sound again.

My name is uttered again, but the sound is so far off I can't place which direction it's coming from in the darkness.

I force myself to sit up, fumbling around until I twist my body and place my feet on the floor. I hold my breath again, cocking my head in the direction I feel the sound is coming from.

Then I hear it again; this time, it's my name and a whole string of curses.

Agatha.

I rise, giving myself a few moments to steady myself as the darkness swims before me. Then I turn slowly in the direction I feel the voice is coming from. "Agatha?" I whisper. "Say something else so I can find you."

She laughs, then rambles out a steady stream of various curse words. I continue shuffling in her direction, eventually running into a wall, so I stop there, listening to the sound of her voice to determine which direction she is in. "Are you against the wall?"

Her voice comes from the darkness, clearer now. "Yes, I think I'm in a corner."

I move to the left, figuring if it's wrong, I still have three more chances to find her. I feel my way along the wall for what feels like days, though I'm sure it's only a few minutes, but then something brushes against my shoulder. I reach my hand out, meeting what feels like an arm suspended next to me. "Do they have you suspended from the ceiling?"

"Sort of. My hands are connected to the wall at such an awkward angle that I can't lift or put them down, but then they have my neck attached to what I guess is the ceiling in the corner. It's fucking annoying."

I slide my hand up her arm until I meet a metal cuff around her wrist. "This feels like a standard lock. Super easy to pick, even in the dark."

"I figured as much. And I have a hairpin we can use when the time comes."

"Do you want me to do it now?"

"No. Not until we have some kind of plan."

I release her arm, then back up against the wall and slide down to the floor at her feet. "Well, this is inconvenient."

She laughs bitterly. "That's an understatement if I've ever heard one."

She's quiet for a few moments, then I hear what sounds like a pained gasp cut through the darkness. I reach my hand out so I'm touching her leg. "Are you okay?"

"No."

"Yeah, me either."

I feel numb. Even the ever-present beast in my chest is silent. I don't dare overthink what happened in that warehouse. Briefly, it's bad—excruciatingly so.

Her normally authoritative voice is small as she asks, "Do you think they're alive?"

"They must be. I can't even entertain the alternative."

"Same. I keep reminding myself that it would take more than that idiot motherfucker to cut them down."

I clear my throat, taking a deep breath as I push down the pressure building in my chest. "What the fuck happened? How did we end up here?"

She laughs, the sound broken and brittle. "Oh, it was quite the spectacle. I gotta give you credit, Darius. It took eight of them fuckers to bring you down, and for a moment there, I thought you were going to win. And even after all that, they had to outright tranq you like a giant fucking horse. Of course, then I was worried you were dead. I think they didn't chain you up when they brought us in here because they thought you were dead, too. Eight big brutes climbed on top of you, and somebody stuck a needle through somewhere, and that was it...you were out like a light. Then it was them fuckers complaining that you're a heavy bastard."

"Did I at least take some of them fuckers out?"

"Oh, yeah. You were making easy work of them until you were out-numbered. They couldn't knock you out with their hands, though, hence the drugs."

"I guess it's too bad that I'm not a fucking hand grenade."

"A hand grenade would have come in quite handy. I feel like if they die, we die."

I tighten my hand on her leg, unsure of how to respond. She's not wrong. If either of us makes it out of our current predicament and doesn't find Antoinette and Lilith alive and well, we may as well be dead. And we will both do our damnedest to eradicate the world of the rats that keep polluting it.

And in the process of this, we will probably meet our own end.

Her voice cut through in a whisper. "Is it true?"

"Which part?"

"The part about Toni being the enemy."

I nod, then realize she can't fucking see me, so I clear my throat and choke out, "Yes."

"You knew?" Surprise laces her voice.

"Yes. I knew."

"You've been protecting her all this time?"

Again, I nod and roll my eyes at myself as, once again, I force myself to speak. "It's not like that. Sure, Toni initially went into that job with the focus of reeling me in, and for quite some time, she did just that. But then, something happened where she had to choose a side once and for all, and she chose us. I think that's why they took her. She was labeled as a disloyal whore, and they were going to sell her off to the sex trade. You get a lot of money for the daughter of a boss, and even more so if that daughter is also tied to me and Lilith. Seems not very many people like either of us."

"So, she knew about our so-called brother, this Vincent?"

"No, I don't think she did. She may have known Vincent, but I don't think she ever knew he was blood-related. I don't think she knew who was pulling the strings or calling the shots. We had little time to get into details because shortly after we came to terms with her background and the shift in our relationship, things changed. They stole her from me."

"So, technically, you've known this Toni longer than the previous Toni?"

"Yes. Sometimes, I worry this Toni will be the only Toni."

"That's a distinct possibility. But that leads us to the other burning question: how the fuck can Lilith be my mother?"

I loudly blow out my breath. "Yeah, my mind is seriously fucking blown over that revelation. Not that I've ever asked Lilith how old she is, but I never got the impression that she's old enough to be your mother."

"She would've been young. I can't even imagine what happened, but I know that our dad, or grandfather, I guess, was a ruthless motherfucker. So, god only knows the story behind that."

I grimace, my jaw clenching at the mere idea of what likely went on with Lilith when she was young. "It seems there are a lot of stories we'll need to get out in the open if we ever get out of here. Maybe if we cross-reference what we each know, we'll find something relevant."

Agatha shakes her leg in my grasp. "Maybe you should start now. Tell me about you and Toni and what happened between you. You protected her, knowing she was working for the enemy. You continued to protect her for all that time, even though she had no idea who you were or what you had. So many paths, yet that's what you did. Why?"

I sigh. "Our history is complicated, and having to put it all out of my mind for long was excruciating. Her doctors told me since her brain wiped clean all the traumatic events in her life, it was in her best interest to allow these events and the people linked to them to remain hidden until the time came when they showed themselves. And since

I was obviously removed from her memory as well, then the best thing I could do for her was protect her from afar."

"You must really care for her."

"Yeah, well. She was mine then, and she's mine now, just as she has been mine for every moment of the time that she has not remembered us. The void in her memory doesn't erase that fact."

Agatha scoffs, shaking her leg in my hands again. "That's it? The whole 'she's mine' line? You've been protecting this woman for ages, and that's all you've got for me? 'She's mine'."

I pause for a moment, attempting to put into words the chronic ache in my chest I feel when she isn't near me. "It's like Elizabeth Barrett Browning said, '*I love thee to the depth and breadth and height my soul can reach when feeling out of sight, for the ends of being and ideal grace*'. She is the depth, breadth, and height of my soul; my soul will call to hers every moment of every day until my dying breath. It's like she stole an immense piece of my being, and everything else around me is darkness. Every moment I lived before her is irrelevant because the man I was then no longer exists, and I'd sooner lay down and die at her feet than even contemplate going back to my previous hollow existence."

Agatha is silent for a moment, but then, as I'm contemplating cracking a bad fucking joke, she says, "Well, fuck. Darius. How did you keep all of that in for so long?"

"Discipline and control?" I respond tentatively, slightly hopeful she won't force me to go into detail, while knowing full well the chance of this happening is zero.

"Nice try, dickhead."

I take a deep breath, holding off for a moment as I gather my thoughts on how to respond. It's embarrassing, really, admitting my complete lack of control during that time. Finally, I say, "I tried to remove all of it from my mind and move forward as if it had never happened, but it was easier said than done. I failed at every turn, had one huge blowup after another until finally Matt stepped in and begged me to ease the rage inside me."

"Oh shit," she responds quietly. "What the fuck did he expect you to do?"

"Hypnosis," I say with a laugh, my hand squeezing her calf as she giggles. "At first, I was dead set against it, but after a freak out or three, I finally relented. It took a couple of tries, but eventually they numbed me enough where I could go about daily life without losing my shit at every turn."

"You really are fucking crazy," Agatha states with a chuckle.

I nod to myself, huffing out a breath in agreement. "Yeah, but mostly out of necessity. Matt didn't realize the effects were wearing off until Toni showed up at his precinct demanding to be taken to me, and he was so mad at me, but I wasn't even fully aware of what was happening, and I had no idea why he was so mad at me. It was complete lunacy." I pause, thinking back to that time and chuckling again as I continue, "Looking back now, I'm certain I started unraveling because I noticed a shift in her...in the little nuances and side comments. The look on her face when I would catch her watching me. Something inside me took it as a sign that there was something there, and I unconsciously attempted to force her into remembering."

"Maybe I jumped the gun. Maybe everything that has happened from the moment I stuffed her in my trunk until now is my fault, and if I had continued to lie low and pretend everything was fine, we wouldn't find ourselves in our current predicament. Maybe none of the dumb shit that has happened would have come to fruition if I had continued to suppress the beast inside me that continuously vibrates with the need to possess her."

Agatha's cackle echoes around me and I can't help but smile as she crows, "You stuffed her in the trunk? Classic romantic move, there, big guy." She pauses, laughing a bit more at my expense and then sobers as she says in a more serious tone, "I don't think any one person is to blame for our current predicament. I think it's likely if any of us had chosen a different course of action, the outcome would remain the same. Maybe we should have left when we had the chance instead of doing your exceedingly stupid idea of going after Carolina. But maybe not. Maybe if we had left, Toni still would've gone barreling in there and ended up face-to-face with the devil, in which case, she would've caught a bullet right in the face. But one thing about it: if we had not gone in there, if we had not gone after Carolina and found out what we found out, we'd still be in the dark. At least now, regardless of what happened in that warehouse after we left, we know what we're up against. Not that it matters if we die in this fucking dark cell. Wouldn't that be fucking poetic? We meet our maker via dehydration."

I can't help but laugh. She's right. Wouldn't this be the most fitting, anti-climactic death for us there ever was? No guns, no glory, just the rats eating our remains in the endless blackness. "Oh, don't fucking say that. I think I'd rather be strung up and tortured than die here in such a boring way. After all the shit I've lived through, I should at least be allowed to die in agony, knowing I didn't spill my guts to the very end."

Agatha's laughter echoes with mine as she says, "At least I'm strung up from the ceiling in a somewhat fitting manner. You were left to roam around the room like you're not even a threat at all. So much for all those years of people trying to bring down the *Beast*."

I snort-laugh, allowing myself a moment to find humor in our ridiculous circumstances. "If it comes down to it, I'll come over there and let you chew out my throat so that it at least looks like I died in battle."

She laughs even louder. "But you know I've never actually done that, right? I don't know what the fuck is wrong with those other two, but the idea of chewing out somebody's throat does not appeal to me, that whole biohazard thing, and all. Maybe that's because I've never been put in a position where that was my only choice, but I don't see that ever happening."

"I have no idea, but the one time I witnessed Lilith chew out a throat, she had all the choices in the world. That was her go-to."

She takes a few deep breaths, her laughter dying down as she says, "Lilith. My fucking mother. I can only imagine the atrocities that molded her into the crazy fucking psycho she is. I'm not even sure I want to know."

I nod in the darkness, standing up and moving in front of her. "I can't imagine it's a pretty tale. Are you sure you don't want me to get these chains off you?"

"Fuck, no. I'll be fine. If they don't come back after a few more hours, I'll think about it. So far, this is child's play."

"Something tells me there's a story behind that line, too."

"There's always a story, Dare. Most of them are not worth the retelling."

I turn around, moving closer to her and pressing my back against her front as I stoop underneath, then stand, lifting her onto my back. "Let me ease some of the strain for a little while, anyway. I've rested long enough; it's the least I can do."

She giggles into my ear, her chin resting on my shoulder. "I won't say no to that. But only for a short time, then you should go back and lay down, continue playing dead."

"I will."

"Dare?" Her whisper cuts through the pitch black.

"Agatha?"

"They're okay."

"Of course they are."

She doesn't say anything else, but I feel her shiver behind me, and I know we're doing the same thing.

Praying.

Chapter Sixteen

Toni

About a year ago

I come awake in stages, my blurry vision clearing more each time I attempt to rouse myself to my surroundings.

I'm not sure what happened or why I'm so disoriented, but I know whatever it is, it can't be good.

Part of me wants to hide, to feign sleep until I'm forced to face whatever awaits me, as if the cause will miraculously disappear, and I'll wake in my bed, this entire episode nothing more than a fragmented memory.

"I know you're awake."

I frown, that gritty voice sending a shiver down my spine, and I grind my teeth against the urge to whimper.

Dare.

I swallow past the lump in my throat, steeling my spine and opening my eyes. I blink a few times, clearing my vision, and there he is, kneeling before me in all his beast-like glory.

He looks me in the eye, his golden gaze glacial, and the heaviness in my chest is suffocating as I watch him watching me.

He knows.

I don't bother saying anything, having learned long ago that you offer no information until you know what information they're seeking. And even then, you offer no information on the punishment of a long and torturous death.

He remains silent, then his hand snaps out without warning and wraps around my throat, squeezing viciously. His other hand comes up, his fingers delving into the hair at the nape of my neck, then tightening painfully as he holds my head in place as he slowly stands. The chair I'm chained to goes back onto two legs, and he uses his two-handed grip to hold me, suspending me in the air, and I'm torn between two very different emotions.

Fear and arousal.

He straddles my legs, his upper body leaning over me until his face is directly in front of mine, and the smile he gives me is cruel, feral even, and I'm relieved for the lack of air preventing me from whimpering in response.

He runs his nose across my cheek to my hairline, his whispered words tickling my ear. "Did you think it would work? Did you think it would be as easy as wooing me with your tits and ass, and I would become a slave to you?"

I still can't speak, his grip on my throat preventing me from taking in any air. I focus on not struggling, adapting to the loss of oxygen, not allowing my body to overcompensate with useless adrenaline.

He licks the side of my face, then bites my cheek—hard. I flinch, his dark chuckle near my ear sending a shiver through me, and I twitch helplessly, unable to control my body's reactions to him. "You dirty, dirty little minx. You get off on the fact you know you're in big, big trouble, don't you?"

I don't bother trying to deny it by attempting to shake my head in his iron grip. He knows me too well to buy any kind of brush-off anyway, and any type of reaction would play into his hands at this point.

I have two options here: attempt to pretend what he knows is untrue or play into what he knows until a better option shows itself.

Of course, the likelihood that a better option will show itself is basically nil, but it doesn't hurt to try.

Either way, I'm dead.

He continues his torturous assault, nipping, licking, and biting my face, my ear, and the corner of my mouth until I'm mere seconds from passing out from arousal and lack of oxygen.

Without comment, he pulls back from me, the chair abruptly crashing forward onto all four legs while his hands release their grip on me. I gasp for air, then cough violently as the influx of oxygen gets stuck in my throat.

While I'm relearning how to breathe properly, I watch him prowl around the room, dingy and dark as it is, until finally, he grabs a chair and places it directly in front of me. He sits down, leaning forward with his forearms braced on his thighs, those golden eyes glittering with malice as he says, "Fuck you for making me want you like this."

The distraught whimper that escapes me catches me off-guard, and I attempt to cover it with a forced coughing fit, but it's too late. He sees me. He knows.

"Why?"

I raise my brows at him but remain silent, and he leans closer to me. "Tell me why, Toni. Tell me why you would do this to me."

I clench my jaw, staring at him intently, watching the micro expressions on his face shift behind the cold indifference prominent on his features. I feel myself crack at the tiny glimpse that flashes before me—agony, betrayal, despair.

I push it back, stuff it right down beneath the concrete edges known as the job, family, loyalty, and obedience. I try to stomp it down, but then he leans in a little closer, those golden eyes boring into mine, and he does something completely unexpected. He lets his mask fall.

Bit by bit, the fractured pieces fall away from him, and all that's left is the tiny edge of rage encapsulating the despair.

The betrayal.

The agony.

It bleeds before me, the catalyst that breaks free the guttural and animalistic response I fear will shatter me into pieces right before his eyes.

Once again, I can't breathe, but this time, it's not because of his hand encircling my throat, physically taking my breath. This time, it's my own vitriol, my own duplicitous nature attempting to choke the life out of me. Words refuse to take form; my inner turmoil a tornado inside of me, and I squeeze my eyes shut to block out the answering storm.

His fingertips touch my cheek, and I flinch away, only to have his hands grip me. His breath touches my face as he says, "You fucking look at me. You open those lying fucking eyes and look at what you've done."

My eyes flutter open, unable to resist the call of his command. His gaze is unblinking; his words are quiet and tinged with pain. "Tell me why you came into my life for the sole purpose of bringing me to my knees. You need to tell me why."

I stare into his eyes for a few moments, inhaling slowly through my nose to gain control of my overwhelming emotions. Then I answer, "No."

His jaw clenches to the point I think his teeth will shatter, and he squeezes my face painfully before shoving away from me. He picks up the chair he'd been sitting in and heaves it across the room.

Then he goes *ballistic*.

I see now where he earned the reputation of the Beast. He wreaks havoc along one side of the room and down the other, demolishing anything not nailed down, and even a few things that were until the entire space looks like a fucking war zone.

He goes quiet for a moment, his chest heaving, his hands fisted at his side. Then, in a blink, his face is directly in front of mine, the wild look in his eyes so completely unhinged I wonder if he's even there anymore.

I open my mouth to say something, but before I can get a word out, his mouth is on mine, his teeth biting my lip until it splits, then his tongue shoves into my mouth. The growl that comes out of him pours into me, igniting me, and I can't stop myself from straining closer. Our lips crash together, our tongues entwining and our teeth biting violently as we each fuel the feral need that's swirling around us.

Just as quickly as he was there, he's gone again, and I gasp for breath, swallowing that metallic taste down, unsure if it's from him or me.

He's standing before me, blood dripping down his chin onto his shirt. His shoulders sag, and he looks down at the ground, taking a few deep, much-needed breaths.

But then he shifts again, his shoulders straightening as his head comes up. He looks at me with his body stiff, his teeth bloody as he bares them at me, and spits out, "Are you waiting for me to be on my fucking knees?"

He drops to his knees in front of me, and I'm shaking my head in denial, completely unsure of what's happening but still incapable of forming any coherent words.

He reaches behind him and takes out a revolver, checking the cylinder for bullets before holding it by his side. "You wanted to see me on my fucking knees, Toni? Is that what you've been waiting for? It would be one thing if you'd come in like the fucking deceitful viper you obviously are and physically knocked me down. But for you to go to such great lengths to snatch my soul and wrap it around your own so fucking intricately, now, that--" He pauses, shaking his head as he laughs bitterly. Then he quiets, his eyes refocusing on my own. "That was the work of a fucking genius. Never in my wildest dreams could I have ever imagined that anyone would dupe me in such an epic way, least of all a woman."

I'm still shaking my head, but the words won't come out. They're still held back by a lifetime of duplicity, by family loyalty. Adherence to the job at hand, that's all that matters. He's a job. He's a fucking job.

As though he's in my head, he repeats it to me, "I'm a job, Toni. I'm a fucking job. I don't know who fucking taught you, but they did a great fucking job. I feel like I should hunt them down and shake their hands, but you know I won't do that. Instead, I'll hunt them down so I can rip out their lungs."

He lifts the hand holding the gun, pointing it at me. "Tell me why, Toni. It's the least you can do after playing me for so long."

I'm still shaking my head, an invisible hand squeezing my throat, choking my denials, my explanations. He's no longer breathing heavily; the maniacal light has deadened into glacial apathy as he continues to stare at me.

"If you don't tell me, I will kill you."

"Go ahead." My voice breaks free finally, and his eyes widen, his hand tightening on the gun. "Do it."

His eyes narrow, but his gun hand remains steady. "You'd rather die than tell me why you set me up? Why you betrayed me?"

I grind my teeth together and avert my gaze from his and await my imminent end. I deserve it. There's no point in dragging it out.

"I don't fucking think so." His voice drags my attention back to him as he lowers the gun, then turns it on himself, pressing the barrel under his chin. "You wanted me dead so badly that you came in here and infiltrated my life. So, I may as well give you what you came here for, so you can get a pat on the back and a kill bonus."

My heart stops in my chest. "Don't."

He raises his brows at me but doesn't drop the gun. "Don't what? Don't do it myself? Were there stipulations to bringing me down? Someone else wants the honor?"

"*Please*. Don't."

"You don't want me to shoot myself? Then tell me why?"

I shake my head again, and the fury burns in his eyes. He removes the gun from beneath his chin. "Let's play a game, then." He opens the cylinder, pushes the bullets out onto the ground, then picks up one and slides it back into the chamber. He stares at me, giving the cylinder a spin before waving it between us.

"One for you and one for me."

I grit my teeth. I can see he's serious, the familiar, determined glint in his eye taunting me to intervene. He points the gun at me, and I raise my chin, meeting his flinty gaze with a matching one of my own as I say, "Just do it. Stop with the unnecessary theatrics and fucking kill me. Just get it over with."

He cocks his head, lowering the gun as he replies, "You'd like that, wouldn't you? For me to allow you to get off easy by ending it now. You won't get that fucking lucky."

He turns the gun back on himself, and as much as I try to school my features, as hard as I attempt to keep my body in a neutral position, I can't do it. He knows me too well.

I see the minuscule widening of his eyes as understanding dawns on him. He gives me a bitter smile, his words just as glacial as he says, "So, you're okay with dying, but you don't want to watch me die. How interesting."

He presses the barrel of the gun more firmly under his chin, and I clench my teeth. My heart pounds in my chest so violently, I hear the blood pushing through my veins. I inhale slowly through my nose, but I feel the slight tremor in my lips, even with them pressed so tightly together. The job. Family. Loyalty.

Click.

He stares at me, unblinking. "That's one. Where do you think the bullet is? Do you think it's number two? Maybe number four? Shall we find out?"

A small whimper escapes through my clenched teeth. Fire burns behind my eyes, the heaviness in my chest suffocating me.

Family. Loyalty. The job.

I try to focus on the mantra of my entire being, but the meaning behind them becomes smaller and smaller as Darius continues to study me, the barrel of his gun still pressed firmly beneath his chin.

Click.

"Well, that's number two. Isn't this poetic? You get to complete your job without getting your hands dirty."

My whole body is shaking.

This isn't what I want.

Loyalty. The job. Family. It all shifts inside me, imploding inward until I don't even know what they mean through the sheer agony sending my heart into overdrive.

I shake my head. "No. No. No."

He narrows his eyes at me, his grip on the gun tightening, and my eyes squeeze shut as I continue to chant, "No. No. No. No. No."

Every time the denial falls from my lips, it gets louder. I'm thrashing my head around furiously. I feel the fiery burn of tears trailing down my cheeks as I pull against the restraints, begging and pleading for it to stop.

Family. Loyalty. The job. None of it fucking matters.

But this needs to stop.

I hear his voice cut through my hysterics, and it's still calm and cold. "What are you saying no to? You don't want me to die? This is what it's come to; the least you can do is have the decency to open your eyes and watch what you've done. You open those lying fucking eyes and enjoy how you did what no one else has ever managed to do: bring the Beast to his fucking knees!"

"No. No. No. No. No." The words fall from my lips, broken and guttural, my head shaking with such force I'm rattling my brain in my skull. I'm struggling, forcefully trying to release myself from the restraints so I can physically remove the gun from his hand, even if it means turning it on myself to make it all stop.

Fuck family. Fuck loyalty. Fuck the job.

Click.

He shrugs, sighing as he says, "Oh, that's three. We're almost there now."

"Stop it. Stop it. Stop it. No. No. No. No. No." I'm choking on the words now; the sobs in my chest break loose, and tears flow freely from my eyes, which are squeezed shut for fear of seeing him completely wrecked before me.

The sounds falling from me are that of a wounded animal, and it feels like my heart and guts are being ripped right out of my body because he won't stop, and I can't get free.

I squeeze my eyes even tighter against the chaos before me, and soon, I'm screaming and sobbing incoherently, begging for him to stop, pleading for him to let me take it back, to let me fix it. He's no longer talking. I can't hear him moving through the wails of my voice echoing through the room, and I brace myself for the imminent sound of the gun going off.

Click. Click.

Boom.

I'm screaming, choking on family and loyalty and the fucking job. Choking on my tears, my breath, and the bile in my throat. I squeeze my eyes shut so tightly the tears can no longer escape, my breath caught up in my chest as I don't even dare to breathe.

And then, after a few moments, I force my eyes open, bracing myself for the bloody mess I will find in front of me.

But there's no mess.

He wipes his mouth, then holds his hand up in front of me, now smeared with red of his own blood, his eyes hard on mine as he says, "I am on my fucking knees before you, the blood of your enemy drying on my hands yet still you refuse to let me in. Tell me, what the fuck do I have to do?"

I sob with relief, hesitating as my eyes meet his furious ones. My body sags in the chair, whispering, "Let me go."

He shakes his head, throwing the gun to the side, his hands resting on the top of his thighs as he whispers vehemently, "Never."

He slowly stands, then walks over until he's in front of me. He cups my cheeks, both of his hands holding my head in place as he stares into my eyes and leans in close. "Is that all I am to you? A job?"

A small whimper escapes, but my response is clear. "No."

He nods sharply, but says nothing as he moves behind me, releasing my hands from their restraints. He does the same with my ankles, and then I sit there in the chair, my entire body shaking with tears still streaming down my face as the pressure in my chest releases.

He sits on the floor in front of me, grabbing my hand and pulling me until I slide into his lap. He jostles me around until I'm lying sideways across him, my head against his shoulder, my face pressed against his heart, pounding powerfully in his chest.

He's rocking me gently, his arms like steel bands around me, and I instinctively struggle a bit, asking, "What are you doing?"

He lowers his head until he's looking into my eyes, and my breath catches in my throat at the calm fire in his as he replies, "Taking care of you."

I frown but don't say anything in response. I squirm closer until he shifts, his head lifting, so I'm staring at his chest instead of his eyes.

I'm shaking so hard my teeth chatter, but the tears are slowing, and he presses his face against my ear, whispering, "It's okay. I've got you."

I clutch at him, once again grappling to get closer. "I don't know what the fuck I'm doing anymore."

His arms tighten around me, squeezing me to the point it should be uncomfortable, but it's not enough, and I whimper again. Then he says, "None of us do. All we can do is our best."

A bitter laugh falls from my lips. "What if my best isn't good enough?"

"You're enough. You'll always be enough."

"What if I'm not strong enough?"

"You are. You are."

I lean into him, allowing him to hold me up. "Don't let go. Please don't let go."

He exhales, his arms around me tightening until I can barely breathe, but I don't care. I sink in deeper as I let myself cry, his words a whispered promise against my ear.

"I'll never let go."

Chapter Seventeen

Matt

ANTOINETTE HAS BEEN OUT for a while.

She lost a lot of blood from the bullet wound that almost went overlooked during the initial chaos.

I called in the doctor we keep on the payroll, who said she's lucky it was through-and-through, a flesh wound that will probably annoy for a while. He cleaned it out and then stitched her up, putting in a small drain he says we can remove in a day or two once the drainage has dissipated.

Tony has been prowling around like a caged animal, and I've been actively preventing him from putting together his own version of an elite special forces team to go after Darius and Agatha. It's been difficult to keep him in check because he's furious at everyone involved, but mostly at himself.

Losing Lilith is going to be immense. We're not entirely sure what happened, and we won't know until Antoinette wakes up and briefs us. That's the biggest reason I'm not giving him free rein to go utterly apeshit on the world. We can't go blindly into this because that will only get more people killed.

But Tony is so deep into the blame game right now that he's not thinking clearly. So far, he has blamed everyone you can think of in this scenario, but mostly, he's blaming us. Because lord fucking knows if the two of us had gotten there sooner, none of this would've ever happened. Because he would have prevented it. Because he's fucking superman.

He's also an asshole.

I look over and see Toni's eyes are open. She's looking in my direction but not directly at me, her unfocused gaze lost.

I rise from my seat and move closer to her, kneeling on the floor beside the bed. "Toni? Are you okay?"

She blinks, then her eyes meet mine, but she says nothing as she shrugs her shoulders and shakes her head simultaneously. So, I ask, "Do you want me to sit with you?"

She nods, but when I move to grab the chair from the other side of the room, her hand on my arm stops me. I look at her questioningly, and she says, "Sit here with me, please. I have so much to say."

I frown but move around to the other side of the bed, piling the pillows up so I can sit beside her more easily. I climb up beside her, and she tries to turn toward me but winces, so I lean over, moving the pillows around, helping her get situated so she's reclining but able to look at me without straining herself.

She gives me a sad look, her eyes haunted. "What is it, Toni?"

"Is Tony here?"

I shake my head. "No, he stepped out for a few minutes. Do you want him to come back? Now?"

She nods, so I pull my phone out of my pocket and send him a message, telling him to come back now because Antoinette is asking for him.

We sit silently for a few minutes, and then Tony comes barreling into the room like the human hurricane he is. He strides to the side of the bed and leans over her, looking her over thoroughly.

Finally, he pulls back, crossing his arms over his chest as he looks at her sternly. He goes to open his mouth, but she raises her hand and stops him as she says, "Not now, Tony. You can berate me later all you want, but first, we have other things to talk about."

Tony scowls at her. "What could possibly be more important than what just happened?"

"I remember."

"You remember what, exactly?"

"Everything. My entire existence."

His eyes widen, and I feel my eyes mirroring his as I say, "Fuck."

I wish she had told me this before I had Tony come back. There are a few things Tony doesn't know, and it's going to piss him off even more. I know little more than Tony does, but there's one thing that fell into my lap completely by coincidence, and Darius insisted we not tell him.

I totally get why, but I have a feeling it's all about to come out now.

Tony walks to the other side of the room and grabs a chair, dragging it over by the bed where he sits, eyeing her expectantly. "So, how far back do you think you need to go to begin with?"

"I don't think it matters how far back I go. I need you to promise me you won't say anything until I'm done. And I also need to speak to Mickey. Once I've said everything I need to say, and Mickey has filled in the gaps, only then can you speak."

His eyes narrow, but he nods, then asks, "Do you need Mickey here now?"

"That would be ideal, but video will do, given the circumstances."

"He's actually here," Tony replies. "He got in an hour ago and went to a hotel nearby."

"Please call him and have him head this way," Antoinette says, relief clear in her voice and on her features. "I'll start the story while we wait for him."

Tony pulls his phone out, putting in a quick call. Mickey must've been by his phone because he barely says two words before he hangs up and says, "He's on his way."

The look of sadness on Antoinette's face deepens, and she takes a deep breath through her nose. I can see she's pushing the distress back, so I reach my hand out, squeezing her arm gently. She turns her head, her eyes meeting mine. "It's okay, Toni. Say what you gotta say."

"First, the man who has Dare and Agatha is my younger brother, Vincent. I knew nothing about him. No one knew anything about him that I'm aware of. That part of the story will have to come from Mickey."

Tony looks at me, and I raise a shoulder and shake my head. This is unrelated to any of the things I know that might piss him off. Tony nods at her to continue.

"I didn't know he was my brother. I didn't really know them at all. Most of the orders I've received throughout my existence came from unknown entities. I lived with my family, who, deep down, I knew wasn't my family, but we never questioned it. If you were born into the family, your purpose was to do as you're told. Loyalty. Obligation. The job. Family. It's all a fucking joke. You become so accustomed to being abused in one manner or another that it's all the same. Nothing fazes you. You have no memories. You have no feelings. You have no soul. Any of us could slit the throat of one of our so-called brothers or sisters and not even blink. We learned not to care."

Tony leans forward, resting his forearms on his knees, giving her an impatient look. "What the fuck are you talking about, Nettie? You were brought up in the suburbs of California, the upper-middle-class spoiled princess of a Dr. Philip and Diane Moreau."

She laughs humorlessly, shaking her head as she replies, "Yes, that's the story. And they did a good fucking job with it, considering you, of all people, still believe it. I guess that answers my question about whether Darius ever told you the complete truth. I know Matt knows because he's the one who told Darius of his suspicions that forced him to confront me. But then, shortly after that night, I was taken to that warehouse, and everything went to shit. So, I wasn't sure what happened from there."

Tony's narrowed eyes focus on me as he grits out, "What the fuck is she talking about, Matt?"

"That's for Antoinette to talk about. I did my part by telling Darius what I knew and letting him take it from there. He told me to take it to my grave, and I will."

Tony's furious gaze focuses back in on Antoinette. "Tell me."

She glares right back at him. "Don't forget your promise, asshole."

He grinds his teeth together but then sits up, resting his palms on his thighs like that makes him appear any more relaxed than he is. He inclines his head at her to proceed.

She shifts on the bed, wincing as her hand presses on the bandage over the bullet wound on her side. "My last job was Darius. I got orders I was to work at this company to get close to Darius Hughes, a.k.a. the Beast. It's kind of funny, though, because I knew little about the inner workings of the underground or the down-and-dirty, bloodthirsty criminal's comings and goings."

"So, when I first went in and got a look at Darius, I thought I had the wrong person. It wasn't until the first time I badgered him, and he put his hands on me, that I realized what a fucking volcano he was. The way he wears those starched white shirts and carefully pressed trousers, his spit-shined shoes, and those stupid fucking paisley socks. He was so soft-spoken and well-mannered that it was hard to picture him truly unhinged. But then, one time, I'd gone into his office to give him a daily dose of annoying, and he came out from behind that desk and picked me up by my throat, and holy fucking shit. For a few moments there, I really thought that I'd gone too far, and he was going to snap my neck."

I laugh softly, interrupting her. "I remember that. You made him fucking batshit most of the time. He worked hard to get himself out of the criminal world, to remove himself and become Darius Hughes, and then there you were, poking his buttons all the time in the office. He was not accustomed to anyone teasing him or going out of their way to be annoying. Throughout his adult life, people mostly stayed out of his way. They feared him. People still do fear him because he has a habit of coming out on top, regardless of how bad the odds are against him. But other than you being fucking irritating, he kept most of your interactions close to his chest. That's how I knew he really had a thing for you."

She gives me a small smile. "How did you find out I was the enemy?"

"It wasn't so much I found out as I fell into it. I saw you out one day, and I was going to speak to you, but no sooner had I turned toward you had somebody else joined you. Some man I didn't know at the time, but you had a heated discussion, and he grabbed you. I was going to intervene, but then I heard him say something about the job."

She nods. "He told me to keep my eye on the job. He could sense my focus was off, and he was reminding me what would happen if I lost sight. Because if you fail a job, they're not going to kill you; that would be a waste in their eyes. There's always some kind of monetary gain to be had. That's why, once they realized I was likely compromised, they took me. They were going to sell me. They'd get a good price for someone of my standing in the skin trade—"

Tony interrupts, his voice full of rage and the look on his face incredulous. "So, you're telling me you're the enemy? And all of this happened because of you?"

"Well, I guess, in a nutshell. I mean, it's a little more complicated than that. But yes."

"Complicated? How? You're gonna have to give me a little more information than that if you expect to live through this conversation."

Antoinette doesn't even flinch. She gives him a bland look and rolls her eyes. "Shut the fuck up. You're not gonna kill me. I understand that you're angry, but it wasn't my decision to keep you in the dark about this. And it's not like I could've fucking told you since I didn't remember any of it."

He goes to say something else, but instead, he snaps his mouth shut, clenching his jaw. I understand why he's mad. But he also should understand that none of us can tell Darius what to do. He told me not to say anything, which means I would've said nothing. That's how we work.

Antoinette grabs the glass of water off the bedside table, takes a drink, and places it back on the table before continuing, "I remember when Darius confronted me. I'll never forget that look of betrayal in his eyes. He asked me why. Why would I do that to him? There was no good answer, but then he pushed me and pushed me until the why didn't matter anymore because it no longer existed to me. The only thing that existed for me at that moment was him. And any world where he didn't exist was no good to me. Even now, I don't want to live in a world where he doesn't exist. You don't have to believe me, and I wouldn't blame you for not believing me, but try to remember that you don't even know me. All you know is Nettie."

Tony's jaw clenches even harder. He blinks rapidly, looking away from her. I can tell he's conflicted. Tony doesn't like very many people. He loves even less. I know he loves Nettie, but that doesn't mean he won't kill Antoinette.

Antoinette gets a strange look on her face, so I ask, "What is it?"

She blinks but doesn't turn her gaze on me as she replies. "Dare reenacted some of our previous interactions. He must've hoped they would trigger my memories without causing harm." She pauses, her eyes meeting mine questioningly. "Did you know about that?"

I groan and squeeze my eyes shut, but then Tony's angry voice cuts through, forcing them open again. "Yeah, Matt. Did you know anything about that?"

I glare at Tony, then say, "Yes and no. It isn't a simple answer."

"Well, maybe you can summarize it a bit without getting into trouble with your boyfriend." Tony sneers, his face twisted with rage and what may be hurt.

I sigh and rub my hands over my face. There isn't an easy or fast way for me to explain what went on with Darius in the aftermath of Antoinette's attack. I look between the two of them, both staring at me expectantly, then sigh deeply, my eyes meeting Tony's as I respond, "Listen, Tony. Darius was a complete train wreck for weeks after Antoinette lost her memory. I'm sure he would've explained the full story to you if things had been different, but there didn't seem to be a time, given she was a mere shadow of her former self. Maybe you don't remem—"

Tony cuts me off, his words fueled by anger as he snaps, "Of course, I remember one of my closest friends morphing into a fucking animalistic cyborg. I'm not fucking blind, Matt. I was going to intercede, but then he seemed to get control of himself, and I didn't think there was anything to be concerned about. Was I wrong in this judgment?"

I sigh again, shrugging as I shake my head. "You weren't wrong, but that change wasn't because Darius suddenly learned how to cap his rage. He tried repeatedly and couldn't get himself under control, so we had to go to extreme measures."

Tony raises his eyebrows at me, but it's Antoinette who asks, "Extreme measures?"

"Hypnosis."

"Fuck," they both say at the same time.

I nod, sighing even deeper as I think back on when Darius finally agreed to have someone hypnotize him into forgetting what pained him. "It took a few tries before it worked, and it wasn't always entirely effective, but it took that sharp edge off his emotions and allowed him to carry on with some semblance of calm."

Tony sits back in his chair with a troubled expression but doesn't say anything. Antoinette is staring at me in shock, so I give her a small smile, which she returns. Then her hand grasps the top of mine and squeezes once before releasing me, clearing her throat as she composes herself.

There's a knock on the door, and I look up to see Mickey standing in the doorway. He looks like shit. He nods in greeting, then walks into the room.

Tony rises, indicating for Mickey to take his chair close to Antoinette, and then he walks around the other side of the bed to sit in the chair closer to me.

Mickey sits, reaching his hand out and taking Antoinette's in his. He bends over, resting his forehead on top of her hand, and his shoulders shake.

It's a difficult thing, watching a grown man cry.

Antoinette rests her free hand on top of his head, the tears she's held back until now stream freely down her face.

I look away, fighting back the burning behind my own eyes, and when I glance over at Tony, I can see he's doing the same.

You don't have to love someone to mourn them. You don't have to be in love with someone to feel the loss of them. Sometimes, you don't even have to like someone to feel the sadness that they're gone.

Mickey loved Lilith. Antoinette loved Lilith. And I liked and respected her well enough to feel the ricochet of her loss reverberating throughout the room.

And Tony? The black death shining in his eyes speaks volumes about what he won't tell any of us.

After a few moments, Mickey straightens, giving Antoinette's hand a last squeeze before he releases her, pulling a handkerchief from his pocket and wiping his face and nose. Then he looks at her, taking a deep breath as he begins, "Your name is Antonia Rossi. You are the eldest daughter of Antonio Rossi. Lilith was very young when she was tasked with seducing the head of the Rossi family. It was known that Antonio had a thing for younger women, but I believe that if not for the alcohol and the lighting, he never would've touched her. When he found out what happened, he was furious, but there wasn't much he could do about it at that point. He couldn't marry her because it wasn't legal, and if anything had been brought to light on it, he likely would've gone to jail. So, Antonio and your grandfather made a deal that you would be raised here, then at some point in the future, you would go to him to learn how to take over."

Antoinette frowns at him, asking, "What do you mean 'eldest'? What about Agatha?"

Mickey shakes his head. "You and Agatha are not twins. I know the resemblance is uncanny, and you're very close in age, but you're not twins. Agatha's given name is Agatha Moretti. Not long after you were born, your grandfather sent Lilith back out again. This time, to the bed of Angelo Moretti, the eldest son of Paulo Moretti. He was one of Italy's most powerful and ruthless men, and the fact that Paulo didn't eliminate the entire Ferro family line was a testament to the sheer level of strategic planning on your grandfather's part. He coerced both powerful men into going along with his plans and didn't suffer any repercussions until years after, and that was by the hands of his own daughter."

Antoinette makes a pained noise, and I glance over at her, my hand reaching out to rest on her arm. She looks at me and says, "Can you imagine? She was a child, having to whore herself out." She looks back at Mickey, her brows drawn down as she asks, "To what end? What was the point of it?"

"Power. Your grandfather sent Lilith in as a glorified broodmare to the most powerful men in the world with the idea he would have direct ties in all corners of the criminal world. It was a terrible thing to do to her, but from the perspective of someone hoping to attain more power—"

He doesn't have to elaborate any further; we already know. Power breeds power. It was a truly despicable way to treat your own child, but in the grand scheme of reprehensible acts, it doesn't even come close to the worst of all. So, I ask, "How many times did he have her do this?"

"Vincent was the last. She almost died giving birth to him. They lied and said the baby died when, really, they took him away so they could shape him into the monster he is now. And while she was ill, they took Agatha and shipped her off, telling Lilith that Agatha had died. Then, they took her last remaining child and shipped her off in a separate direction. Lilith found you, but she had to keep this knowledge a secret so they wouldn't move you again."

"Vincent has a different father?"

Mickey nods. "Yes, his father is a Russian, Dmitri Petrov. This job went south quickly, though, as Dmitri is a truly vile man who has little regard for anything beyond power and money. Lilith never told me everything that happened while she was over there, but I got the impression Dmitri was abusive and cruel. There were even questions on whether Vincent was Dmitri's child because of rumors he used to pass her around as punishment. It took your grandfather months to get her back, and by then, she was a shell of her former self. She never truly recovered from the experience, and Dmitri never got over the fact Lilith betrayed him, even if she was only acting on orders from her own father. He would have tortured her to death if they had given him the chance."

I grimace, and Antoinette makes a pained sound in her throat. "Did he make her do it again after that?"

"I believe that once Lilith was over the age of consent, your grand-father would've stopped using her in that way because, without the threat of backlash or criminality, they wouldn't have had any real leverage. But after everything that happened with Dmitri and losing Vincent, it wouldn't have worked anyway since she couldn't have any more children."

"But she ended up getting married?"

Mickey scoffs. "Marrying Jimmy was a means to an end. She was fond of him, but there was no genuine love there. She certainly didn't have any hesitation in getting rid of him. I don't think she ever would've wanted to have more children, though. She spent her entire life fighting to survive; she wouldn't have willingly subjected more innocents to that life."

Antoinette laughs, bitterness lacing her words as she asks, "But why does Vincent hate me so much? I'm not anything to him. We don't even come from the same lineage. He can have his fucking Russian empire; I don't give a shit."

Mickey replies, "Oh, Vincent would never be pacified with only the Russian empire. He's so stupid that he thinks he can take over the entire world. He doesn't understand that no one person can rule the world. It doesn't matter if it's the New York underground, Chicago, Miami, Paris, Rome, or Moscow–they all need their own network. They all need separate oversight to run fluidly, or else you end up with anarchy."

"What the fuck does Darius have to do with any of this? Why would they send me to get him?"

"Well, other than Darius and his team single-handedly taking down a fair number of people in positions of power across all networks, Vincent knows that Darius Hughes wasn't always Darius Hughes."

Antoinette groans, holding her hand up to stop him from continuing. "I don't even wanna know. Every time I fucking turn around, some new weird shit happens, and I lose my mind, and then some insane memory gets triggered, and someone dies. I can't take anymore *what the fuck* right now."

Tony speaks up beside me. "That's fair."

I nod in agreement but keep my mouth shut. I'm also having a hard time keeping up with the tangled web all these deceitful fuckers have weaved over the years. I've known Darius for a long time, and I don't know what Mickey is talking about. I look over at Tony and ask, "Do you know what he's talking about?"

Tony shakes his head. "Not a fucking clue. And frankly, I don't even know if I want to know either. If Darius knows and he chose not to tell us, that's fucking good enough for me."

I look at Mickey and ask, "Is this something we need to know now?"

Mickey shrugs. "I don't know. All I know is that Vincent won't just kill him. He'll try to use him for some kind of gain first. He likely thinks Antoinette is dead, so that'll help us, especially since she is a little under the weather."

Antoinette speaks up, "Well, I guess if he would use Dare as a pawn, then we should figure out who he would use him against and start there?"

Tony and I look at each other, then nod in silent agreement. It's not a bad idea. And it's not like we have much else to go on right now.

Antoinette leans forward, wincing slightly and gingerly reaching her hand out to place it on Mickey's arm. She looks him in the eyes and asks, "We're not related, right? Me and Dare?"

This time, Mickey does laugh. "No! Toni, Lilith never would've let that happen."

Antoinette leans back against the pillows, a look of relief on her face. "Thank fuck for something."

Chapter Eighteen

Dare

WE'RE GOING TO DIE here.

It's amazing how strangely time moves when you're sitting around in complete darkness.

Agatha stayed chained in the corner for almost a full day before she finally relented and allowed me to pull the bobby pin from her hair to pick the lock on the cuffs around her wrists and neck. She puts them back on intermittently, but the time in between is growing longer and longer as time goes by. She figures if she's going to die here; she won't die chained.

The only good thing about not having any food is that it makes the whole bathroom issue a little less frequent. I found a sink and a toilet, much like you'd find in a prison cell, off in the far corner, so though it has been a little awkward, we've made do.

Agatha has already said that we will never speak of it.

We've played every type of word game you can dream up. The darkness is almost maddening, though, I suspect we're both well-versed in living in darkness.

We're both lying on the narrow bed, a shitty excuse for one as it may be. Then Agatha says, "I wonder what time it is."

It takes a few moments for me to remember the watch on my wrist. I press the button on the side that tells me it's 1:38 AM. Which means we're working on our third day here.

She sits up so suddenly it jars me as she grabs my arm and exclaims, "You've had a watch this whole time?!"

"Yes, sorry," I say sheepishly. "It's been so long since I've worn it, I completely forgot I was wearing it."

"Is that the watch from Toni?"

"Yes. She gave it back to me right before they got me in the parking garage."

And then she laughs. She laughs and laughs and laughs until I'm sure she must have tears streaming down her face. And I'm confused because I have no fucking idea what could be so funny about a watch. "What the fuck is so funny?"

She laughs for a few more moments, pausing a few times as she tries to get control of herself. And then she finally says, "You don't know?"

Now, I feel stupid, considering whatever is funny must be something I should know. Which means the joke is on me. "Apparently not, so by all means, let me in on the joke."

"That's the watch Antoinette gave you, correct?"

Fuck. "Yes."

She laughs again, so I lay back and let her get it out of her system. Eventually, she settles back beside me, letting out an occasional giggle. She grabs my wrist, turns the watch face toward herself, and pushes the button, and the soft glow of light shines on her face. It's almost startling, considering all I've seen is darkness for so long, but she's grinning at me in a creepy Agatha way.

Her smile gets even wider, and the light goes out, so she presses the button again and looks right at me. "Antoinette put a tracker in that watch. That's how they found us the last time."

"No fucking way. She gave me that watch ages ago."

Agatha laughs again. "She sure did. Back when I was trying to get my hands on you, we pulled in a couple of people who worked with her, and one let us in on that tidbit. That's why, when you got on that plane so many months ago, we took your watch away from you, but we left it for her with a note telling her to drop it or else."

I shake my head, frowning. "A tracker? That fucking bitch was tracking me?"

"And thank fucking god for that. But now, I feel like I shouldn't have told you, and I'm gonna get in trouble."

"You won't get in any trouble, assuming we even get out of this fucking place alive. Do you think they've been able to pinpoint your tracker yet?"

She presses the button on my watch again, and I see her shake her head. "No. If they could locate me, they would've already come to free us. I'm assuming this metal prison fucks with the signal, so either we get out of here at some point, and they'll be able to pinpoint where we are, or we'll just rot here for all of eternity."

"Always the optimist, Aggie."

She drops my wrist as we fall back into darkness again. "I'm not afraid to die. I think my biggest fear would be dying last. Better to die first and not have to watch your loved ones pass on."

"I get that. I don't even know that many people I truly give a shit about, but the few I do, I couldn't watch them suffer. I couldn't live without them either."

We fall into silence again, and all I can think about is Toni. I've done my damnedest to put it out of my mind while we've been here, but the silent, seemingly endless darkness echoes those thoughts back to me. I truly feel that if she was gone, I would know. That the emptiness inside me would become so finite it would draw me down into the earth itself. I worry for Lilith, too, though, that's mainly for Antoinette and Agatha. And then there's Matt and Tony. I didn't see them in that warehouse, and that's extremely concerning.

Regardless of whatever has happened, I'm sure everyone is playing their own version of the blame game—myself included. So, it's all for nothing. Regardless of the choices any of us have made over the last year, it's likely we all still would've ended up in the same place. Just like if it's our time to die in this room, surrounded by darkness, then we'll die here.

There's a strange rattling on the far wall, and Agatha springs up and rushes to the far corner of the room. She's been doing intermittent speed drills with those restraints for most of the entire time we've been in here. Now, I'm curious if she can get those things back on before someone opens the door. *If* someone even opens the door, since the last few times we heard something out there, nothing came of it.

This time, I hear voices or what sounds like several people having a heated argument. It quietens, and I hear the slide of deadbolts being drawn back. The door cracks open, light filtering through the pitch black. I squeeze my eyes shut as pain lances across them. I turn my body away from the doorway, squinting across the room at Agatha, relieved to see that she's once again in position. We couldn't come up with any kind of workable plan, so I figure I'll play possum, and maybe I'll overhear something useful.

They haven't come into the room yet, but I hear their panicked voices scrambling from the hallway, and it sounds like someone's in trouble. I'm trying to decide who they're going to pin it on when I hear them talking about "that fucker" and someone "being dead", and I assume they're referring to me. I guess they're lucky I'm not fucking dead.

Footsteps enter the room, and then someone says, "Well, he doesn't look dead."

An unknown voice says, "Doesn't matter what it fucking looks like. Check him for a pulse."

The first voice comes back with, "I'm not fucking touching him. You do it."

Then all the voices argue at the same time about who is and who will not check me for a pulse. It's so annoying that finally, I say, "I'm not fucking dead. Shut the fuck up."

They all fall silent, and I feel their eyes on me. Slowly, I open one eye, checking out the group of fucking idiots in front of me. After a few moments, I open both of my eyes and since they're still not saying anything; I move to sit up. They all jump back, and I can't hold back my laugh as I say, "Oh, for fuck sake. I don't bite."

The big blond one who barely looks old enough to legally drink speaks up. "Yes, you do. I've seen it."

I smile at him humorlessly. "Well, only if they ask nicely."

He takes another step back but says nothing. Dark-beard guy next to him pipes in, "I don't know, I don't think I ever saw anybody ask for it."

Blond guy jabs his elbow into the bearded guy's rib. "I don't think that's what he meant, you fucking moron."

I laugh then, and they all flinch back. This is comical but also strange. "I take it you lot are not with Vincent. Either that or he hires some questionable men."

The blond guy speaks up again. "I don't know any Vincent. All

I know is we came across the shipping ticket about tending to the occupants of this room one time daily and realized that it was dated almost three days ago. So, we were a little concerned."

"Then how would you know anything about my reputation?"

The bearded guy's eyes widen. "Everyone knows the Beast."

I roll my eyes. I'm so fucking sick of that name.

I move to stand up, shaking my head as they all step back again. What's funny is that not one of them has noticed Agatha in the corner, unrestrained and ready to party.

She's abandoned the pretending-to-be-restrained look and is nonchalantly leaning back against the wall. If she wanted to, she could've snapped at least two of their necks before the other three even noticed. I'm surprised she hasn't, but I suppose she probably senses their level of incompetence amongst them. From the looks of her, she's having a pretty good laugh. Likely at my expense, the bitch.

"I guess the real question here is, how much is it going to cost me to get you to drop us at a new location?"

Chapter Nineteen

Dare

THEY ALL STARE AT me as if I've got multiple heads, but no one says anything. So, I try again, "Name your price. I'm good for it."

"I'm afraid there is no price." A new voice from the doorway draws my attention. "As much as I like money, my reputation is priceless."

The new person is standing in the shadows, and I squint my still-light-sensitive eyes as I stare in that direction. I recognize that voice. "Jayme Devereaux, is that you?"

He steps through the doorway, a grim smile on his face as he turns to me and replies, "In the flesh. I can't say I'm overjoyed to see your stupid face under these circumstances."

I laugh. "Honestly, seeing your stupid face doesn't bring me any joy, either. Especially knowing I can't buy you off, even given our colorful history."

He shrugs, inclining his head at me in acknowledgment of these facts. "Last I checked, we were even-stevens, so it's not like I owe you anything. I certainly don't owe you my reputation."

He walks further into the room, waving his hand above his head and pulling on a short cord that illuminates the room with a click. Agatha's agitated voice from the corner draws all their attention. "Motherfucker. There was a light in here the whole time."

"Nearly impossible to find, even if we had tried harder," I reply. We had checked every inch of the walls to see if there was a switch, and we waved our hands around to see if maybe there was some type of string hanging, but it was obviously too short to find.

Jayme stares at Agatha with interest. She glares at him and spits out, "What are you looking at?"

Amusement flares in his eyes, and he gives her a winning smile. "I would think that'd be obvious."

She curls her lip at him. "Don't get any ideas unless you wanna lose those eyes."

He throws his head back and laughs, and she bristles even more. After a few moments, he sobers and says, "Finally, a woman after my heart. I have to say I'm kind of disappointed that I'm required to offload you at the end of the journey."

Agatha continues to glare at him, her arms crossing over her chest. "I guess we'll see about that, won't we?"

The other guys in the room are watching their exchange with interest. Then the bearded one says, "These two don't seem so bad. Why do we have to deliver them if they're more valuable to us having them in hand?"

The dark-haired one answers, "If you get a reputation as someone who doesn't deliver as promised, you won't get any more contracts. So, no more money."

I walk over to Jayme, extending my hand, which he accepts easily. I look him in the eye and smile, and when he returns my smile, I give him a pat on the back and a bro hug. I pull back and say, "Circumstances notwithstanding, it's good to see you."

I don't question Jayme's need to protect his reputation. He likely has more money than god now, but I know he continuously funnels his cash back into good causes, so I don't begrudge him his full payment for delivering me wherever the fuck he's supposed to bring me. "At least we'll get to catch up before you meet your end. Come along. I'm sure you two would like a shower and some fresh clothes. Unless you'd like to eat first?"

Agatha and I both respond. "Shower first."

He leads us out of the room into a hallway, where we take a left. A few doors down, he stops, opening a door on our left, showing a small single-bed cabin with a narrow ensuite. He motions for Agatha to enter, and she gives him a suspicious look, which he returns almost playfully. "You have nothing to fear on my ship. You're welcome to jump overboard, but just know that we're thousands of miles from anything in either direction. It would be a very slim chance that you would make it. Assuming you didn't get picked up by pirates. Most of them are not as hospitable as I am."

She makes a face. "There's no chance of me jumping overboard. Literally zero chance."

"I'm glad to hear it. You can lock the door while you get changed. There are clothes in the wardrobe, likely too big, but they're clean. Take your time. We'll come back for you when it's time to eat, but there are snacks and drinks on the sidebar."

Her eyes light up at the mention of snacks and drinks. She walks into the room and closes the door behind her without so much as a backward glance. I don't hear that she locked it, and I can't say I'm surprised because god save anyone stupid enough to try anything with her.

We continue down the narrow hallway, taking a right toward a dead-end. Jayme opens the door at the end of the hallway, motioning for me to enter before him, then he follows me inside. He closes the door, flipping the lock as I turn back to him and say, "I don't get any privacy?"

He gives me a bland look. "And chance you silently killing my entire crew and taking my ship?"

I laugh at the idea. I'm sure I wouldn't have any problem killing almost everyone stealthily or not; however, he would give me a run for my money for sure. And then there's the fact I don't have the first clue how to drive a ship. I can barely manage a canoe. "There's one thing you should know about me, Jayme. I don't do boats. Just like there's zero chance Agatha will jump into the ocean, there's also zero chance I will steal your ship."

He squints at me thoughtfully, tilting his head as he replies, "Oh, yeah. You're the one who could never maneuver Tony's pontoon boat with any type of accuracy. I forgot about that."

"Does that mean I'm gonna get some privacy, then?"

He shakes his head. "Not a fucking chance."

I shrug, accustomed to having no privacy for the last few months. I strip down, leaving my dirty clothes on the floor as I walk into the bathroom. I don't bother warming up the water. I step into the shower and turn on the taps, groaning as cold water hits me and then slowly warms.

Jayme's voice from right outside the shower interrupts my leisurely wash-up. "So, are you gonna tell me what the fuck's going on or what?"

"I see little point. You have a job to do. End of story."

He's quiet for a moment, but then says, "This is true. But that doesn't mean I'm not nosy enough to inquire."

I snort in response, continuing to wash without further comment. Then he says, rather nonchalantly, "Haven't I seen you in the papers running around with that actress?"

I pause while soaping up my torso. I'm genuinely surprised he would've been reading anything talking about celebrity gossip. So, I ask, "Where'd you see that?"

Jayme doesn't reply, so I quickly finish my shower, turning the taps off and opening the shower door. He's no longer in the room, so I grab a towel and dry off a bit before securing it around my waist and exiting the bathroom.

He's sitting in the chair in the room's corner with a pensive expression. He raises his hand, pointing toward the bed where clothes are laid out for me. I walk over to the bed, dropping the towel and grabbing the clothes as Jayme asks, "You been working out, man?"

I glare at him over my shoulder. "Stop fucking eyeing me up."

He laughs. "Oh, get over yourself. You know I like pussy."

I shake my head, pulling the jeans on, relieved they're only slightly too small. I'm not much taller than Jayme, but it's obvious I've spent more time in the weight room recently. How I found the time for gains is not the point. "You jealous that there is now one hundred percent chance I could kick your ass?"

He rolls his eyes at me. "Eighty percent, tops."

I give him a half-smile, then sit on the edge of the bed to put on clean socks. "Are you going to tell me what the fuck's going on, Jayme? Is it a complete coincidence that I ended up on your ship? Or did you arrange it?"

"It's a coincidence. But if I could have arranged it, I absolutely would have."

"Why? You already stated the importance of your reputation."

"Carolina Tennent."

"You know Carolina?" I ask in surprise.

He nods, then leans forward, resting his forearms on his thighs as he answers, "She's my little sister. And she's in big fucking trouble."

I sigh, rubbing my hand over my face in agitation. Why can't anything be fucking simple? Every time I turn around, there's some additional complication in an already twisted fucking story. "I didn't know you had a sister."

"I didn't know either until recently. Turns out my father had an affair, and she resulted from it. Unfortunately, his problems became her problems, and I can't seem to get close enough to her to fix them."

"And fixing her problems is a big priority for you? The man who gives fuck all about anyone or anything?"

He narrows his eyes at me, but nods. "Yes. She's the only family I have left, and she never stood a chance growing up the way she did. I owe it to her to at least try to salvage her future."

"Only family you have left? What happened to your father?"

"He became shark bait soon after I found out about Carolina," he laughs humorlessly. "Everything came to a head, and he became an unneeded complication."

I'm not surprised by this revelation, given Jayme isn't known for his kindness and understanding—or his forgiving nature. And his father has been a useless fucking twat for decades, so it's surprising it took as long as it did for Jayme to snap. "So, what's the story with Carolina?"

"You tell me."

I lift a shoulder tiredly, sighing as I say, "Apparently, she was planted to play the role of my girlfriend, hoping to snag me and or Toni. They did a good job with her background information and Agatha didn't know she was playing us until she blew her cover to save us."

"She saved you?"

"Yes. I mean, if it wasn't for her interference, it's likely Vincent would've sent a more competent team to bring me in. And she went back in to take the hit for us getting away, but I was too stupid to leave her behind after she stuck her neck out for me."

"Who is she working for?"

I inhale deeply through my nose, taking my time exhaling as I think about my response. I don't know how much Jayme knows about what's been going on in my neck of the woods, and I'm uncertain how much he needs to know, given he has every intention of handing us over at the end of this journey. "I don't know if it's so much a case of working for someone as her doing the bidding of her husband, Vincent."

"Her husband? The Russian?"

"He didn't appear to be Russian, but we didn't really have time for a heart-to-heart, so it could be. I'm still mostly in the dark outside of recent events, and even the information he shared with us may be false."

"But she went with him willingly?"

"No, he knocked the shit out of her, and then someone else carried her out."

"He puts his hands on her?" he asks, his expression darkening.

"I would say yes, and often. And likely not only him."

His expression darkens further, his hands fisting on his lap. "But she helped you rather than let you be taken?"

"Sure did. But we had little time to trade notes since we were focused on getting to Agatha before something happened to her. So, I have little information about her circumstances."

"Why doesn't she try to escape? She could have told you; you would have helped her get out. I know you would have."

I nod, then explain, "She said he has her daughter."

His jaw tightens. "I have a niece?"

"Apparently. And she will literally do anything to protect her."

He sighs, rubbing his hands over his face before looking up and staring me in the eyes. "Can you help me get her back?"

"That depends on you. Can you help me not die upon delivery to the enemy?"

He raises his shoulders noncommittally, then half-nods. "Maybe. You know there's no guarantee in these types of deals. I can certainly finagle delivery in your favor and come up with some contingencies once I hand you over. My men report this Vincent doesn't have many loyal followers, and most of his operation is staffed by forced loyalty. It should be easy to find someone on the inside who'll work for us, even if it's trading information."

"That's a start. I guess we'll have to wait and see how it pans out. If I live, you'll have my help in locating Carolina and her daughter."

He straightens, exhaling as he sits back in the chair. He's giving me an odd look, his jaw clenching rhythmically as he mulls something over. "What are you thinking?"

"You know what I'm thinking."

I eye him skeptically, then a smile forms on my lips as I say, "Really? You're gonna go there?"

He groans but nods, and I laugh. "You're gonna have to say it."

He narrows his eyes at me, opening his mouth to reply, but then stops, and I laugh some more.

After a few moments of deep contemplation, he inhales sharply, then says clearly. "Let's go fuck around and find out."

I beam at him. "Yes, indeed."

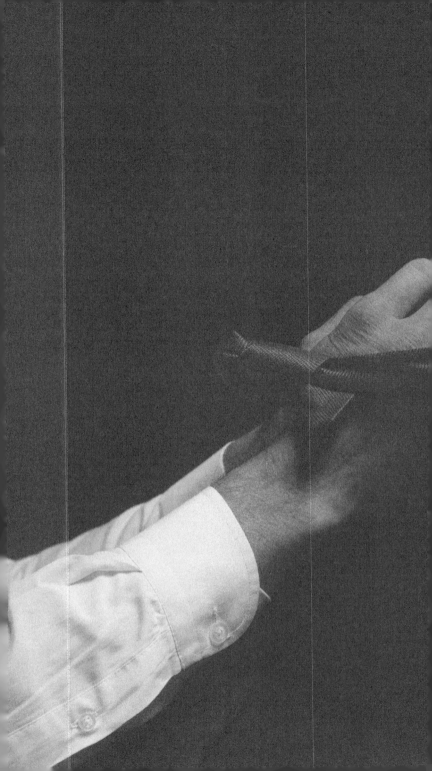

Chapter Twenty

Dare

I did it. I finally made her crack, for her to show me once and for all where we stand.

It wasn't easy, and for a few moments, I thought for sure it was going to fail, and I'd have no choice but to remove her from her current life.

I mean, I wouldn't have killed her, but I had every intention of locking her away indefinitely to serve my every whim as punishment for her treachery.

Now, she's in my lap, clutching me as if afraid I'll vanish from her grasp. Tears still stream down her face, and every few breaths sounds more like a hiccup. I tighten my arms around her, and she squirms closer, her ass grinding against my dick, and I can't stop my body's automatic reaction to her nearness.

I shift beneath her, trying to move my hardening cock away from her, and her breath catches, a breathy giggle falling from her lips as she realizes what I'm doing. "Ignore it," I whisper. "It'll go away."

She pulls back, her gaze coming up to my own as she says, "Maybe I don't want it to go away?"

My cock hardens further at her words, and I press my hips up, groaning at the friction of my dick rubbing against her ass. "I'd say that's not an appropriate response to the trauma you've just suffered at my wicked hands."

She wiggles her ass against me in response, and my hands move to her waist, stopping her movements as I work on controlling my urge to flip her onto her back and fuck her senseless.

We've had our dalliances. We've fucked around spontaneously whenever she's pushed my control to the breaking point. But we've never fucked. And as much as it pains me, this is likely the worst time for us to go there. "Now isn't the time for that, Antoinette."

She shivers in my lap, pressing closer as she says, "If not now, then when?"

"I don't know, but now, in this place, doesn't feel right. You deserve more."

She snorts. "Deserve more of what, exactly?"

"Romance? Tender loving care?"

"Sounds boring," she replies with a laugh, her warm breath on my neck causing me to shiver as she goes on, "Maybe I don't want romance and tender loving care. Maybe I want the animal, that deep urge to possess and be possessed."

My blood is so hot in my veins it feels as if my heart is going to implode in my chest. She doesn't know what she's saying. So, I tell her. "You don't know what you're saying, Antoinette. What you're asking."

She frowns at me. "Don't tell me what I know, Darius. I'm not a child; I know what I want and don't want. I don't want the type of romance where all I get is roses and sweet nothings. I want you. The real you. The you who looks at me as if he wants to swallow me whole. The you who wants to fight and fuck me at the same time. The you who touches me with such deep intensity, I fear you've imprinted yourself on my very being."

She stares into my eyes, and I see the truth behind her words. Her eyes are glassy from her tears, her cheeks still damp, her hair a wild tangle, and I've seen nothing so beautiful in my entire life.

I roll my eyes at myself, annoyed at what I feel I have to say. "You say that, but maybe you're not ready for the me who will consume you for the rest of your days. Sometimes, it's best to ease into it, to take a few steps at a time before laying yourself out at my mercy."

She gives me a soft look, her lips curving up into a small smile. "You mean, give you little bits of me at a time so I get used to your feral ways?"

I grin back, nodding. "Exactly. Because once I possess you, there's no going back. You'll be mine. The depth, breadth, and height of my soul, a soul that will call to yours every moment of every day until my dying breath. So, if that's not what you want, you need to say so now because there won't be any going back."

She leans closer until her forehead presses against mine, her eyes boring into my eyes, her words a whisper against my lips. "Did you paraphrase Elizabeth Barrett Browning to me?" I shrug and nod and she laughs. "And you say you're not a romantic?"

"I'm really not," I say matter-of-factly. "But I have no problem communicating intense feelings when needed."

She smiles at me, then sighs. "But you're saying my odds of getting laid are nil?"

I smile back at her, squeezing her around the waist as she wiggles against my still-hard cock. "That is entirely your call. I'll do whatever you're comfortable with. Just know there's no going back once I get inside you."

She presses her lips softly against mine, and I kiss her back just as gently. I want her to make her own decision, even as I physically force back the grunting beast inside of me, demanding I shove her down onto her front and rut into her like the animal I am.

She pulls back, looking at my face as she asks, "Would you let me tie you up?"

I blink at her a few times, surprised by her request. "Is that what you want?"

She falls quiet, obviously lost in her own contemplative thoughts, and I remain still, waiting for her to answer.

She raises her eyes to mine as she replies, "Yes. I think I would if you're okay with it."

I stare at her for a few moments, watching the quickening rise and fall of her chest and the racing pulse in her neck. "We should probably discuss some things first to clear the air."

She shakes her head. "It'll keep, Darius. All that shit will still be waiting for us in an hour, a day, or even a week. Let's keep now for us and pretend for one moment in time that nothing else matters."

Nothing else matters at all. She should know that by now.

"Okay."

Her eyes widen, her excitement shining back at me, and my breath catches in my throat. I've never let anyone take control from me, and the possibility that she may still be playing me enters my mind. If she's still playing me, once I'm tied down, that's it.

Game over.

Fuck it.

If she's truly toying with me, and none of this is real, then I'll die by her hand with no regrets.

I help her rise, then stand beside her, taking her hand and leading her across the room and out the door to the stairs. We enter the living space of my hideaway, and she looks around with great interest. "What is this place?"

"It's where I go when I don't want to be found."

"And where you bring people you want to never be found?"

I shake my head. "No. No one else has ever been here before now."

She gives me an almost shy smile, and I turn away from her, walking across the room toward the loft stairs. "This way."

She follows behind me, and awareness flickers over me as her hands reach out, stroking lightly over my back. I stop at the bottom of the stairs, motioning for her to proceed me up the steep staircase. I watch her scramble up the ladder, second-guessing my decision to go along with her plan to tie me up.

Her voice draws my attention, and I look up to see her peering down at me from above, beaming with anticipation. "You coming?"

I smile back at her. "Of course."

If this turns out to be a giant fucking error in judgment, then I deserve whatever bloody end I may come to.

I scramble up the stairs after her, raising my brows when I find her standing in the middle of the room, her arms wrapped around her waist protectively. I walk over, pulling her close as I say, "It's okay if you're having second thoughts. We don't have to do anything right now."

She shakes her head, pushing me away to look me in the eye as she says, "Nope. I'm in. We're doing this."

I grin at her conviction, pushing down my inclination to argue with her. If this is a trap, I can only hope she lets me finish before ending me.

I must have a strange look on my face at the thought because her eyes narrow slightly, and then she says, "What? What's that look for?"

I shake my head, but honesty falls from my lips. "I was thinking that if this is a trap, I hope you let me finish before slitting my throat. Take that as my dying wish, if that's where this is headed."

She gapes at me. "You're going to let me tie you up, thinking it could be a trap? Are you insane?"

"Clearly."

"You don't have to be tied up," she says breathlessly. "It's not a requirement, just a thought."

I shake my head, walking over to the dresser and grabbing a belt and a couple of ties from the top drawer. "I don't have any official restraints here, so we'll have to improvise."

She scoffs. "The darkly eclectic Darius Hughes, with no type of bondage gear? What would people say?"

I raise my eyebrows at her. "Darkly eclectic? Really?"

She shrugs before explaining, "I don't think unhinged really suits you. While you're certifiable, you're clearly not insane."

I walk over to the bed, securing the belt around the headboard, then turn toward her. "How would you like me?"

She looks at me, then looks at the bed, a blush staining her cheeks as she replies, "On your back, hands over your head."

"Should I undress first?"

She shakes her head as she walks over until she's standing in front of me, almost close enough to touch. "I'll do it. I want to unwrap you like a present."

The heat in her gaze has a shiver running up my spine, and I lean in, brushing my lips over hers before stepping back and climbing onto the bed. I secure the ties around my wrists, then lie back, stretching my arms over my head. "You'll have to secure the ties to the belt. I'll likely be able to get out of them in a pinch, but certainly not fast enough to save my life."

She gives me a dirty look. "For fuck sake, Dare. Stop joking about your own murder."

"Oh, but what a way to go."

She tsks at me, climbing onto the bed and securing my bound hands to the belt wrapped around the headboard. She scrambles off the bed, quickly stripping her clothes off before climbing back on and straddling my upper thighs.

My eyes skim over her naked form before moving back up to her face, and my breath catches at the pained expression on her face. "Go ahead, baby girl. This is your show. As fast or as slow as you want. The only rule is that you take everything."

She takes a shuddering breath, then reaches both hands out, grasping both sides of my ruined white shirt and wrenching them apart violently. Buttons fly everywhere, and my cock hardens in my pants, drawing her gaze down. She licks her lips, her eyes glinting with excitement.

I pull at my restraints, again recognizing what a bad fucking idea this was, given I'm not the type of man wired to hand over control to someone else. I brace my feet beneath me, bucking my hips to shift her until her pussy is pressing against my dick.

I push my hips up rhythmically, and she throws her head back, her eyes closing. I thrust a few more times, but then she leans forward, pressing her hands against my chest and sliding her lower body off me.

I groan in response, and she gives me a playful look and asks, "Do you need a safeword?"

I give her a dirty look in response.

Do I need a fucking safeword? Has she lost her fucking mind?

She leans over me, licking a line from my belly button up over my pec to my collarbone. She licks along my neck, her tongue snaking over my lips, but then she laughs against my mouth before pulling back. "I'm going to need your words, Darius."

That sassy fucking minx.

I growl, "No, I don't need a fucking safeword."

She laughs, the gleeful sound igniting a sudden warmth in my chest. It's as disconcerting as it is exhilarating. She could strike me down at this very moment, and I could survive a million lifetimes in hell based on this feeling alone.

She crawls up my body to sit on my chest with her knees on either side of my head. She leans forward, tests my bonds before sitting back, staring down at me with a wanton look.

I smell her arousal, the heated sweat on her skin, and the fear and distress from our previous altercation, making my balls tighten. I strain my head forward as I say, "Get that cunt on my face. Let me taste you."

She freezes, her eyes widening in distress as she says, "I'm not exactly fresh right now."

I raise a brow at her, my tongue snaking out to lick my lips as I say, "I don't fucking care. Sit that pretty pussy on my face, and I'll eat it like the starved man I am."

She shifts herself a little closer to me without pressing herself fully against me as I ordered her to. "Closer," I growl.

She doesn't move, so I glance up again, and she gives a little shake of her head, a small smile playing on her lips. I blow out a breath onto her glistening cunt, and she shivers in response.

Suddenly, she stands, and my head falls back onto the mattress as I watch her turn around so she's straddling me, facing my dick. She sinks down, pressing her wet pussy against my bare chest, and then I feel her hands on my pants, unbuttoning and unzipping, pushing them down with my boxer briefs to the tops of my thighs.

She pauses for a few moments with me lying there, tied up with my dick out, so I ask, "Are you okay?"

She nods her head, then looks at me over her shoulder, licking her lips as she replies, "Oh, yeah. I'm good."

I bark out a laugh that quickly turns into a moan as I feel her hot breath fan my cock. She licks a line down my shaft, and I squeeze my eyes shut to keep myself under control. The need to break free, grab her by the back of her head, and force her down onto my dick is almost overwhelming.

I want to face fuck her into submission. I want to fuck her raw in every orifice until she's begging and pleading for me to relent while crying for me to never stop.

She takes my cock in her mouth, and I thrust up sharply, catching her off-guard. She pulls back, narrowing her eyes at me over her shoulder, "Control yourself, big boy, or I may drag this out a little longer."

I bark out another laugh, already contemplating doing some begging and pleading of my own. She adjusts herself over me, seeking a better angle to suck my cock from, and once again, her knees are straddling my head, her pussy right above my face.

"For the love of fuck." I strain closer, but she's just out of reach. I curse under my breath, pulling on my bound hands as she slowly sinks down closer, and I run my tongue up her pussy lips and over her clit. I pull back, licking my lips as I say, "Sit on my face. Give me that sweet pussy."

She takes my dick into her hot mouth at the same time she presses her wet cunt against my face. I moan against her, licking, sucking, and biting her pussy lips before spearing my tongue into her hole as deeply as I can manage from this angle. She stiffens above me, and I feel her saliva dripping down my dick onto my balls as the sensations paralyze her.

I lick my way back down to her clit, and she shifts back against me, grinding herself on my lips and tongue as she swallows my dick. She grips the base of my dick in one hand, working me over in tandem with her hot mouth, and I buck up into her again, unable to control my response to her as I eat her pussy.

She sits up, moving her body back down until her hips are straddling mine, then she sits on me, rubbing her slick cunt on my dick, still wet from her spit. She rubs herself against me; her swollen flesh gliding over me erotically, and I feel the tension coiling, hear her breathy noises and panting moans.

"Holy fuck, what are you doing to me?" I know I sound desperate, and her next moan is almost a broken laugh as she grinds herself on me. "There are condoms in the bedside drawer."

She writhes over me, turning her body so I see her hand on her breast, squeezing and tweaking her nipple as she gasps. "Are you saying I need one?"

"Fuck no."

"Then why offer?"

I lick my lips, my hips pressing up as I respond, "Making sure you're taken care of, baby girl. It's entirely your call."

She turns her body back around so she's facing away from me as she grasps the base of my cock and positions herself just so. She sinks down slowly, taking me in, inch by inch, until there's no space between her ass and my abs. Then she rocks her hips, pressing herself down against me as her head falls back on a moan.

I pull harder on the ties around my wrists, the beast in my chest vibrating with need as I feel the pressure give. She's still undulating slowly over me, occasionally sliding up and down my shaft before grinding down onto me as deeply as possible. "Stop fucking playing with me, Antoinette."

She laughs breathlessly, slowing her already leisurely pace until she's barely moving at all, her round ass teasing me. "What are you going to do about it?"

I growl, yanking on the restraints even harder as she resumes her sliding and grinding, her head falling back as she brings one of her hands around to rub her clit. Every time her hands brush the base of my cock, I twitch, moaning and cursing for more movement, more friction.

I close my eyes, muttering curses to myself, but her self-satisfied laughter makes me open my eyes. She's staring at me over her shoulder, her eyes half-closed, and I feel the tension coiling inside her, her mouth falling open on a moan. I watch the pleasure wash over her features, feel her pussy twitching around my dick, and that's it.

I'm done.

I yank on my bound hands with enough force they come loose, and I sit up, wrapping my arms around her torso and lifting her as I use my momentum to force her onto her stomach, my dick buried deep inside her. She's still in the throes of her orgasm, her face pressed into the mattress, and I bend over her, grinding my cock into her as I lick and bite her neck, my words a whisper against her ear. "I warned you not to fucking play with me."

She smiles at me almost sleepily, and I pull my hips back, ramming my cock back into her with enough force it jars her back to reality. Her eyes open, and she whispers, "What are you doing?"

I give her a smile that's all teeth, the wildness inside me calling for me to take her, claim her. I yank the silk ties from around my wrists as I reply, "I'm taking my fucking turn."

Her eyes widen, but she doesn't say anything, so I reach my hand down, gripping her by the front of her throat and squeezing with enough force to make it slightly uncomfortable. She doesn't fight, though, or give any sign she's in distress, so I use my grip on her neck to pull her back against me, thrusting my cock in and out of her in punishing strokes. "You're mine, Antoinette. Any chance you had of ever escaping me is no longer valid. Say it. Tell me you're mine."

She chokes against my grip, so I loosen my fingers, and she drags in a ragged breath. "I'm not yours. You can't force me to be with you."

The beast in me thrashes, begging to be unleashed, so I drape my front over her back, my teeth sinking into her neck before licking a trail up to the side of her face. "Oh, but I can. I'll go to any lengths to force my will on you day in and day out for the rest of your life. Just try me."

She thrashes beneath me, trying to throw me off, but I ease more of my weight on top of her, effectively stopping her attempts to get away from me. I snake a hand beneath her, pinching her clit, then rubbing it in time with my cock moving in and out of her pussy, and she gasps, "Oh, fuck. Oh, fuck. Oh, fuck."

"That's right, Antoinette. Take my cock. Beg for it." I stroke her clit, driving my cock into her faster, harder, and deeper until she's moaning incoherently beneath me.

I remove my hand from between her legs, shifting so I can grab her by her hair and yank her head up and back, my face right in front of hers as I growl, "Open your eyes. You open your eyes and look at me as you take my cock."

She opens her eyes, those blue depths sucking me in, consuming me, but I can't look away—I won't. Instead, I release her hair, my hand going back to her clit, and I rub and stroke, my cock rutting into her hard and fast. "That's right; you're mine. You look into my eyes and know that you're mine."

I slam into her short hammering thrusts, and my fingers work her clit faster, more firmly, as I feel her unravelling. Her mouth falls open on a moan, and I press my lips against hers, my tongue invading her mouth as I eat her sounds of pleasure, drawing my name from her lips as I ravage her.

But we never look away.

Her orgasm rolls over her, drawing my release from my body, and even through the euphoria that overwhelms us, we don't look away.

We ride the waves of pleasure, unblinking and unable to find words. Our panting breath echoes throughout the room, and we sink into the mattress, the exhaustion imminent after all that's happened.

We lie there on the bed, facing each other, our hands stroking gently, and our legs intertwined, the sweat cooling on our bodies.

And still, we can't look away.

Chapter Twenty-One

Dare

PRESENT DAY.

"When are you going to tell me about your new girlfriend?"

The question comes out of the left field, and when I look at Jayme, he's looking at me with mischievous eyes.

I glance at Agatha, who smirks as she says, "Yes, Darius. Why don't you tell us all about your new girlfriend?"

I glare at her, then turn back to Jayme. "What do you wanna know?"

"I want to know how it is you got yourself tangled up with the spawn of the enemy."

I shrug. "They sent her to destroy me. I decided to keep her."

Jayme laughs, shaking his head as he replies, "You're telling me that all we had to do to bring down the beast was send the right woman?"

"It's not as simple as that, asshole."

He raises his brows at me, his hands coming up as if he's asking for some evidence as he says, "Well, that's how it looks. They sent a woman to destroy you, and rather than kill her, you start of a relationship with her. How is that even possible?"

I narrow my eyes at him, sitting back in my chair as I contemplate my answer. I've spent so much time over the last year pushing back any truth concerning our relationship; sometimes, it's hard for me to refocus. And it's difficult to put it into words because no one else will ever understand. Finally, I say, "Yes, they sent her to take me down. They had groomed her from a young age to focus on obligation, family loyalty, and the job. But I changed all that for her. And we changed each other."

Jayme scoffs, his fist coming out and knocking on the table. "Bullshit. There's no way the Beast gets taken for a ride by some duplicitous bitch and he allows her to live. That just doesn't happen."

"You watch your fucking mouth. You say whatever you want about me, but you shut your fucking mouth about her."

His eyes widen in surprise. "Well, shit. It really is serious."

I grind my teeth together, my urge to leap over the table and pound the shit out of him extreme. No one has to understand anything about my relationship with Antoinette. All they need to understand is that I will literally burn anyone and anything that threatens her. "You could say that. She confessed, and I forgave her. That's all you need to know."

Agatha interjects, "She confessed? She told you who she was and why she was sent to destroy you?"

I shake my head, sighing deeply before I reply, "She confessed they sent her to set me up. But we never had time to go into any of the details."

"Didn't have time? What the fuck does that even mean?"

"She was taken shortly after I found out."

Agatha and Jayme both frown at me. They keep staring at me expectantly until, finally, I say, "It's a long fucking story."

Agatha and Jayme look at each other, then Agatha turns to me. "We have time. Start at the beginning."

As much as I don't want to fucking talk about it, I don't see them letting me off the hook. It's been so long since I thought about that time. So many months, twisting the tale, always adjusting the different variations of the story to suit whoever was listening. I've run through the story so many times as a lie, it's difficult for me to piece it back together in real time.

Just the thought of it makes me tense, and I feel the heavy weight on my chest.

My words catch in my throat. I clear it a few times, then look between them, and take a few deep breaths.

Then I open my mouth and let the words fall.

About a year ago

I'm so fucking bored I'm considering stabbing myself just to feel the racing of my heart.

I look across the table at my so-called date. Her mouth is moving. It hasn't stopped fucking moving since we got here. I'm sure she's talking some nonsense about an ex-boyfriend or girlfriend or whatever. I could not care less.

I'm only here because I'm waiting to lay eyes on the only woman who does it for me. I brought the fake date, though she doesn't know she's a fake date, just to make it look like I wasn't spying.

But, of course, I'm fucking spying.

After our night of revelations, Antoinette told me she'd have to continue to date to keep up her end of her cover story. And she definitely would need to keep this date, given the short notice.

I didn't like the plan at all, but it's difficult for me to argue, not knowing the full extent of what's been going on behind the scenes. She said she'd meet up with me afterward to give me the full story, but I couldn't just sit back and wait around for her. So, here I am. Creeper Central.

I hear her before I see her. What others might find to be genuine laughter, I hear as false. For someone who doesn't know her very well, they would think she was having a spectacular time, but when I glance over, all I see is the disdain outlining her smiling face.

I should have insisted on getting more of the backstory, but we were too busy fucking each other to worry about business. I even let her take a little video of us reveling in our post-orgasmic bliss. It was cute to watch her watching it, her cheeks blushing and a satisfied smile on her face. I smile to myself just thinking about it.

The woman across from me says my name sharply, and I glance up to see she's giving me a dirty look. I don't even bother pretending to give a shit. I toss some bills onto the table, then give her a mock salute as I depart.

I know. I'm an asshole. And I can't find the energy to search for one fuck at this point.

I walk toward the main entrance, then take a quick right, looping around to the far corner of the restaurant where Antoinette and her jackoff date are sitting. I take a seat off by the wall, ignoring the reserved sign on the table.

I have an excellent view of the two of them, but I also see the dirty look the waitress is giving me as she makes her way to the table. I pull out a couple of hundred-dollar bills. "I just need to borrow it for a bit, Dee. I'll be out of your hair before you know it."

She gives me a skeptical look, then takes the money with a quick nod. "Sazerac?"

"Please. That would be lovely."

She rolls her eyes at me, then gives me a half-smile as she walks away. I turn my focus back on Antoinette, and she's motioning toward the back of the restaurant as she stands up. She grabs her bag, then walks toward the restrooms.

Once she is out of sight, I turn my attention back to jackoff. That smarmy fucker is sitting there with this incredibly superior look on his face. He glances over his shoulder a few times before reaching into the inside pocket of his jacket. He pulls out a small bottle, opens it quickly, and pours something out into his hand.

Jackoff returns the bottle to his pocket, then grabs two spoons, crushing whatever he got from the bottle between them. He glances around once more, then taps the spoon over her drink.

That is one dead motherfucker.

I move to get up, but then stop myself. I can't go over there and confront him because that could put her at risk. And this is where I'm kicking myself for not getting all the information before now, because this means I'll have to bide my time and grab him where there are fewer witnesses.

Antoinette returns to her seat and sits down, sipping her drink. He laughs, blatantly flirting with her. She smiles, laughing along with him, but I see the distant look in her eyes. Still, she picks up her drink and chugs it down like a good sport, completely unaware of the danger.

They both rise from the table. She gathers her bag and proceeds him toward the back exit. I move to follow them, but then Dee is back with my drink, standing in my way. I throw more money on the table, pushing her to the side as I stride quickly across the room to the hallway. I hear the door click and rush the rest of the way to the exit, opening it quietly so as not to draw attention to myself. I figure I can grab him in the parking lot, then take care of him later once I know Antoinette is okay.

But when I walk into the parking lot, no one's there. I look to the right just in time to see the tail end of a black SUV turning down the street. I run toward it, but by the time I reach the street, it has turned the corner and is already gone.

Fuck.

I walk back toward the restaurant entrance, taking out my burner phone and dialing Antoinette's number. It goes directly to voicemail. I pull out my personal phone and bring up my tracking app, but she's not there.

Now, my heart is pounding in my chest, the beast inside me vibrating, demanding we go find her. My stomach is in my throat, so I call her number again, but it still goes directly to voicemail.

I pull up Matt's number and call him, but he doesn't answer, so I send him a 911 text message and the corresponding code for our rendezvous point.

I consider attempting to locate the vehicle, but the number of black SUVs in New York City is insurmountable. Instead, I rush to my car, falling into the driver's seat, and hurriedly leaving the parking lot, heading toward the warehouse to meet Matt. I'm trying to keep it together, to not let the beast take over.

I send a message to Tony, knowing it will probably remain unread for a while because he gives no fucks about the tail I may be chasing.

It's best if I get to Matt first, since he knows more of the backstory than Tony does. I contemplated telling Tony about my recent revelations about Antoinette, but recognized it would be a mistake. He would consider her a weakness, a liability, and he would have zero problem eliminating her.

Matt pulls into the warehouse at the same time I do, and he meets me at the door, asking, "What's going on? What happened?"

"I ran into Antoinette tonight when she was out with some jackoff she dates sometimes."

He raises an eyebrow at me, giving me a skeptical look. "Just happened to, or you were spying?"

"Is this relevant?"

He shrugs. "Not really, but I still want you to admit it."

"Fine, I was spying. But it's a good fucking thing I was because I watched him drug her drink."

His eyes widen. "And you let him live?"

I shake my head. "I was going to grab him once I got outside, but by the time I got out there, they were gone."

"Gone? What the fuck do you mean they were gone?"

"In the time it took me to walk around my waitress and out the back exit, they were gone. There was a black SUV turning out of the parking lot when I exited the building. When I got to the road, it was gone."

Matt frowns. "So, someone obviously set her up. Someone must've been out there waiting."

This is really fucking bad. It's becoming more and more obvious that jackoff set Antoinette up to be taken. He drugged her so she would be incapable of putting up a fight and then had a vehicle waiting for a speedy exit.

My stomach clenches, bile rising my throat at the implication of why they would take her. I choke, hunching over as I attempt to reel myself in, to get control of the panic rising inside me.

Matt's hand squeezing my shoulder pulls me out of my spiral. I look up, meeting his eyes, and he says, "We'll find her, man. We'll find her."

I nod, walking with him to his wall of monitors. He flips switches and pushing buttons, and I lean against the bench and pull my phone out to text Tony again as Matt says, "Did you tell Tony?"

I hold up my phone. "If he would only fucking respond."

Matt sighs, pulling out his own phone to send a message, likely telling him it's not a drill. Not that either of us expects Tony to give a fuck, as he is one of those guys who doesn't have any fucks left to give beyond his small circle. He certainly doesn't know enough about my relationship with Antoinette to be too bothered by what happens to her.

Of course, now I must communicate this without telling him about her initial duplicity. My tangled web is growing, and it seems as if I'm stuck right in the middle of it.

Tony finally strolls in, not a care in the world, and I'm glaring daggers at him. I allow Matt to brief him, and he keeps eying me suspiciously. It's all I can do to hold myself back from pounding the shit out of him for acting like such a fucklicker. He doesn't understand my attachment to her, but he could at least have the decency to check in with his band of merry miscreants.

Once we've gone over everything and Tony has given me enough guff about my attitude, he takes off on a fuck-around-and-find-out mission. He even grabs his special bag and favorite gloves, which means nothing good for the rats scurrying around the underground, but you reap what you sow.

Matt and I attempt to keep my shit together. There are very few people I have an emotional investment in, and even those few relationships pale compared to this one. It was all so new, and we've already been through so much; the thought of having it snuffed out so soon is enough to turn my stomach.

Beyond that, regardless of any relationship we may foster in the future, she has to be okay. She didn't survive whatever she has survived so far, only to be taken out by some jackoff with an agenda.

Eventually, Tony returns, and he's a fucking mess. He detours to the showers, returning clean and dressed in record time. As he's walking in, an alarm blares. Matt confirms it's her phone that someone turned it on, and we're getting a location.

It's a warehouse not too far from us, one owned by someone other than me, which is unusual in this area. We don't waste any time discussing what needs to be done; we grab our weapons and head toward the exit.

Tony and I head over on foot, and he keeps bitching at me to slow down. He's not wrong, but I'm not feeling exactly reasonable. Matt should get there a few minutes ahead of us to scout out the perimeter. By the time we hear him on the COMs, we're closing in on the building, making our way on silently. The updates from Matt are now a constant companion in our ears.

We make our way inside the building, moving cautiously and listening for any signs of life. Then there's a scream and shouted cursing, so we run down the hallway, stopping at the intersection, and listening. There's shouting coming from the stairs, then more cursing and yelling, and hurried footsteps, so we stop tiptoeing and rush up the stairs as fast as we can.

We burst out onto the rooftop. It's raining now, a sudden storm letting loose on us. I see a group of men standing on the other side of the roof and two lone figures standing on the ledge. Tony and I don't have to say anything to each other. We sneak into the mix and start slashing throats. It takes a few moments for anyone to notice that something is amiss, but once they do, they turn on us in a swarm.

I hear Antoinette's voice coming from the ledge. She's screaming, and the other figure is shouting back at her. Then, the next thing I know, I hear laughing, the maniacal sound sending an icy shiver down my spine.

I'm yelling to her, bellowing for her to wait, not to move because I'm here, I'm coming for her.

Tony and I are trying to push forward, but the crush of people makes it all seem futile. I barge ahead with renewed vigor, pulling out my gun, and aiming at the man still standing on the ledge. But then Antoinette stops laughing. She says something incoherent, shouts words lost on the wind, and then lurches forward, grabbing onto the shadow with her arms and legs as she uses her momentum to pull him closer to her.

And then they're gone.

I hear screaming, and after a few beats, I realize it's coming from me. Pain slices my side, and I attempt to refocus on the here and now, on the enemy still surrounding us. Tony has done a fair job cutting them down, so I hack my way through the rest, engaging until there's no one left standing but Tony and me.

I stand there, gasping for breath, lost in a void. The weight hanging over me feels infinite, the darkness so thick I can't blink it away.

A sudden blinding pain shoots through my face, and I blink to find Tony standing in front of me, yelling at me to move. To keep it fucking together. It's not over.

I come back to myself and rush to the edge, leaning over and bellowing for her, but all I see is pitch black. I still hear Matt on the COMS, listening to him as he engages with somebody down on the ground.

Tony pulls me from the edge, forcefully pushing me toward the exit and back down the stairs. I'm running on autopilot, barely able to spit out the blood running from my broken nose to my mouth.

We run outside, sprinting around the building to the side where they disappeared. I see the bodies on the pavement, and the sight makes me slow my pace as my heart stops in my chest. Once again, bile rises in my throat, and I swallow it down, continuing forward in a trance.

I kneel beside her. She's face down, sprawled awkwardly on top of jackoff, who is splattered all over the pavement.

There's a deep, guttural vibration coming from deep in my chest, and even knowing it's coming from my body, it sounds completely foreign to me.

I put my hands out to touch her, but then Tony is there, pulling me back. I fight against his hold, trying to claw my way back to her, but then I hear him yelling in my ear that it's not over. It's not over. It's not over.

Matt motions to us, but I can't hear his words through the roaring in my ears, the sound of my blood pumping through my veins, the beast inside me thrashing to be set free.

I push it down, giving my head a severe shake as I once again attempt to reel myself in, to gain control over my actions and reactions.

Tony must sense it because he releases me, and we move closer to her as Matt motions us over. Tony helps Matt carefully flip her over, then shift her until she's reclining on me, her back to my front, her head supported on my shoulder.

She's lifeless, but I allow myself a tiny moment of relief to see her eyes are closed rather than half-open and vacant. It's still pouring down rain, and she's so beat up it's hard to tell if it's from before the fall or after.

Matt's voice is yelling directly into my ear, dragging my attention from her face, and I stare up at him, frowning in confusion at his words.

I blink a few times, allowing the words to sink in, but I don't dare hear him. He tries again, this time grasping my face in his two hands and yelling it directly into my face. "She's alive."

Our medics are on the way.

I'm not sure how long I sit there cradling her against me before the van shows up and the medic team descends upon us, and Tony has to hold me back when they attempt to take her from me. I know I'm acting unreasonable, irrational even, but this deep fear in me is blinding, driving me mad.

I finally rise from the ground, watching as they work on her, securing her to a backboard and eventually lifting her into the back of the van. I turn to Tony, saying, "You make certain that fucker never breathes again."

He nods, knowing the drill. "I got this. Go."

I nod to him and then to Matt. Then I bang my hand on the side of the van, letting the driver know it's time to move, and shut myself inside.

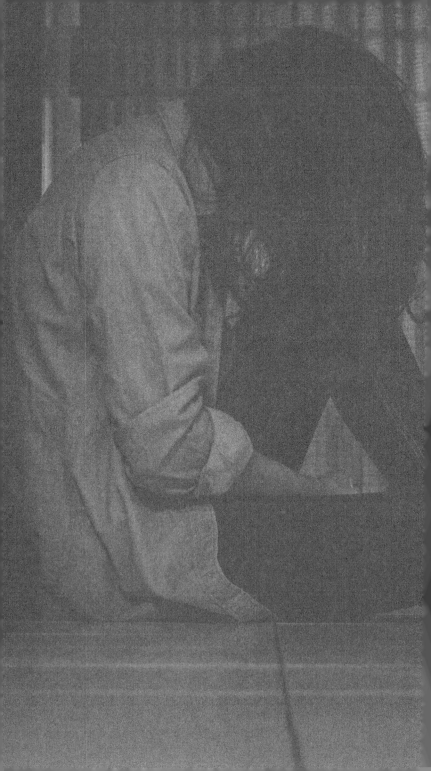

Chapter Twenty-Two

Toni

IT'S INCREDIBLE HOW CLEARLY you see things once the fog settles.

It's like having your eyesight checked when the doctor puts those blurred lenses in front of you, clicking buttons until suddenly your vision becomes clear. Unbeknownst to me, some of my memories had a blurry filter over them, and now that everything is put into its proper place, I can see everything clearly again.

Even the memories I had that I felt were clear and accurate clicked into place and, with those clicks, spun reality. I'm shocked by how many of these so-called memories were cued by other people with only a few words. How many of these distorted recollections were put into place so I would see a narrative that was not my own? So, the bones of my memories in that warehouse were true, but the many layers of the memory were hidden.

I was the enemy.

They sent me on a mission to take down a beast, and I came close to accomplishing the job, but I threw the fight. I was compromised, no longer adhering to family loyalty, obligation, and the job.

It's like a veil lifting from my eyes, and for the first time in my life, I can see clearly how much I've been manipulated. How they broke me down just so they could try to rebuild me back up in their own image.

The fact I haven't spoken freely to Darius about any of it weighs heavily on me. Between our revelation and my being taken, there hadn't been enough time. Hindsight being what it is, we should've taken the time, but we gave in to our wants and allowed ourselves to revel in the short-lived bubble around us.

All I can do is take comfort in the fact it isn't over. There's still time.

The last known location for Darius is a shipyard in Spain. So many ships go in and out of that port that it's nearly impossible to determine which one he ended up on. Matt said that once they put him on board the ship, it's likely he was put into a secure container, which means the signal wouldn't be strong enough to ping.

Agatha's men have also had little success in pinpointing her. Matt got in touch with them while I was comatose. I still get some amusement from the fact that we're micro-chipped like dogs, but given the number of times this has become useful, I'm resigned to keeping it that way.

Of course, there's also the chance that they tossed his watch overboard, but it's more likely somebody would try to steal and keep it. I've got good taste, after all.

Now, we're coming into our third day here with no sign of them, and all of us are getting discouraged. My bullet wound is healing well, or as well as expected. It wouldn't be ideal for me to overdo it, but I'd live if I had to.

I finally get myself out of bed and cleaned up, and I'm just finishing putting a clean dressing on both sides of my wound when I hear Matt yelling in the living room. I rush out there, where he has a mini-recon station set up, and he's pointing toward his monitor. "We got him."

There's a knock on the door, and I move to open it, but Tony gets in my way, shaking his head. I allow him to take the lead, and standing on the other side of the door are two of Agatha's men, one of them holding up a hand device. "We got her."

Tony motions for them to enter, then shuts the door and secures it. Everyone mills around Matt and his computers, and they compare notes on locations to confirm that they are indeed together. Then they all look at each other, and finally, I get sick of waiting for someone to elaborate. "Well, where are they?"

Matt makes a face, leaning closer to his monitor as he replies, "Apparently, in the middle of the Atlantic Ocean."

I groan. This is not ideal. This is about as far from ideal as one can get without including mythical creatures. "How the fuck are we supposed to get to them if we don't know where they're going?"

Tony and Matt look at each other, then share the same look with Agatha's men. Eventually, Tony says, "We meet them on the high seas."

"You cannot be serious."

"Oh, I'm serious. We will project their most likely course, and one of us will get dropped off along the way and attempt to board."

This is a horrible plan. But given there isn't a long list of workable plans, I guess this is it. "Fine. When do I leave?"

They all start shaking their heads, each of them listing off reasons the person who goes cannot be me. I interject, "Listen, I am more than qualified to swim a few miles and stealthily board a moving ship."

Tony crosses his arms over his chest. "Absolutely not."

I narrow my eyes at him. "And why not?"

"What if you fail? End up drowning in the Atlantic?"

"Well, then you'd get your way without having to get your hands dirty?"

He scowls at me. "What the fuck is that supposed to mean, Nettie?"

Nettie. He hasn't called me Nettie since he found out I'm the enemy. That I *was* the enemy. I force myself not to cringe, straightening my shoulders and meeting his glare with one of my own. "You know what that means, you asshole. You want me dead anyway, so my failure would work in favor of your wishes."

Matt takes a step toward me. "Antoinette, Tony has said nothing about—"

I cut him off, putting my hand up to stop him from saying anything further. "He doesn't have to say anything. I know how he operates. I know how his mind works in terms of friend or foe, and I am unequivocally a foe. The best way to control a foe is to end them."

Everyone is silent as Tony and I continue to stare each other down. Shockingly, he's the first to look away, but it doesn't feel like much of a victory as he walks closer to me. He stops in front of me, his hands reaching out and grasping me by my upper arms. I tense at his touch, but rather than shake me as I first thought he would, he gently pulls me against his chest until he's hugging me.

"I don't want you dead. I want you to prove to me that letting you live is the right choice," he whispers against my ear, and I feel the sting behind my eyes as he squeezes me closer.

"Then let me do this," I whisper back.

He sighs, pulling back and dropping his hands as he looks down at me. "You truly feel you can handle this?"

I nod. "Yes, I can."

He sighs again, his gaze jumping to Matt before settling on my face again. "Okay."

I gape at him for a moment, truly surprised he gave in so easily.

He holds up a hand, continuing, "But we have to make sure we do this right. We will come up with a plan and then several solid contingency plans in order to ensure this has the best outcome possible because if Dare comes back and finds out we let you get yourself killed, we will never hear the end of it."

Before he can change his mind, I smile at him, nodding my head like a nut job. "Is this where I say it?"

Matt and Tony both laugh and then Matt says, "Yes, seems as good a moment as any. Go right ahead."

"Well, boys," I say with a smile and a swagger. "Looks like it's my turn to go fuck around and find out."

They all groan, then Tony laughs. "That was terrible. Never do that again."

I laugh, knowing it was terrible, but not caring at all. "How are we going to do this?"

Matt pulls out his tablet, taps a few times, then shows me the screen as he explains, "As far as we can tell, the ship Dare is on is headed for New York. There's no way we can catch up with them by ship, so we're going to take a helicopter and kind of hopscotch out to them using some contacts of Tony's. Once we're close enough for a relatively safe swim, it should be easy to intercept the ship and sneak aboard."

I raise my brows at him and snort. "Simple, huh? How many miles are we talking?"

Matt grimaces, then swipes the screen on the tablet to a map filled with lines and numbers. "Between two and eight, I suspect."

"Between two and eight? Fucking hell, Matt. Can't you narrow it down a bit?" Tony asks angrily as he walks closer and yanks the tablet from Matt's hands.

Matt snatches it back. "Well, yes, once we're out there, I'll have a much narrower margin of error, but this pre-planning is mostly working with hypotheticals, so give me a break."

"Why can't we fly directly out to them and drop me nearby?"

"Easily attainable helicopters don't have the flight range to make that kind of journey in one go. It's also best if we have a safe home base where we can refuel and regroup before sending you out there. We'll have more equipment, too, given this friend of Tony's has a thing for extreme sports of all kinds. He'll have all the fun bells and whistles to aid you in your mission."

"Seems simple enough, in theory." I pause, looking between the two of them before continuing. "And once I get on board, then what? Do we know anything about this ship? Will I have to fight my way to him? Will I have a weapon? And once I've found him and told him what's up, then what? Do I stick with him until they make port, and we duke it out on land, or do I drag him and Agatha overboard with me? How will you know when to come find me? How will you know where to find me? That ocean is big, right?"

I stop talking and take a breath. Matt is staring at me wide-eyed, but Tony seems amused. Finally, he asks, "You okay, Nettie?"

I nod, though I'm sure I must have a deranged expression. "I'm fine. Everything's fine."

"I'm sure it is," he replies, amusement lacing his words as he tilts his head at me. "We'll work out all the finer details on our journey out there. Don't worry. We'll have a contingency plan for every plan to ensure you're not left out in the open water as shark bait."

The fucker smiles at me, so I return his smile, though I'm sure my smile is more akin to a deranged grin than any type of reassuring camaraderie. "So, now what?"

Matt cuts in, "Now, we go fuck around."

Chapter Twenty-Three

Dare

I WAS A BIT rattled after sharing my side of Antoinette's story with
Agatha and Jayme. It was almost freeing to finally shed the last rem-
nants of the lie, but it also brought to light the possibility that our
story may already be over.

The likelihood that neither Lilith nor Antoinette made it out of
that warehouse is high, and whether or not I like it, it may be quite a
while before I know. I asked Jayme if there was a way for us to inquire
about their fate, but he said there was no way for him to do so without
risking Vincent or some other enemy finding out.

I was not happy about his decision, but I also know he's not wrong.

After some rather intense interrogation from both of them, they
finally allowed me to escape to my room. I dozed off for a while, only
rousing myself once my hunger got strong enough to override my
laziness.

I'm walking back to my room after gorging myself on anything and everything I could find in the galley when I hear a splat, like soggy clothing hitting the floor. I stop, craning my head and listening intently, but the noise seems to be gone, or I'm losing it, which is highly possible at this point.

Shaking my head at myself, I continue down the hallway toward my room. I'm just walking through the doorway when I'm suddenly pushed from behind. I catch myself before falling on my face, but when I attempt to face my attacker, they somehow slip by me and, this time, push me against the now-closed door. I feel something hard and narrow press against my ribs, and I freeze, waiting to see what my attacker will do next.

Instead of speaking, they push closer until their front is pressed tightly to my back. From their size, I'm assuming I'm dealing with a slight man or a woman, but it's difficult to be sure when I can't see, hear, or smell them.

The person leans in even closer until they're pressed so tightly against me they're pushing my front into the door forcefully. Then I feel a warm breath against my neck and whispered words that send all my senses into a tailspin. "Well, hey there, baby." She, that's definitely a female voice—an almost familiar one. "I thought you were bad boy enough to handle me."

My eyes widen, my breath catching in my throat as I whisper, "Antoinette?"

She laughs against my ear, her breath tickling me as she replies, "In the flesh."

I'm stunned into silence, the relief flooding my body almost painful as I try to wrap my head around her being here, on this ship, with me. I press both palms against the door, pushing myself away from it with enough force to push her backwards.

She attempts to step forward again, but I'm right there, in her space and in her face; my hands are on both sides of her head, squeezing slightly harder than necessary for fear she will vanish in front of my eyes. "Toni." Her name falls from my lips with a pained gasp, our locked eyes speaking volumes since we seem to be out of words.

I unravel, then. All the fear and frustration boil over until I can't contain it. I yank her closer to me, my lips crashing against hers painfully, but she doesn't flinch or attempt to get away. Instead, she meets me with the same crazed intensity, practically crawling up my body as I pick her up and turn us around until I press her back against the door.

We're eating at each other with such ferocity, one of us bleeding from the coppery taste on my tongue. I squeeze her ass with one hand while the other fists in her hair. She wraps her arms around my neck; her legs coming around my waist, and she squeezes me tighter, like she's afraid I'm going to get away.

I pull back, dragging my lips and tongue along her jaw to her neck, where I bite down, sucking hard on her pulse point. She tastes salty. Like, extremely salty.

I pull back until my eyes meet hers, then I notice her hair is wet. I narrow my eyes at her, and she grins at me. "Why are you looking at me like that?"

"You taste like the ocean."

She laughs breathlessly. "Well, that makes sense, since I literally just climbed out of it."

"How did you get here?" I ask, pulling her back into me, burying my face in her cold, salty hair.

"I swam."

My eyes widen, and I freeze for a moment before jerking away from her. I stare at her face, frowning as I ask, "You swam here?"

She nods. "Yes, they dumped me off a few miles out, and I swam toward the dot until I intercepted you."

"Swam toward the dot?"

"Well yes. Though I suppose it was a bit more complicated than that," she says with a shrug, seemingly unconcerned.

My blood pressure increases significantly at her nonchalant delivery. "A bit more complicated? You somehow boarded a moving ship in the middle of the goddamn night, and all you can say is it was complicated?"

She opens her mouth to speak, then snaps her mouth shut as she gives me a look over. Her lips purse, and she squints at me, then replies, "I don't see any point in going into the finer details right now in the middle of our grand reunion and all, but apparently, you'd rather have a pissing contest about something you can't change."

My hands tighten on her arms, and I shake her. "What the fuck were you thinking, putting yourself in danger like that?"

Her eyes narrow, and she releases her hold on me, then steps backward, yanking her arms from my grasp. "Excuse me? What was I thinking?"

I know I should probably shut my mouth, but I'm livid and completely appalled that they dropped her into the middle of the ocean and tasked with swimming until she either found the ship I'm on or perished. "Yes, what the fuck were you thinking? Or were you thinking? Obviously, you must not have been, because that is the most preposterous, insane idea I've ever heard."

"You don't say," she says blandly, her arms crossing over her chest.

"You may not put your life in danger under any circumstances, for any reason. It is not allowed."

She gapes at me for a moment, and then her jaw snaps shut. She glares at me and gives me a big shove backwards, which only moves me a couple of inches. And then she says, "Allowed? I'm not fucking allowed?"

I lean my body in closer until my face is barely an inch from hers and whisper, "That's right. You're not fucking allowed."

She blinks at me a few times as my words sink in, and then she laughs. She laughs and laughs and laughs until tears are streaming down her face. I raise my hands to my hips. "What could possibly be so funny?"

She points at me, then says through her laughter, "You're funny. Fucking delusional, but funny."

That's when it occurs to me. There's something different about her. Not just the fact that she swam miles in the ocean to get to me, but the way she carries herself, the way she's speaking. The way she looks at me with such belligerent warmth.

Suddenly, the weight on my chest triples, my breath catching in my throat. I push my body closer to her until she's forced to stand upright, and I have her body pressed back against the door. My hands come up, once again gripping the sides of her head, keeping her in place as I stare into her eyes.

She sobers, her laughter slowly dying off until she's staring back at me with a somewhat evil grin on her face. I lean closer and whisper, "Antoinette?"

Her eyes widen a little, and she replies, "Darius?"

"It's you. You're you. You're back." I'm babbling now, and she gives me a rather peculiar look; her hands come up and grasp my wrists as she leans forward, her nose brushing along my cheek.

I feel her breath on the corner of my mouth as she whispers, "It's me. I'm me. I'm here."

If any breath could escape my lungs, it would've come out as a sob. If there ever was a moment in my entire adult life where I might cry like a baby, this would be it. And even knowing I rarely allow myself the luxury of tears doesn't stop that distinct burning behind my eyes, and soon, I feel the hot slide of a tear trailing down the skin of my cheek. Then I feel her tongue there, and she laps it up with a low chuckle. "Did I finally break the Beast? You poor thing."

I do laugh this time, though it comes out watery. I drop my hands from her face, wrapping my arms around her back and pulling her into my chest. I press my face into her neck, my teeth once again sinking in until she flinches. I don't want to hurt her, but I have this distinct need inside to mark her again, to mark her permanently, so no one will ever question who she belongs to.

She must sense my sudden change in demeanor and feel the shift in my immediate desire because she wraps her arms around my shoulders, and I heft her up, pulling her thighs up and around me. I squeeze her ass in both my hands, suddenly very aware that she's not fully clothed. "Where the fuck are your pants?"

She's licking and nibbling on my neck and then up to my ear. "I was in the middle of changing when I saw you. I figured it was easier to follow you without pants than try to figure out where you went after I dressed myself." She pulls back, her eyes meeting mine as she asks, "How is it you're roaming around freely? Aren't you a prisoner?"

I lean into her and groan against her lips as I mutter, "It's a long story. I'll have to tell you later." I kiss her neck, nuzzling her ear, and she rocks against me, so I ask, "Is that an invitation?"

She laughs against my neck, her arms pulling me tighter, and her hips rotate in my grip. "Since when do you need an invitation?"

I growl, placing another bite mark on her neck before straightening. I adjust my grip on her ass, then grind myself against her as I brush my mouth against hers. She's smiling softly, and I lick her lips, sucking and nibbling, coaxing her to open for me.

With all the different puzzle pieces shifting back into place where they belong, I wonder if she'll now recognize that many of our intimate interactions since they took her were snippets from our brief history. I didn't even realize I was doing it, but once all the pieces shifted back together for me, I realized that even after being programmed to not remember, those memories never truly quieted.

The first time I saw that bratty look in her eyes back so many months ago, when she was telling me I wasn't bad boy enough to handle her, that was the first unconscious sign that maybe she needed a little more prodding, the little zing that queued my locked-up memory into action. And occasionally, in the heat of the moment, I would feel like I was reaching for something unknown, but then as soon as the excitement faded, she went right back to the Toni, who couldn't remember, and I went back to the Darius who was locked in an abbreviated version of our reality.

She leans her upper body back against the door, her hands coming between us. She undoes my belt and pants, pushing the fabric out of the way as she pulls my cock free. I watch her face as her hand comes up, and she dribbles saliva into her open palm, then lowers her hand to the head of my dick. She slicks her spit over the tip, and my eyes close, my head falling back at how good her hands feel on me.

She strokes me for a few moments, then I feel her adjusting herself in my hands; when my eyes open, I look down, watching her rub the head of my cock against her pussy.

I shove my hips forward at the same time as I pull her closer to me, pushing my cock inside her. She hisses at the sudden intrusion, and I pause, my dick half inside her. "Are you okay? Am I hurting you?"

She gives a breathless laugh, shaking her head. Then her arms are back around my shoulders, giving herself some leverage to rock her hips and push herself onto me further. "Stop asking so many fucking questions. Take me. Take what you want."

I growl again, pulling my hips back so the first couple inches of my dick is still inside her and then shoving back in with enough force that her back slams against the door. She grunts, her arms tightening, pulling me closer. I pull out and then shove back in, setting a punishing rhythm, in and out, the sounds of our bodies slapping together echoing throughout the room.

She's moaning against my ear; there are little sobs of pleasure and occasional curses, and I feel the heat in my spine, the tingling in my lower pelvis. The oppressive weight in my chest eases, overwhelming me with such a state of euphoria I lose my breath and rhythm.

I pause, my dick shoved inside her as I use my hips to pin her against the wall. I take a shuddering breath in, then whisper against her neck, "I thought I lost you."

I feel her nodding, her lips against my ear as she says, "I know, baby. But you didn't."

"You can't keep fucking doing that to me." I know I'm being entirely irrational, that it's a ridiculous statement, but I can't help it. The thought of losing her completely wrecks me.

She's still nodding, her hands grabbing my hair and pulling on me like she can't get close enough. I'm overwhelmed by relief, but I can't find the words to fully communicate my feelings to her. I pull back, my eyes seeking hers, and the emotion I see in those blue depths rips me to shreds.

She brushes her lips against mine, muttering little whispers I can't quite comprehend, and I lower my head to deepen the kiss. She pulls back, so she's just out of reach, and a growl rumbles deep in my chest. I push her back harder against the door, using my pelvis and chest now so she can't get away from me, and then I attack her, my lips and teeth savage, my tongue urging as I demand an equally savage response from her.

She doesn't succumb so much as retaliate, her hands grasping onto my neck, her nails digging in, scoring me. I pull back a few inches, the bite of her teeth on my lips spurring me to push all the way inside her, the slap of my hips against hers loud in the otherwise silent room. She whimpers into my mouth, and I ease out of her only to slam back in, grinding the base of my dick against her clit, drinking the broken sob that falls from her lips.

She wraps an arm around my neck, pulling herself up and rolling her hips to meet my forward momentum. For a moment, I worry I might hurt her, but she digs her nails into my back, biting at my lips, encouraging me to take, take, take. Her hot breath is in my ear, and she's whispering, "That's right. You fuck your good little slut. Take what's yours."

As if the beast inside me needed any encouragement, her words increase the heat building in my groin, that familiar tingle at the base of my spine returning. I try to slow down, but she's writhing against me from above like she's trying to force my orgasm from me. "Slow down, baby girl. Slow down, or I'm gonna cum."

She barks out a laugh, then her mouth is back against mine, and she's drinking down my grunts and moans, her body slamming down on me insistently. I push off the wall, staggering over to the bed, where I unceremoniously dump her on her back. She glares up at me, sprawled, pantless, and panting. "I said slow down, you naughty little minx."

I quickly strip myself of my clothing, then reach out and snag one of her ankles, yanking her to the edge of the bed, where I pull her damp shirt over her head. She lies back, utterly bare to me, her hair spread out on the white comforter, and I feel the increasingly familiar sting behind my eyes. She has a bandage on her torso, and I touch it gently and give her a questioning look. She gives a slight shake of her head and says, "Later."

I go to respond, but the words get caught in my throat, so instead, I crawl over her, cupping her face in my palms as I kiss her cheeks, the corners of her eyes, her eyelids, and then her lips.

Her eyes meet mine, and she smiles softly, pulling me closer. "I know, baby. I know."

She wraps her arms around my shoulders, pulling me down on top of her as she hooks her ankles at the base of my spine. I wrap an arm beneath her hips, pressing myself up with the other so I can shift us up on the bed. "Hold onto me, baby girl. Don't let go."

Her grip on me tightens, and I slide us toward the headboard, pulling a pillow under her. I pull her arms from my shoulders, then sit back on my haunches and allow myself a moment to revel in having her spread out before me. I swallow the lump in my throat, my hands stroking her thighs as I nudge her entrance with the tip of my dick.

She bucks her hips, her breath catching as my cock nudges her clit. I pool saliva in my mouth, then dip my head, dribbling it over where my cock is pressed against her, moaning at the slide of my hard flesh with her slick heat. She smiles, then says, "Will it always be like this?"

"Probably not."

Her eyes widen, and she slaps my arm before I can move out of her reach. I laugh, pushing my cock inside her slowly as she shakes her head at me, gasping, "You could at least lie to me in the heat of the moment."

"Never. I'll never lie to you."

"Fine. Then maybe try to pretty up the truth a bit."

I shake my head, flexing my hips until my cock is seated fully inside her, my lower pelvis pushing against her clit. "Nope. All you'll ever get from me is the brutal," thrust "hard," thrust "unforgiving," thrust "truth."

I'm grinding against her, going back and forth between watching the slide and press of my cock inside her and the rapturous emotions flitting across her beautiful face. "This is how I want to die. Buried deep inside you, your sexy noises and smells surrounding me."

She chokes on a moan, her hands coming up to pinch and pull on her nipples, her hips rotating on my dick. "Really, Dare? You choose this moment to speak of dying?"

"If this is what dying feels like, I'm a fan."

"Oh my god. Shut up."

I chuckle but do as I'm told before I completely embarrass myself. This is what she does to me. She renders me completely ridiculous, a besotted caricature of my typically unflappable cold self. And I don't give a fuck.

I pull my hips back, slamming forward sharply. "Touch yourself. Let me see your fingers on your greedy little clit."

She doesn't hesitate, her hand moving between her legs and stroking over her clit with purpose. "You saying you can't handle it, big boy?"

She's taunting me, and I'm hard-pressed not to edge her a few times out of principle. I narrow my eyes at her, shoving inside her until I can't press in any farther. "Are you looking to get punished, minx?"

She looks up and away from me as if she's contemplating the question, and I chuckle again, not at all surprised that she might still want to play with me. Finally, she refocuses on my face and shakes her head. "Not this time. Right now, you need to fuck me like you mean it."

My hands move to her hips, gripping her so tightly she'll be sporting my fingertip bruises for days. I pull back, and she moans at the slow slide of my cock retreating from her, her hands moving against her clit faster, more firmly. I thrust into her slowly, sharply, dragging the head of my dick along her inner walls with purpose until she's writhing beneath me. Soon, she's moaning, begging me to give her the final push she needs to come, so I use my grip on her hips to pull her up against me, my dick battering her G-spot in a quick staccato that sends her sobbing and cursing over the edge.

I rut into her a last time, my dick throbbing as I release inside her, our eyes locked as we both take in the rapture clear on each other's features. We're panting, gasping for breath, and I'm not sure if it's from the physical exertion or the emotional wreckage we are for each other.

We stare at each other, still connected intimately, and the pressure in my chest increases with each passing moment until I can hardly breathe from the words stuck in my throat.

"I can't fucking stand how much I love you."

"Ditto. It's the fucking worst."

We smile at each other in understanding, allowing ourselves to enjoy the peacefulness of the moment, knowing it will most likely be short-lived.

Chapter Twenty-Four

Dare

"How did you end up out here?"

She's sprawled over me, her face pressed against my neck, her hands stroking over my chest. I pull her closer, sighing into her neck as I respond, "Vincent contracted our transport out, and we were fortunate enough to end up on the ship of someone I knew personally."

"Seriously? Of all the ships in the world, you end up on the ship operated by one of your cronies?"

It is kind of crazy when worded like that. "Well, yes. Exactly that."

She shakes her head, a humorless laugh escaping her lips. "And you feel you can trust this guy?"

"To an extent, yes."

She's quiet for a moment, obviously lost in her own thoughts since she doesn't continue picking my brain about my old crony. I can only assume what kind of inner turmoil would take precedence over her need to know every little detail, but I have a sneaking suspicion my assumptions are spot on.

"Are you ready to talk about it?"

She tenses, and I tighten my hold on her, craning my neck around so I can look at her face. She's silent for a moment, her eyes wide on mine, her lips trembling. I feel the shudder in her body as she inhales deeply, so I pull her closer, pressing my face into her neck and placing a kiss below her ear. "It's okay, Toni. Whenever you're ready."

I know whatever went down in that warehouse is horrific. Since Toni obviously got lucky and appears to be mostly unscathed, most likely Lilith wasn't so fortunate. She doesn't have to tell me if she doesn't want to. Just the fact that it's a struggle tells me most everything I need to know.

She clears her throat, her eyelids fluttering as she blinks back tears. "She's gone. The fucker took her from me." She pauses, her jaw clenching a few times before she continues, "And for what? Greed? Power? What the fuck is the point?"

"For some people, that's all there is. Especially someone like Vincent, who was likely raised to live and die for power. And who knows what kind of bullshit they fed him his entire life about you and Lilith. Most likely, he feels like they denied him some kind of silver spoon treatment, even though that's obviously as far from accurate as you can get. Just think about yourself and your views of the world or your opinion of me from the beginning versus now."

She attempts to push away from me, but I tighten my hold, forcing her to stay where she is. She tips her head back, glaring at me. "Are you seriously making fucking excuses for him?"

I bark out a laugh, then lower my face to hers, kissing away the stray tears on her cheeks. "Hardly. I just know that it's easy to lose sight of other people's perspective."

"People on the edge have a different perspective."

I smile. "And birds are entangled by their feet and men by their tongues."

"You remember," she says with a little smile, her body relaxing against me, her eyes softening as she looks up at me.

"Of course, I remember. I still have them in my wallet."

"No, you don't!"

I nod, shrugging my shoulders but not saying anything. It's silly, and I know it's silly. I never thought I'd be the type of man to keep little anecdotes and trinkets that remind me of a woman—or anyone. But here I am, carrying around old fortunes in my wallet. Tony and Matt would have a field day if they knew, accusing me of getting soft, and in some ways, they wouldn't be wrong.

"So, in all of this and everything that's happened, was it even you they were after? Or me? Lilith?"

"Probably all of us in some fashion. Many people want me out of the way because I interfere with their mission to make more money off the backs of innocent people. I've lost a lot of people, a lot of money over the years, and plan on taking even more from them in the future."

"So, you're always going to have a target on your forehead?"

"Yes. Even when I attempted to remove myself from the picture, they still came for me. I'm not sure if there will ever be a way for me to leave the life completely without always looking over my shoulder."

She's quiet for a moment, her fingers rubbing patterns on my chest. Then she says, "So you're saying we're gonna have to pull a Wyatt Earp?"

"Wyatt *Earp*? What do you mean?"

"You know, Wyatt Earp and the Cowboys. Anyone wearing a red bandanna will be shot on sight kind of thing. Anyone who wants to stand up against us is fair game—no questions, no problem."

"Sounds kind of drastic."

She shrugs, her lips twisting as she replies, "Well, the fuckers won't leave you alone, so what are we supposed to do? Spend our entire existence looking over our shoulders?"

She's not wrong, but that kind of anarchy would take a lot of time and energy, and we'll likely end up with a few more of our own dead. "You have a point, but we may be better served removing the heads of a few at the top and then negotiating with the rest."

Her features harden as she stares off into space. "Negotiate? Since when does the Beast negotiate?"

"Have I mentioned how much I hate that fucking nickname? It's so stupid."

"You mean you didn't start it?"

I scoff, shaking my head. "Absolutely not. I wouldn't give myself a nickname at all. It's so tacky."

"Tony did it, didn't he?"

"He sure did. He still thinks it's funny, too. Sometimes, I feel like half the shit I hear about myself isn't even true."

She giggles, the sound sending a rush of warmth through my chest, and I smile in response. Then she says, "So, you're saying you're not the murderous, bloodthirsty, rampaging beast they all say you are?"

"I probably am, to a certain degree. But I don't go around killing people indiscriminately. And I don't care about power or money."

"That power thing may not be entirely true," she says dryly.

"There's a difference between wanting power regardless of the lengths you must go to keep it. That's the difference between me and people like Vincent. Most power-hungry people can't handle the responsibility needed to wield it appropriately. And they're so desperate to keep it, to always crave more, they don't care who they step on. My aim is to help those who would be stepped on to be a bigger hurdle."

"Sounds like a thankless, impossible task."

"It's never thankless, but it does often feel impossible. And if it was just me against the world, then it would be. But there are scores of people like me out there, people who have made it their life's work to infiltrate organizations that seek to cause harm and dismantle them from the inside. Good will always overcome evil, Toni. It has to."

"I'm not good."

"Yes, you are. Deep down, beneath the bullshit they fed you for your entire life, you are good. You could have taken me down, you could have destroyed me and then taken out every good thing I'd ever done, but you didn't."

"I wanted to. I came here determined I was going to succeed, that I would be the one to finally take down the infamous Beast." She sighs, pressing her face into my chest for a moment before pulling back and continuing, "I was drawn to you from the start. At first, I thought it was the pull of the job and the thrill of the chase. And knowing that I might actually pull off a feat that no one else had even come close to. It's surreal, almost impossible to fully explain."

"Try."

"I don't know. It was like the more you pushed back at me, the more difficult you made the task—chasing you became like a drug. And then, in those rare moments where you would flip the switch and show me the real you when you turned your intentions on me fully, good fucking lord, you were so hot."

The corners of my lips lift slightly, my eyebrows raising as I peer down at her knowingly. "Hmm, I was irresistible?"

She barks out a laugh, slapping me on the chest as she rolls her eyes. "Not hardly. You were such a fucking prick, but there was just something about you."

"I'm sure I was a total bastard sometimes, but you put me on edge.

I couldn't figure out your game, and that's what made me finally strike out. It was my need to know what you were about."

"Even when I lost my memories, I still had a glimmer of those moments, and it scared me shitless. In the beginning, my changing emotions didn't change the fact you were a job, and all my deeply ingrained beliefs about family, loyalty, and obedience were tough to overcome. And then, you twisted me around in the basement of your hideaway, and it just didn't matter. I didn't care about any of it, even knowing what they would do to me when they found out–I didn't care. There was something about you in that moment that stirred my soul, and no matter how much I tried to push it down, I couldn't. In that moment when I thought you had ended it by shooting yourself, my soul tore apart, dying right there with you."

I squeeze my arms around her, pressing my face into her neck. "I wouldn't have actually shot myself; you know that, right?"

"I didn't. I was having an actual heart attack. So, if that was your mission, it totally worked."

"My mission was to get you to admit you were besotted with me."

"Besotted? Really?"

I chuckle against her neck and feel the shiver run through her. "Yes, besotted. You didn't exactly admit to it then, but you gave me enough to realize I wouldn't have to go to plan B."

"What exactly was plan B?"

"The box."

She laughs, shaking her head as she asks, "And what exactly is the box?"

"There's a big drawer under the bed in the loft that pulls out. You'd fit in there perfectly."

"Oh, my god. No, thank you."

"I wouldn't have kept you in there all the time. Just when I wasn't around to use you."

"You would've stored me in this box whenever you weren't with me, and then whenever you showed up, you'd take me out just to use me for your whims?"

I nod, my teeth nipping her neck. "Oh, yes. I don't think you truly understand the sheer depths of my depravity for you. If things had gone differently and you had shown me you felt nothing for me, no one ever would've found you again. But I would always know where you were because regardless of how you feel, you will always be mine."

"No 'if you love someone, set them free' for you?"

"Not a fucking chance."

I would have done it. I would have put her in that box and kept her there for the rest of my days.

"Can I ask you a question?" Her voice is quiet, hesitant.

"You can ask me anything."

"Were there any others? You know when I wasn't myself for all those months?"

"Any other what?"

She clears her throat, her voice small. "Women."

I stiffen and immediately sit up, shifting back until I'm leaning against the headboard. I pull her up beside me, turning her so she's facing me, and I can watch her face as I explain my answer, likely in more detail than she planned.

"I tried to."

Her jaw clenches, and I see anger cross her features before she quickly buries it. She inhales sharply through her nose, then gives me a curt nod. "I appreciate you being honest with me. I understand."

I reach out and grab her hand, pulling it onto my lap and holding it between both of mine. "No, Toni. You don't understand. And I don't know if me explaining it will make you understand or not, but I'm going to try."

Her eyes are wide, and she looks nervous, but finally, she responds, "Okay. I'm listening."

I settle back against the headboard, keeping her hand between mine as I speak. "When you were first injured, I went out of my mind. Of course, the only one who knew the complete story of our relationship was Matt, and even though he watched me like a hawk, sometimes things would get out of hand too quickly for him to contain. You had a vague idea of who I was, and we planted as much benign information as we could to keep you pacified, but it was a constant struggle to keep the lines clear."

"I tried my best to toe the line between what I wanted to do and what the doctor said was best for you, but now and then, things would become too much, and I would completely lose it. There was one time, after a certain instance of complete insanity, that Matt finally cornered me and mentioned the idea of hypnosis. At first, I was completely against it, thinking it was stupid. I thought I could figure it out and keep the rage down—and the hurt and the fear—but I had to accept I couldn't. My entire life, they knew me as the man who could control everything, but being unable to control what was going on with you ate me alive. I was the Beast, but I was more like the Beast on steroids, and it was not pretty. To make it even worse, this behavior from me was also dangerous and confusing for you, and that's what finally made me change my mind."

She reached her hand out, resting it on top of mine. "Matt mentioned the hypnosis when I first got my memory back, but he didn't go into any detail. But it helped you forget us?"

"I know it sounds silly, and I thought it was completely ludicrous, and that's probably why it took a few times before it worked. It wasn't a clear cutoff or anything; it mostly took the edge off the overwhelming feelings I had for you that needed to be kept at bay for fear of permanently altering your memories. And even then, it only worked to a point. My pull to you was so strong that even after they used hypnosis to make me believe you were nothing more than a pain-in-my-ass coworker who I was insanely attracted to, I still had moments where I would kind of pop back into my normal overbearing, possessive, jackass self."

"Matt literally had to put trackers in my car, in my clothing because he couldn't trust me to behave myself. I think if he could've micro-chipped me like a dog, he would have done so because keeping track of me ended up being a full-time job for him. And, of course, the more time that went on, the more often I slipped. It was like the bones of the hypnosis were still there, keeping me upright, but eventually, small bits of truth sneak through, sending me into a tailspin."

She looks up at me, and then glances away, her lips pressed together in a thin line. I can tell she wants to ask me something, so I squeeze her hand and say, "Ask me whatever you want, Toni. I'll tell you anything. Even things I know might hurt you in the moment. I won't keep anything from you."

"Did I do something?"

"What do you mean 'did you do something'?"

She shrugs, attempting to pull her hand from mine, but I hold it tighter, not allowing her to pull away. "Was it something I did that made you want someone else?"

I laugh, and she gives me a dirty look. "Is that funny? Do you think you fucking other women is funny?"

She tries to pull away again, but this time, I grab her by both her wrists, pulling her so she's leaned into me as I reply, "No, baby girl. What's funny is that you think that I just went out and fucked other women when you were injured and needed me."

"You said you tried to have other women?"

"I said that, but it's not as simple as that. They had to use hypnosis to get me to forget about our intimate relationship and the depth of my feelings for you. But even after that, I still had a calling to you. Even though, in my brain, I couldn't for the life of me figure out why, because you were a mouthy pain in my fucking ass, and I constantly wanted to throttle you. Or, at least, throttle you while fucking the shit out of you. So, to take the edge off of all that, Tony decided we would go on a double date. It was fucking painful."

"Double dates usually are painful, regardless of whether you have a super-secret girlfriend with amnesia or not."

"That's fair. He made it even more painful because he intentionally set me up with a woman I was typically attracted to, but also a woman who would have no problem with just getting into bed with me. Which, under normal circumstances, would be great, but I only became increasingly frustrated because I wasn't interested, and in my head, I didn't know why. Of course, Tony didn't make it any easier on me because he thought it was hilarious. And Matt, who knew what was going on but couldn't explain why, would pat me on the back and tell me I'd figure it out eventually when the time is right."

She gives me a small smile, relaxing and shifting closer. "So, you're saying nothing happened?"

"I'll be completely honest and tell you exactly what happened. She attempted to put her lips on me, and I made a face that she found incredibly offensive, so she slapped me and left."

Now she laughs. "She slapped you?"

"Right across the face. It was a good hit, too."

"Well, I guess it serves you right, then."

"I figured the same, but that slap worked me up quickly, and I started right back, asking questions. Tony didn't have any answers, and once Matt gets a job in his head, you can forget him going back on the deal."

"At what point did they undo this hypnosis?"

"It wasn't so much an undoing, but after you forced Matt to arrest me, things changed rapidly. Matt wasn't fully aware that I had gone off the rails until you showed up that last time and strong-armed him into taking you to me. After you left with Tony and he cuffed and stuffed me like the good friend he is, we had a heart-to-heart on the side of the road, and he realized I was slowly unraveling. At first, he was going to have it undone entirely, but after speaking to the hypnotherapist, they waited to see if it would wear off on its own—which it did. But by then, I was locked up with Agatha, and there wasn't anything I could do with the recent revelations. I was impressed with myself on how many old memories I could incorporate into our new dalliances, though."

She beams at me. "I didn't know at least, not that I was fully aware of, but as soon as it all came back to me, and my old and new memories meshed back together, I saw the overlap. And I was shocked."

"Shocked by what?"

She raises her brows at me, inclining her head as if I should already know. "Shocked by your incredible attention to detail, even if it wasn't entirely intentional. The amount of stuff you unwittingly remembered from our one time together is insane. *You're* fucking insane."

I smile back at her and nod. "Come on now. You know I'm darkly eclectic."

She rolls her eyes at me, pulling her hands free and smacking me on the chest playfully. "You're fucking unhinged, and you know it."

"I admit nothing." I grab her hands again, pulling her until she's lying on my chest. I kiss the top of her head and then chuckle when I hear her say, "I smell terrible."

"I've smelled worse."

"You're disgusting. Sometimes, I forget men are disgusting."

"You lived with Tony and Matt, and you forgot men are disgusting? How's that even possible?"

"They must've been on their best behavior."

I pull her closer so she's lying on me almost awkwardly, and I have my face pressing into her neck again. She doesn't struggle or anything; she lays there on top of me, allowing me to hold her close. And she says, "Anything else I need to know?"

"I don't know. You'll probably have to ask me questions as they come. I don't know how things would've panned out if things had gone a little differently, but once Lilith showed up, things escalated quickly."

She tenses against me, so I pull back to see her face. "What is it? What's wrong?"

She grimaces, her eyes tearing up before she squeezes them shut and presses her face against my chest. "I can't believe she's gone."

"I know, baby girl. I'm sorry."

She takes a shuddering breath, and I feel her hot tears on my bare skin. I wrap my arms around her, pulling her into me until she's sitting in my lap. She cries quietly, occasionally attempting to break free from me, but then she allows herself to lean into me. I didn't have any serious attachment to Lilith, but that doesn't mean I don't feel the loss of her, that I don't understand how a part of Antoinette went with her.

After a few minutes, her tears slow until finally, she's lying there quietly. She shifts against me again, and I see her wince, so I pull back, my eyes scanning down her body until I come to the now-red bandage on her torso. She shrugs. "Looks like I overdid it."

"That from the warehouse?"

"Yeah, I caught a bullet. Lilith ended up with the rest of them."

Her eyes tear again, but this time, she blinks them away, giving her head a shake. "Luckily, it was just a flesh wound. I have some bandages in my kit, though I'm hoping they're still dry."

I move off the bed, pulling her with me and scooping her into my arms before heading to the bathroom. I set her down in the middle of the small room, making sure she's steady on her feet before moving away and turning on the shower. I step inside, giving myself a quick clean-up before leaning out the shower door, indicating for her to join me.

She smirks as she walks toward me. "Gonna be kind of a tight fit, isn't it?"

"We'll make it work."

She squeezes into the small shower stall with me, then allows me to help her wash up. I gently pull the bandages off her, making a mental note that her bullet wound appears to be fine. I help her rinse the wound, running warm, soapy water over the angry skin.

"I feel like it's my fault."

I frown, but I get it. "No one plays the blame game more often than I do, but there's no one person to blame. And in this specific circumstance, it's equal shares of blame to everyone involved, though condemning people changes nothing. All it does is make the pain fester, the questions of what if and if only setting you on a tortuous existence. The fact of the matter is, we can shoulda, coulda, woulda ourselves into oblivion, but we would still be right here, where we are now."

"Well, Tony has no problem blaming someone."

"Oh, really? And who is Tony blaming now?"

"Once he heard more of the story from me, his blame is being put directly on Carolina. Or, as he likes to call her, the deceitful whore bag."

"Sounds like Tony. He often forgets that some people have legitimate motives for doing shitty things."

"And did she?"

I nod as I massage the shampoo into her scalp. "I believe she did. But really, she's the least of our problems right now."

"Not according to Tony. He's gonna make it his life's mission to find her and make her pay."

"That's gonna be a problem."

She raises her head, looking up at me as she shifts back into the water so I can rinse her hair. "Why is that?"

I stare down at her, reaching behind her to turn the water off. I open the shower stall door, motioning for her to move back so I can reach around and grab the towels that are hanging there. I quickly dry myself off, wrapping the towel around my waist before turning back to her. She holds her hand out, giving me an expectant look that I ignore, instead pulling her out to stand on the rug so I can dry her myself. I'm sure she's rolling her eyes at me, something else I'm going to ignore for now. "Let's get you bandaged and dressed, and then we'll go find Jayme."

She lifts a brow at me, pulling the towel from my hand so she can do a better job getting the water out of her hair than I did. "Who is Jayme?"

I sigh deeply, reaching into the cabinet under the sink and pulling out a first aid kit. Then I turn to her and say, "You're about to find out."

Chapter Twenty-Five

Toni

I'M SO TIRED. I was aware I'm not in tip-top condition to be pulling off secret ocean missions, but I'm still shocked by my level of exhaustion. I'm certain it's only my tenacity that got me through the swim, that, and my refusal to let Tony win if I failed. But after that, plus my reunion with Dare and our deep conversations and animalistic sex, I'm completely spent.

Unfortunately, it doesn't seem like I'm going to get a nap anytime soon because, once I'm dressed, Darius hustles me out the door. The sun is peeking over the horizon, and I stare out at the stillness of the water, mesmerized by how beautiful it is. Dare stands with me for a few moments, but then, the next thing I know, I hear a voice from behind us asking, "Where the fuck did you come from?"

I peer around Darius and see Agatha standing there with her mouth dropped open in shock. Can't say I blame her, considering it's not every day someone swims across the Atlantic. She laughs. "Every time I want to believe that maybe we're not related, you prove me wrong."

Dare steps back from me, and I move away from the rail, turning toward her. She walks toward me so quickly I can't help but startle, but then she's got her arms wrapped around me, and she's hugging me tightly to her, whispering into my ear, "I'm glad you didn't fucking die."

A squeak falls from my lips. She's squeezing me so tightly I can barely breathe, never mind speak. Then, as quickly as she had grabbed me, she releases me, her hands coming to my shoulders as she pulls back and stares me in the face. "I'm telling you right now, if you had died, this guy would have to be put down. He's fucking insufferable and would be completely useless."

I look over at Darius, who shrugs at me but doesn't seem to disagree. Then, he says, "We spent a good amount of time lying around in the dark when we first got here. There may have been a lot of words said. I was delirious."

Agatha releases me, snorting as she takes a step toward him, giving him a good punch in the chest. "Like fuck you were delirious."

She goes to say something further, but he interrupts her. "Would you like to go back into that room and stand in the corner for a while longer, or do you want to stop talking?"

Her mouth snaps shut, but she appears to be seriously thinking about the question. "I'll quit talking for now. But I reserve the right to change my mind."

I look between the two of them, a little confused. I'd forgotten how much time they've spent together, most often under intensely stressful conditions. Their interactions remind me of siblings or how I presume siblings act in a so-called normal family situation. That I can consider anything that has happened to them in recent times to be a normal anything is preposterous, but it is what it is.

"Where were you headed, Agatha?"

"I was coming to find you. We're getting closer to our destination, so we figure we best try to come up with some kind of plan." She glances at me, then back at Dare, smiling widely as she says, "Won't Jayme be surprised to find we have a new person on board?"

She turns abruptly, walking along the rail before taking a left, moving deeper into the ship. Dare grabs my hand, pulling me as he follows behind her. I'm surprised by the massiveness of the ship. It's my understanding that it's not a commercial freight liner, but it would be unusual for a single person to own a ship of this size.

We finally enter an area that looks like a galley, and then I smell food. My stomach rumbles, and suddenly, I'm dying of thirst.

We walk through the cafeteria area and then into the kitchen, where a group of men are working at a long counter. Darius and Agatha enter first, and everyone greets them at once, apparently all on good terms, given the shady circumstances that landed them here.

Then I enter the room behind them, and the place falls silent. A tall man with blond hair freezes mid-sentence, staring at me with narrowed eyes. "Where the fuck did you come from?"

I give him a cocky smile, pointing over my shoulder as I reply, "The Atlantic. It was a long swim."

The man looks at Darius, then Agatha, and then back at me, resting his hands on the counter and leaning on it, shaking his head. "Apparently, I need to think about upping the security on my ship. Though, I don't think we ever really considered the odds that someone would decide to swim to it."

Darius pipes in. "Jayme Devereaux. This is Antoinette. I may have forgotten to mention the tracking device. Though, I honestly didn't consider that anyone would swim to the ship either."

Jayme squeezes his eyes shut, inhaling deeply through his nose. He does this a few times before finally opening them and eyeing Darius. "Tracking device?"

Darius nods, "In my watch. I had no idea either, until Agatha told me."

"There's also a tracking device in me," Agatha states, waving her hands over her body as if she doesn't know exactly where it is.

"Well, isn't that great? I have half a mind to toss all three of you overboard."

Darius laughs. "I'd like to see you try."

They stare at each other, all humor gone. Agatha looks back at me and rolls her eyes, and I can't help but laugh as she interrupts their staring contest. "No one's getting thrown overboard. Stop being ridiculous."

Jayme sighs again, turning to the man on the other side of him and telling him to finish up the food prep they were doing. He walks toward me, but then steps around and out the door. "I guess we've got some stuff to talk about."

The three of us follow him to the other side of the large room, where a beverage bar is set up. He grabs a mug and then pours himself some coffee, motioning for us to grab whatever we'd like. I get a large cup of water, immediately downing it before refilling it. Then I grab another cup, adding ice and a couple inches of cranberry juice before topping it off with sparkling water. I follow Jayme over to a table and sit across from him as we wait for Darius and Agatha to join us.

Jayme is eyeing me suspiciously, and I can't seem to wipe the smile off my face, which I'm sure is obnoxious. Finally, I ask, "So, how do you know Darius?"

He lifts his eyebrows at me. "Who doesn't know the Beast?"

I mirror his expression. "Well, I'm sure at one point or another, somebody doesn't know him. I'll rephrase: when exactly did you first cross paths with him?"

He sighs again, resting his forearms on the table and leaning toward me. "I've known Darius since we were kids. Our families were friends, so we got to commiserate about how shitty they were."

I know nothing about Darius' family. Much like me, there's a big split between Darius, the accountant, and Dare the Beast. And there hasn't been enough time to review every little detail about both of us. "Well, are you friend or foe?"

He levels his cool stare at me, his arms coming up and crossing over his chest as he assesses me. "I could go either way. It's a sliding scale most days."

I nod, looking around the galley as I run out of questions I want to ask him before anyone else comes over.

"How did you end up on my ship?" His words are low and cold, and his eyes match his tone as he watches me.

"Helicopter. I was dumped off a ways out, then swam toward the marker until I crossed paths with you all."

"What would you have done if the marker was off? Or if it had been a trap and Dare wasn't even on this ship?"

I raise my eyebrows at him, knowing he's testing how prepared we were for extenuating circumstances. "Well, there were two markers on that map, so I had two shots at someone being here."

I figure he'll ask me what I mean by markers, but I'm saved when Darius and Agatha finally join us. Agatha pushes a bagel toward me, which I accept gratefully. It's everything I can do not to inhale it like a mannerless cretin. Instead, I take an almost too-large bite, keeping my head down while I chew it. Agatha does the same, though, with a little more vigor, likely being a good sport and drawing some attention off me. I take another bite, and a small moan slips from my lips, and my hand comes up, covering my mouth. Darius is watching me, smiling, and I feel a slight blush creep up my neck.

I glance over and see Jayme watching us, then he says, "Jesus fucking Christ, tell me it ain't so."

Darius glances at him. "What are you talking about?"

"The Great Beast succumbs to love." This comes out more as a statement than a question, and Darius laughs, giving him a small shrug. But he doesn't say anything, and Jayme continues, "I never thought I'd see the day the beast is finally tamed."

I roll my eyes, swallowing my giant bite of bagel before replying, "I don't know if I would go so far as tamed, but I have made him purr a few times."

Jayme makes a face, and Agatha laughs next to him, jabbing him with her elbow as she jokes. "What's the matter, Devereaux? No one ever made you purr before?"

He turns his gaze to her, his eyes lighting up with interest as he looks her up and down, then focuses on her face. "I don't know. Maybe you should find out."

"In your dreams, baby."

"Every night, Agatha. Every night."

Darius and I both glance between the two of them with interest. I feel the energy crackling in the air, and I look over at Dare, jabbing him with my elbow so he looks at me. I give him a questioning look, and he smirks in return, the corners of his mouth twitching as he tries not to smile. Finally, he turns back to Jayme and says, "Let's just keep it down all right. We don't have time for canoodling right now."

Agatha scoffs, "Are you saying you didn't canoodle before bothering to let us know we have a new guest on board?"

I feel the heat rising in my face again, but Dare doesn't even blink; he turns his gaze to her and says, "Touché. But regardless of that, the canoodling is over. We need to get back to business because I'm sick of dealing with this shit. I'm tired. I want a vacation. Then I can do all the canoodling I want."

Agatha and Jayme both nod, adjusting themselves so they're facing us. With only a slight amount of mockery, they both square their shoulders and place their hands on the table in front of them, their focus entirely on Darius. Jayme says, "So let's get down to business. What's next?"

"Antoinette needs to fill us in on a few things, and then we can try to determine our best plan of action." He says this as he looks at me, and I push the last bit of my food away, quickly losing my appetite. I take a slow drink of my cranberry concoction, then set it down in front of me and push it away, too, so I won't fidget with it. I'm not entirely sure what to say, so I ask. "What do you want to know?"

Jayme speaks up first. "Since I don't feel like we have much time here, maybe start at the beginning, but give us the highlights. Who are you? Where do you come from? Are you friend or foe?"

"I've only learned recently who I am. I was always called Toni, and all my documents showed Antoinette Moreau. I was raised in a group home setting, where survival of the fittest lead most days. They taught us everything we need to know about living a lie. That's how I ended up getting assigned to Darius, though I'm not entirely sure why they chose me to do it, considering I don't get the impression he really has a type. We'd all heard the rumors on how he wanted out of the life, that he had turned over a new leaf and had moved on as the accountant, Darius Hughes. It was whispered that he had the perfect cover for someone wanting to clean or hide money or whatever you wanted to do with illegal money. He was also known for constantly thwarting the illegal dealings of many powerful men, so eliminating him was high on everyone's to-do list. He was so different from the man on paper that it was quite confusing at first, but after a while, he grew on me."

"You're the enemy?" Jayme's words are quiet, cold.

I meet his gaze head-on, unflinching. "I was. But I'm not now."

He narrows his eyes at me, then looks over at Darius. I don't look away from him, so I don't know what passes between the two of them, but finally, Jayme turns back to me and nods. "Fine. Continue."

I clear my throat. "It obviously shocked me to learn I was the enemy in that warehouse with Vincent. Shit, everything he said was a fucking shock, really."

Agatha speaks up. "It sure was to me. And I bet Lilith must've been super pissed that Vincent ran his mouth like that before she could explain it to us herself."

I tense, a stabbing pain coming through my chest at the mention of her name. Agatha looks at me expectantly, but she must see the look on my face because she frowns, then leans forward, staring into my face as she asks, "Toni? What is it?"

The stabbing pain is there again, and my response gets stuck in my throat as my guts twist. I squeeze my eyes shut, but then Dare's hand is on the back of my neck, squeezing hard enough for it to be slightly uncomfortable. I lean back into his grip, taking a shuddering breath in as he leans close, pressing his face against my ear, whispering, "Are you okay? Do you want me to tell her?"

I shake my head, forcing myself to swallow the lump in my throat as I open my eyes and turn my head toward him. He pulls back and looks at me as I reply, "I'll do it. I can do it."

With a last squeeze on the back of my neck, he releases me and sits back in his chair. I give him a small smile and then turn back to Agatha, who's staring at me with a stony expression on her face. "Lilith is dead. She died in that warehouse protecting me."

Agatha's eyes search mine for a few moments, then she gives a curt nod and sits back in her chair. I don't know what to do. It's not like I know her at all or that I even know how to comfort anyone. "She didn't have time to tell me much, but she told me that Mickey would know everything, and he seemed to. Do you want to know?"

She nods, so I give them a summary of how Lilith's father abused her when she was barely a teenager. And how she had fought every day of her life to keep us safe. I explained our individual parentage and how each of us ended up on a different path. I did my best to explain how much we meant to her. I probably did a shit job, but I never said I was good with words.

Agatha's eyes look glassy, but she keeps her emotions in check. We all sit silently for a few moments, and finally, she asks, "So you're saying we have different fathers?"

I nod. "That's what Mickey said. I think he made a joke once about us being Irish twins, but we definitely do not have the same father."

She tilts her head at me as if she's studying my features. We have the same eyes, which, of course, we got from Lilith, but her bone structure is a little more refined, and she's shorter than me, willowier, as they say.

Jayme interrupts, laughing. "You certainly look like twins at a glance, but those similarities become less the more you look at the two of you next to each other. I figure you both got your looks from your mama, and all that other shit came from whoever your father was. Kind of like me."

Darius snorts. "Pretty sure you got all the shit from both sides."

Jayme squints at him. "You say that now, but I recall a few times where you were eyeballing my mom. Shall I remind you of the things that you've said about her?"

Agatha laughs, and I turn to him, my mouth falling open in shock. "Darius Hughes, you dirty dog. You had a thing for the reverse-age-gap?"

He turns and looks at me, confusion painting his face. "Reverse age gap? What are you talking about?"

"Oh, I do like a good reverse age gap," Agatha says, waggling her brows.

Dare and Jayme look at each other, perplexed, so I take pity on them and explain. "A reverse age gap is when the woman is significantly older than the man. As opposed to the age gap where the man is significantly older than the woman."

Dare shakes his head at me. "I always forget about you and your porn books. You don't seem the type."

Agatha scoffs. "What exactly is the porn-book type? You men could learn a lot from them."

Jayme shakes his head. "No way. What could a romance book possibly teach a man of the world like me?"

"First, it might teach you when to shut the fuck up. That would be a start." Agatha flips him the bird.

Then, I add, "Also, dirty talk. The importance of foreplay and clitoral stimulation."

Agatha cackles loudly. "That's a good one. What else...Oh, cheating is a no. Possessiveness is a go."

Dare interjects, "How about stalking? Is stalking okay?"

Agatha shakes her head, staring at him like he's crazy as she replies. "Stalking is only good in fiction. Outside of fiction, it is a hard no."

Jayme asks, "How about somnophilia? Is that good?"

Agatha and I both say, "Only if previously consented to."

Darius and Jayme look at each other, then Darius shrugs. "You got me, man. If Antoinette took a survey of my rights and wrongs, I'd be in deep shit, for sure."

"Possibly in jail." Jayme laughs. "I would definitely be in jail."

Dare chuckles. "It's likely we would both be dead. Jail would be a luxury."

I sit back and enjoy the moment of camaraderie, but I can't help but feel the vacancy inside me where Lilith is. She would've loved this conversation; she would have had so much to add.

Agatha's voice across the table drives me out of my thoughts, and I blink a few times before asking, "What was that?"

"Vincent thinks you're dead. You have an opportunity here to stay that way if you want to."

I blink at her, confused by what she's saying. Dare reaches his hand out, squeezing my leg so I turn to him, and he says, "She's right. If you ever wanted to be done with this life, this is the perfect opportunity. You can start all over again, somewhere else."

I frown at him, placing my hand on top of his and squeezing. "With you?"

He shakes his head. "No, baby girl. I have no choice but to see this through."

"I won't leave you."

"Are you sure? I wouldn't blame you if you wanted to be done with it all. You've been through so much; it would only be fair for you to take the out and walk away."

I scowl at him, then turn my unhappy expression on Agatha and Jayme before replying, "No. I won't leave you. Never."

No one says anything for a few moments, so I finally ask, "So, I guess the real question is, what do we do now?"

Dare and Jayme look at each other for a few moments, as if they're trying to communicate telepathically. I look over at Agatha at the same time as she looks at me, and we both raise our eyebrows and roll our eyes at this bromance. Finally, Agatha chimes in, "I have a few ideas."

Jayme shifts his gaze to her, his mouth twisting as he goes to reply, but she puts her hands up to cut him off. "Don't even bother. It's obvious what we need to do here, so let's stop fucking around and get to it because I'm tired of this shit, too. I want to go home, and it doesn't even fucking matter that I'm not sure where home is. I'll make a new one. This shit needs to end."

I nod in agreement. "I'm with you. What are we going to do to put an end to it once and for all?"

Agatha looks at Dare, who finally nods, so she continues, "Jayme needs to deliver us wherever it is he's supposed to deliver us. Which means Toni needs to get her ass back in the ocean and off our ship."

"Absolutely fucking not." Dare shakes his head as he leans forward, his forearms resting on the table in front of him, his fists clenching. "There must be a better way. She's not getting back in the fucking ocean."

I smile at Dare's little show of sullen disapproval, patting him on the shoulder before turning to Agatha. "You're right. I need to get the hell off the ship before we get close enough for somebody to see me. The only leverage we have right now is Vincent assuming I'm dead. If I'm a ghost, we have a leg up on him, especially since I'll be able to take back the information on where you're going so that we can be prepared."

Dare is still shaking his head, and he looks at Jayme. "Come on, man. There has to be another way."

Jayme leans back in his chair with a little shrug. "There really isn't. We make it into port with her on the ship, then she's going to either be stuck here, or she'll get caught trying to leave. The best way to get her into position on the other end is for her to go now. Or, at least, soon."

"Matt and Tony are waiting for me to make a move. They figured I wouldn't be able to go into port with you, so they're trailing behind us a safe distance away, monitoring my location every moment. They have the resources needed, and they'll know when to come for me."

Dare pushes himself back from the table furiously, then sits in his chair stiffly, his hands fisted on his legs, his jaw clenching and clenching. He looks at me, and I see the desperation in his eyes, the fear. I rise from my seat, shifting over so I'm sitting in his lap, my hands cupping his cheeks as I search his golden gaze.

It seems my beast is feeling emotional, but I know once we get the ball moving, he'll come back around. So, instead of responding to him with snark and fire, I lean in and brush my lips against his, releasing the breath I'd been holding as his arms come up around me. He squeezes me so tightly my breath catches, but when I squirm a bit in protest, he eases his grip so I can pull back and meet his eyes. "I got this. We got this."

He stares at me, his eyes on fire and his lips pressed together tightly. Finally, he sighs and says, "It's not that I don't think you can handle it. I just can't lose you. You know what'll happen if I lose you."

I nod because I know, and everyone at this table also knows how completely off the rails he'll go if I meet my end. "You know what they say, Darius. What doesn't kill us…"

He scowls at me. "What? It makes us stronger." His words are mocking.

I don't let it get to me; I just smile at him. "Well, yes. But it's more than that. What doesn't kill us brings to the forefront what we have to live for. What's the point of money and power if you've sacrificed everyone who has ever been important to you to gain and keep it?"

He squints at me, his left eye twitching, his lips twisting a bit as he replies, "Going soft on me, baby girl?"

I laugh. "Hardly. But I'm becoming quite fond of this whole fuck-around-and-find-out mentality. It grows on you after a while."

He smiles in response, his golden eyes warm on my face as he leans closer, nipping at my earlobe, his breath warm against my ear as he whispers, "I've got something that'll grow for you."

I can't stop the giggle that erupts, and I squirm against his hold. Then, I hear Jayme's voice behind me, "Oh, for fuck sake. Would you two get a room?"

Agatha snorts, and I hear a chair push back as she says, "They are disgusting. I may as well go take a nap."

Dare stands suddenly, hefting me up into his arms, and I yelp, my hands clutching at him as he says, "You two do whatever you want; just don't bother us until it's time to toss Toni overboard. We can make her walk the plank."

Dare heads toward the exit, still carrying me, and I push against his chest to break free. "I can walk."

Dare hefts me higher, giving me a little bounce so I'm more secure in his arms. "Don't care. Shut your face."

I'm slightly annoyed but I'm not unhappy about it, so I shut my face and let him take me wherever he wants.

Chapter Twenty-Six

Dare

I DIDN'T ENJOY TOSSING Antoinette overboard, but it also wasn't a great hardship once I wrapped my head around the idea. I heard her cursing and snarling on her drop into the water, along with the cackling of Agatha as she watched. It was immensely satisfying, given how much shit she has given me since we met.

Of course, now, I'm wandering around the ship rather morosely, with that deep fear that she won't make it out alive, leaving a hollow feeling in my chest. She explained Matt would have eyes on her tracker at all times, and the time she'd spend in the water would be minimal, but I know how easy it is to lose sight of someone in the middle of the ocean at night. And though she had a flare in her kit, the odds that she would risk using it were nil.

Regardless, I constantly scan the sky for her distress signal, relieved and annoyed when nothing comes of it.

I'm on what feels like my hundredth lap of the ship when I see Agatha and Jayme approaching me, matching serious expressions on their faces. They stop when they reach me, and we spend a few moments staring out at the ocean as daybreak peeks over the horizon. I know why they're here; they don't even have to say it.

It's time.

Agatha inhales deeply through her nose, then turns to me. "Are you ready for this?"

"Ready as I'll ever be."

She gives me an assessing look, then reaches her hand out, squeezing my forearm as she says, "She'll be fine, Dare. I promise."

I raise my eyebrows at her, then eye her hand on my arm before replying, "Kind of a bold promise, don't you think?"

She doesn't waiver. "It's facts. You know Antoinette, but you don't know Toni. She is the reckoning. You'll see."

She's right. What I know of Toni is minimal, given the chaotic evolution of our relationship. I know her intimately. I feel her soul entwined with my own, but the inner workings of her character and upbringing are foreign to me. But it still grates on my nerves that someone may know her better than I do. "I didn't get the impression you knew her all that well, either."

"I don't, but I've heard people talk, and countless people would swear up and down that she's the most dangerous sister. And since this would have included Lilith, that's saying something."

I have an idea how dangerous Toni may be if provoked, especially after hearing how she took out some of her attackers after she was assaulted. She understands the kill-or-be-killed mentality, and she's not afraid to get her hands dirty when needed. "Let's hope these rumors are accurate because she's going to need that bloodthirsty tenacity to get us out of this mess in one piece."

"Did you tell her Tony isn't allowed to hunt down Carolina?"

I nod as we walk toward the room where we were previously being held. "I did. She said she'd do her best, but we all know how Tony is once he gets something in his head. Luckily, he won't focus on her too much right now, but we'll have to rein him in once all this is over."

"Do you think he'd just kill her outright?"

I shrug, opening the door to our makeshift prison and motioning for her to enter before me. "Possibly. But I feel like he'd play with her first just because it's fun for him."

Her eyes widen as she walks to the corner where the shackles are still hanging from the walls. She bends down, picking up an old dirty bottle of sand, handing it to me. "Jayme said we better get gross, or they'll be suspicious."

"What is it?" I ask skeptically, holding the bottle gingerly.

"Rancid oil." She moves to the other side of the room, grabbing the clothing that's on the floor beside the bed. "And our old dirty clothes."

I groan, opening the top of the bottle as she walks over, carrying the dirty clothing from the days we spent in the dark. I hold my breath and pour some of the rancid oil in my hair, shaking my head in disgust, though I'm also relieved Jayme thought of it. I hand the oil to Agatha, then grab my clothes and make quick work of changing. By the time I'm redressed, she's passing the bottle to me, a nice grimy sheen in all the right places. I finish making myself appropriately disgusting, and by the time I turn back, she's dressed and ready for the shackles.

She has her back pressed against the corner of the room, waiting for me to secure her into place, and as I lock the metal cuff around her neck, her eyes meet mine. She doesn't seem afraid or nervous, just resigned to whatever comes next. I bend down, grabbing the wrist shackles, and she takes one from me, securing it herself as I stand there waiting.

I move to secure her other wrist, but her hand grips mine tightly. I raise my eyes to hers, those blue eyes so similar to Toni's that it makes my breath catch. Then she says, "This is what they trained her for, Dare."

I frown down at her, securing the shackle on her wrist as I ask, "What are you talking about?"

"Toni," she explains, her eyes burning like blue fire at me. "She was always meant to be the hero."

I choke out a humorless laugh, my forehead pressing against hers until those blue eyes are one giant orb in my vision. But we don't say anything else; we take a few breaths together, then get back into position.

And we wait.

Chapter Twenty-Seven

Dare

IT FEELS LIKE WE'VE been waiting for years for something to happen, though I'm sure it has only been a few hours.

I did not miss the dark, that's for sure.

Finally, we hear a commotion near the door, and I force myself not to tense up as the door opens, light sneaking in behind the silhouette of someone who appears to be on the large side. I see an arm reach up, and then, with a click, the light comes on.

It's Jayme.

"Jesus fucking Christ, Jayme," I snarl, sitting up and running my hands through my gross hair. "Did you have to make such a dramatic entrance?"

He smiles at me, shrugging as he moves toward Agatha, holding a small key. "I didn't have to, but I definitely enjoyed it."

Agatha gives him a bored look, straightening in her shackles as he approaches. "What's going on?"

"I have updated instructions to deliver you to a specific location, and since they paid a premium for the service, I'm inclined to deliver. You have twenty minutes to get cleaned up, and we're out of here."

I narrow my eyes at him. "Get cleaned up? We were already clean, you fucking asshole."

"Yes, well, I had no idea they would ask for delivery, providing me with the perfect cover for why you're not covered in a week's worth of grime. How was I to know?"

Agatha comes up behind him, and he's so focused on me he doesn't notice the threat until it's too late. She kicks him in the back of the knee at the same time that she puts him in a headlock, and he goes down, face first, with her on top of him. She rubs her hair in his face, taunting, "Do I smell good?"

He curses, using his own strength to extricate himself from her grip, and she rolls off him, spinning to her feet into a grappling stance as he rises, squaring off with her. He narrows his eyes but doesn't make a move to grab her as he says, "You just wait."

Her eyes widen, and I don't miss the gleam of excitement as she responds, "I'll be waiting."

"Fucking children," I mutter as I get to my feet and walk toward the door. I have twenty minutes to get cleaned up, and I'm not going to waste them listening to these idiots flirt. I stop in the doorway, turning and saying, "I'll meet you in the galley."

I don't wait for a response; I hurry down to the room I've been staying in and make quick work of washing the stench from my hair and skin. I steal one of Jayme's suits from the closet, then take a few moments to polish my shoes, feeling more like myself than I have in days.

If it wasn't for the ominous black cloud hanging over my head, I would almost say there was a spring in my step.

Shockingly, Jayme and Agatha are waiting for me when I get back to the galley. Jayme gives me a dirty look. "Nice suit."

"It could be a little roomier in the crotch, but it'll do."

Agatha cackles. "You a little short in the drawers, Jayme?"

"If you're that concerned, maybe you need to look. I can assure you there's nothing short on me."

She opens her mouth to respond, but I interrupt. "Do you two ever fucking stop?"

They both look at me and say, "Nope."

I shake my head, sighing as I respond, "Well, as amusing as this is, how about we shelve it until we know we're not gonna die soon?"

Jayme smiles. "I'm mostly certain I'm not going to die today."

Agatha grins as well, "I figure there's a 75% chance I die. But I've gone into situations with far worse odds, so I'll take it."

I'm not surprised she's so nonchalant about the idea of dying. She has so much faith in her sister that it's borderline concerning, but from listening to her, I can't help but feel like I'm missing a huge part of who Antoinette is. I only know two sides of her: the duplicitous viper who set out to destroy me, and the empty shell who danced around me almost innocently. I figure she's a mix of both people, but right now, we need the viper.

Jayme looks at his watch, then heads toward the door, motioning for us to follow him. "I won't have to restrain you until we get closer to our destination. I told that fucker I'd have to play nice with you to get you out of port inconspicuously, and he bought it."

A group of Jayme's men wait for us on the gangway. Jayme takes a bag from one of them and hands it to me. "The quickest way to get you through the customs checkpoint is legally. Passports are in here."

I open the bag and peek inside. "Passports?"

"It's amazing what you can get when you have a lot of money."

I nod in agreement, then take mine out of the bag and put it in the inside pocket of my suit jacket. I hand Agatha hers and do a double-take as I watch her put it in the inside of her coat. "New wardrobe?"

Her lip curls, and she gives Jayme a dirty look. "Apparently, someone has a woman visitor often enough that she gets her own closet. Very unprofessional, if you ask me."

Jayme gives her a bland look. "Not that I have to explain myself to you, but I have a female crew member who isn't working right now. Those are her clothes."

"Really? That's your story? Where is she?"

The blond-haired guy opens his mouth to answer, but Jayme puts his hand up and says, "Not that it's any of your fucking business, but she's on maternity leave."

"Maternity leave? You've got to be kidding."

He shakes his head, muttering to himself under his breath, and I smile. I bet Antoinette and I were like that not too long ago. Well, to be fair, we probably still act like that sometimes since she still hasn't learned when to shut her fucking mouth.

The two of them continue their bickering as we walk off the ship. There are two customs agents waiting for us at the bottom of the gangway, and Jayme takes one of them to the side, having a brief conversation that has the man nodding. He comes over to me, quickly checking my passport and then Agatha's, and then motions for us to move along.

Most of Jayme's men stay behind to deal with whatever aboveboard goods on the ship need to be managed. There's a car waiting for us, and Jayme motions for Agatha and me to get in the back.

I open the door to see a set of handcuffs and a black bag on the seat. I glance over and see another matching set on the other side for Agatha. We both pick them up and then sit there with them in our laps as if this is an everyday occurrence. Jayme gets in the front passenger seat and looks back at us. "I'll let you know when it's time for those."

Agatha yawns, completely unbothered by the situation, as she asks, "Do I have time for a nap?"

Jayme cranes his head around to look at her. "What is with you and naps? Do you ever stop sleeping?"

"I learned at a young age to take whatever sleep I can get whenever I can get it—that and food. If there's a snack available, eat it."

"Fair," he replies, then points to the middle of the seats as he continues. "There should be some snacks in there if you're hungry, but you don't have time for much of a nap."

Her eyes light up, and she doesn't hesitate to pop open the middle console and dig through the goods she finds there. I shake my head at her, asking, "How could you possibly eat right now?"

She pulls out a bag of chips, not hesitating to open it, quickly shoving some in her mouth. She barely swallows before she replies, "Not eating will change nothing. I guess I'd rather die with a full belly."

"You really are crazy, aren't you?"

The smile she gives me is pure Lilith, and I can't help but smile in response as she says, "All depends on your perspective, Darius. I may not know a lot about love and affection, but I know more than my fair share about survival."

"Survival comes down to naps and snacks? Is that what you're saying?"

She nods, swallowing before answering. "Hey, the first things they deny you in a torture situation are sleep and food. So that should tell you something."

"Sure, but naps and snacks don't save you from pain."

She raises both her eyebrows at me and smiles wickedly. "Yeah, but you know I like pain."

Jayme crows from the front seat, twisting around and looking at her with renewed interest. "Well, well, well. Isn't that some news."

She stops smiling and glares at him. "Not for you, shithead."

They bicker again, and I shake my head and stare out the window. I'm still worried about Toni. Worried about all my people, really. There's no way for me to know if she made it out of that water. She assured me that the guys were watching her every movement, preparing to retrieve her as soon as they noticed her moving away from Agatha and me. But I don't enjoy being out of control, having to count on all the unknowns to assure her safety.

It doesn't take long before Jayme is telling us to get ourselves ready. Agatha hands me her black bag, then cuffs her own hands behind her back. Her eyes meet mine, and she gives me a small smile. "Back into the dark we go."

I nod, returning her smile. "Into the dark we go."

I move to put the bag over her head, but she pulls back, so I drop my hands, waiting for her to speak, a serious expression on her face. "Don't forget what Toni said. What doesn't kill us..."

I give her a tight smile and a nod, then I put the bag over her head, securing it around her neck. She wiggles around in the seat and settles as best she can with her hands cuffed behind her back.

Jayme reaches his hand out, and I give him my bag, then cuff my own hands behind my back. I lean closer to him so that he can easily reach me to put the bag over my head, but before he does, I look him in the eyes. "Do you remember what to do if it all goes south?"

He meets my gaze, nodding. "Burn it all."

Then he places the bag over my head, and everything goes black.

Chapter Twenty-Eight

Dare

AGATHA WAS RIGHT. A nap and a snack would've been a great idea.

Jayme dropped us off not long after the bag went over my head, and a few men led me and Agatha a fair distance before finally strapping us to chairs and leaving the room. I'm not sure how long we've been sitting here, but I'm bored.

Everybody thinks the life of a criminal mastermind is all laughs and parties, but really, it's long, dark hours of nothing. Yeah, sometimes we beat people up, sometimes somebody dies, but we spend most of our lives sitting around, waiting. Waiting for news, waiting for someone else to make a move, waiting and waiting and waiting.

So now, I'm tired and hungry, and when I stupidly mention this to Agatha, she laughs at me. Of course, she can sleep anywhere, so I'm thinking the long-drawn-out moments of silence from her are her taking a cat nap. Meanwhile, all I can think about is how I should have had some of those snacks in the car. She's probably not even hungry yet.

Goddamn it.

I drifted off for a moment when I hear movement across the room. I hear Agatha next to me, but I can't tell how close she is or which direction she is facing through the bags over our heads.

I hear what sounds like a group of people walking toward us, and then the footsteps stop, and I feel someone fiddling with the tie on the bag on my head. It's yanked free, and I blink rapidly as my eyes attempt to adjust to the light in the room.

It takes me a few moments to see clearly, and then I look around. Sure enough, Vincent is standing there surrounded by his cronies, and they all look smug. This seems to be their default expression, and I'd like nothing more than to smash their teeth in right now.

Vincent doesn't give me the chance to speak, deciding to immediately start running his mouth. I'm only half-listening as I glance around the room, annoyed that I seem to be sitting in my own warehouse. Or it could be a different one, and they look very similar, considering a warehouse is a warehouse.

Agatha is off to my right, but she's sitting facing me. They also remove the bag from her head, and she mostly looks bored as normal. I know what she's doing. She's literally sitting there waiting for her sister to come save the day. I can't suppress the smile on my face at the thought, which Vincent notices immediately and wipes it off my face with the butt of his gun. I spit blood onto the floor and then glare at him. "Was that really necessary?"

He gives me that same smug smile, then replies. "No, but it was satisfying."

"Well, are you gonna fucking talk shit all day or get on with it?"

He cocks his head at me. "But Darius, we have so much to talk about."

"I highly doubt that, but you just carry on."

Agatha pipes up next to me. "Maybe we can die of boredom in the meantime."

Vincent turns his gaze to her, his eyes narrowing. "You're going to have a hard time running that mouth with something stuck in it."

She snorts, giving him a disgusted look. "Over my dead fucking body."

"You better shut your fucking mouth, or that can be arranged."

She shakes her head at him, attempting to shrug her shoulders with her cuffed hands secured to the chair. "I don't know why you bother with all this. You know Toni is going to skin you alive when she gets here."

I expect him to go on some tangent about her being long dead in that warehouse in Europe, but he doesn't. Instead, he gets this joyful look on his face and steps closer to us, bending down as he says, "Oh, you didn't hear? It seems your girl had an unfortunate run-in with some sharks."

Agatha's gasp is quiet, but I still hear it, and my blood runs cold. "I have no idea what you're talking about." Somehow, I keep my voice level, even though there's a volcanic tornado brewing in my guts.

He smiles at me, and the beast inside me rumbles. "You all thought you were being so clever. You thought you could outsmart me by staging a rendezvous in the Atlantic. But I don't fucking think so. You wanted to play a game with me, and you lost."

I glance over at Agatha, and she's shaking her head, with her jaw clenched and her eyes glaring daggers at him. Then, she says, "I don't fucking believe you."

I remain quiet, wanting him to continue as I attempt to escape my restraints. But I can't stop the growl that falls from my lips, and he steps even closer to me, leaning forward until he's looking me in the face as he brags, "I'm just sad that they didn't have time to really make her pay before feeding her to the sharks."

I snarl, snapping my head forward and sinking my teeth into his cheek as he's too slow to pull back. I shake my head, yanking against my bound hands as his men leap forward and pull him free. I spit out meat and blood and then bare my bloody teeth at him, snarling, "There's no fucking way."

He curses, pressing a handkerchief to his bleeding cheek and glaring at me. His smile broadens as he looks behind him, taking something from one of his men before turning back to me with a small ball bag in his hand. He tosses it at my feet, and I blink as I recognize it. The black kit I stuffed into Toni's wetsuit myself not too long ago. It's wet, and I see a trickle of light pink water on the dirty gray floor. I squeeze my eyes shut, then open them, hoping Toni's kit won't still be there, staring me in the face, but it's still there.

I straighten in my chair, still shaking my head, looking him in the eye. "You're a fucking dead man. You and anyone you've ever known are fucking dead. I will kill every motherfucking one of you if it's the last thing I do."

Vincent throws his head back and laughs. All of his cronies behind him join him, and soon, all I hear are the echoes of their laughter around me. The beast inside me thrashes again, my gaze drawn to that black bag mocking me from the floor.

There's no fucking way.

I don't want to believe it, but it's difficult to refute the evidence that he's showing me. I feel like I'm being ripped apart from the inside, the beast inside me, bellowing to be set free. If she's gone, then we may as well all be dead.

Vincent's voice draws my attention back to him, and I see he's now standing beside me, pointing a gun at my head. I can't help but roll my eyes. The idea that I'm going to meet my end in this stupid fucking warehouse at the hand of this stupid fucking asshole really twists my pants. "Well, if you're going to do it, just do it. Just for the love of fuck, quit fucking talking."

He smirks at me, that superior look back on his face, and I want to smash all his teeth in even more than before. Of course, he's not the type of guy who knows when it's time to stop talking, so he continues running on. Gloating. Bragging.

Then I hear Agatha behind me, "Oh, for fuck sake, man. Just do it already. I think I'd rather be dead than have to listen to you run your mouth for another fucking second."

He turns his focus on her, raising his brows as he says, "Oh, dear sister. You won't have the luxury of a bullet today. You get to go out into the trade. I already have somebody lined up for your sweet ass."

She doesn't even blink; she grinds out between her clenched teeth, "Whatever. Just don't talk about my ass, you disgusting piece of shit."

He glares at her. "Let's see if you're still running your mouth after you've had a few dozen men sticking their dicks in it."

She rolls her eyes, and I try not to laugh, but a little sneaks out as I feel the hysteria sinking in. I look up at Vincent, meeting his gaze, and I figure I have nothing left to lose, so I taunt him. "Let's stop pretending you have the balls to actually shoot me. You know I still have people out there, people who will hunt you to the end of your days. If what you're saying about Antoinette is true, they're already looking for you. So even if I go straight to hell right this very moment, I can sit back and wait for you because you're going to be next. So, you go right ahead and stick that gun to my head and pull the trigger. The quicker you get this over with, the quicker you get to meet me in hell."

A glimmer of uncertainty passes over his features, but then that condescending look returns. His lip curls, and he sneers, "Oh, your fucking people are dead, too. I blew their little operation out of the fucking Atlantic. I'm just sorry I couldn't get it on video, so I can replay it for you over and over again. Then you'd really beg me to kill you."

I snarl then, spittle flying from my mouth. "You spineless fuck. All you know how to do is sneak up on people when their backs are turned. If you ever had to come face-to-face with an actual threat, you'd piss your pants like the fucking coward you are. I can't wait for someone to rip out your spine and then ass-fuck you with it."

He laughs again, and I hear his group of cronies twittering behind him. As much as I want to get loose, as much as I want to make good on my threats to kill him, I also feel that edge in me seeking relief from the darkness that exploded at the thought of everyone I've ever cared about being gone. I hear Agatha beside me; I hear her words telling me not to believe him, not to give up. It's not over.

And I want to believe her. I want to believe her, but it's this unhinged, maniacal part of me that responds. "Either untie me and fight me, or shoot me. Just get it over with. I don't know what you're waiting for. Just fucking shoot me already. Just get it over with and fucking shoot me. Fucking shoot me. *Shoot me!*"

He has a gun pointed right in my face, and every time I tell him to shoot me, his grip on the gun tightens. I'm staring down the barrel, looking him right in the eyes, daring him to do it.

Finally, he grits out, "I guess I'll see you in hell."

I clench my teeth, but I don't look away. I don't close my eyes.

I'll meet my maker, staring him in the face.

He waits a few seconds, his eyes boring into mine.

Bang.

Chapter Twenty-Nine

Toni

I STILL CAN'T BELIEVE that asshole tossed me overboard. He was almost gleeful about it, making jokes, chuckling, and then waving goodbye to me from the main deck. I was glad to have my little hand-held motor to assist me in my swim because it felt like I was out there for far longer than expected before anyone came along to retrieve me.

By the time the boys locate me, I'm beyond annoyed. Matt's bullshit about being close enough to snag me relatively quickly seems to have gone awry, and the first thing out of my mouth is going to be a demand for an explanation, but when I get into the helicopter, there are a few extra men onboard. And then, within a few seconds, there's an explosion in the distance. None of the men on the helicopter so much as flinch, so I finally give Tony a shove and ask, "What the fuck is going on?"

"Sorry, Nettie. We had a last-minute change of plans and had to run a relay from New York to get these fellas. Somehow, Vincent found out you're not dead, and he was sending a team out to finish the job. Luckily, we caught wind of it and were able to run interference, and in the process, we found out a bunch of information about Vincent, his father, and his entire operation. It's some seriously shady business."

"This doesn't seem like news to me."

Tony makes a face and rolls his eyes a bit as he continues, "Turns out there are far more people on his payroll who would rather not be there than be there. Which means we have an opportunity to pull one over on him—an opportunity we cannot pass up."

I don't like the sound of this, but that won't stop us from taking any advantage we can. "What do we need to do?"

"We need to give these guys something of yours to bring back as proof you're dead. Something Dare would recognize."

A shiver of foreboding runs down my spine as I consider the likelihood that Vincent will brag to Darius about my demise. I'm not sure he'll believe him at first, but he'll have enough information to make it sound workable, and that will 100% send Darius over the edge.

I shake off my unease and reach into my wetsuit, pulling out my kit Dare stuffed in there not too long ago. "Have someone make it look wet and bloody before showing it to him, and Dare should react in a believable manner. What was that explosion?"

"That was one of our rendezvous ships," Matt answers, his lips twisting as he stares out over the horizon. "It was insured."

By the time we make it near land, it's full daylight. The helicopter lands on a yacht anchored offshore, and we have to wait a short time for a close contact of Tony to pick us up on his smaller fishing boat. The helicopter with Vincent's men refuels and heads off to give Vincent the good news of my untimely death.

I'm lucky to find a change of clothes on board, and by the time I'm changed and ready to roll, Tony's buddy is there, and we're on our way. I won't deny that I'm incredibly nervous, maybe even a little scared. Not because I care about what happens to me, but because I can't bear the thought of something happening to Darius.

When we make it into port, we get a message from Jayme stating he dropped Darius and Agatha off over an hour ago. We really left little margin for error in terms of timing, and the unforeseen delay has thrown things off significantly. By the time we make it to where Darius and Agatha are being held, my stomach is in knots. There's no way to tell what's happened if we're too late. I don't believe Vincent intends to kill Agatha because she's worth far more alive, but if he's smart, he'll take out Darius sooner rather than later.

I'm counting on him not being smart. He's a braggart and a blowhard, too intent on patting himself on the back to understand that, sometimes, you're better off getting it over with a bang.

We enter the warehouse stealthily, making our way through the building as swiftly as we can. I hear someone talking up ahead, so we stop to listen. Sure enough, Vincent's running his mouth—again.

We move closer as we listen to him spouting off to Darius that we're all dead. Everyone he ever cared about is dead, and he's going to be next. Darius has some choice words for him, and Agatha is less than convinced. I wish they'd both shut their mouths before he overreacts and does something rash.

We stop outside the doorway, and I peek around the corner. I see them on the other side of the large room. Darius's back is to me, and Vincent is obstructed by an inconveniently placed beam. I glance around, looking for a way to get a better sight of him, but then Vincent raises his gun and points it at Dare.

My heart stops in my chest, my hands squeezing the handles of both pistols that are suddenly in my hands. I look at Tony and Matt, and they both give me a nod, so I turn back and silently enter the room.

There's no hesitation on our part. Tony turns left, Matt turns right, and I step forward, raising both of my guns so I can get Vincent in my line of sight as I move closer. He's still running his mouth, and he still has the gun pointed in Dare's face, who's snarling at him, calling him a coward, daring him to duke it out one-on-one. Of course, we know he'll never do that. Men like Vincent can only get ahead by subterfuge and duplicitousness.

Vincent is so focused on Darius, on taunting him before killing him, that he doesn't see me coming. His gun hand tenses, the barrel raising up and moving closer so it's right in Dare's face, and he's talking about seeing him in hell.

Bang.

He jerks back; the gun going flying as he cradles his now bleeding hand against his chest, and he curses, shouting out in pain and anger.

Bang.

He stops talking.

He blinks a few times.

He stares at his bloody hand in shock, then brings his other hand up and touches his neck, his mouth gaping open and closed like a fish. I stand unmoving, guns still raised but frozen in place, waiting to see if he'll make another move.

He drops to the floor.

I smile and lock eyes with Darius.

Then a bullet ricochets off the beam next to me, and I duck for cover behind the beam I'd stepped around to get a shot at Vincent. The beam is narrow and doesn't exactly cover me, so I try to make myself as narrow as possible as Vincent's men open fire in my direction.

I hear Matt and Tony returning fire, and one by one, bodies start hitting the ground. We didn't have time for any type of COMs between the three of us, so I can only hope that none of the bodies falling belong to us.

I peer around the beam, and I see Agatha free from her restraints, attempting to help Darius out of his cuffs. Vincent's men are swarming into the room like fucking ants on the march, and Agatha falls backwards as if she's been hit.

She quickly rights herself, springing onto her feet and engaging hand-to-hand as the enemy moves in on her. Darius comes out of his chair like a wild animal, jumping into the middle of the fray like the savage fucking beast he is, and I have to force myself not to sit back and watch him.

This is not the fucking time.

I glance beyond them, noticing Tony coming up around on the other side behind them, so I fall back, preparing to loop around to help him. As I turn, more men run in through the same doorway where we entered. I shoot three of them before my guns are knocked from my hands, and then I'm pushed back as several try to overpower me.

I snag a knife, slashing and stabbing, as more people approach me. I'm holding my own, but more men come running in, and my strength is waning. I'm sweating, and my arms are screaming. Matt runs over, helping me cut down the swarm of men as he moves closer to me. Agatha shouts from the other side of the room, and the men suddenly stop coming in from our end and detour around toward Darius and Agatha. Matt looks at me and nods, then takes off back the way he came.

I bend over at the waist, my bloody hands resting on my thighs as I attempt to catch my breath. I look around at the carnage, assessing the situation for what it is. A fucked-up mess. Apparently, cutting off the snake's head didn't work, which most likely means the top snake is waiting in the wings.

Dmitri.

I glance around at the men on the floor in front of me, finally finding one who's still breathing. I grab him, noting the knife stuck in his chest, then lean down close to his face and whisper, "Tell me where he is, and I'll let you live."

He laughs humorlessly, his words pained as he replies, "There are worse things than death."

"We can protect you. If they're so determined to take us down, you must know what we do. We can help you."

He sighs heavily, then swallows a few times. "My life means nothing. I only ever did this to protect my family."

The surrounding chaos is escalating, so I drag him further out of the line of fire. "Tell me where they are. We'll get them to safety."

"You'll remember?"

I nod. "Yes, I will. Tell me."

He rattles off an address, and I repeat it back to him twice, then ask, "What can I tell them to make them trust me?"

He smiles softly, the light in his eyes sparking. "Tell them pink is my favorite color."

I snort out a laugh. "Well, that's not one I've heard before."

"Vincent's father, Dimitri, never got over being duped by Lilith. Even though he ended up with the boy, he vowed to never rest until he had taken her down and stolen the entire kingdom for himself. So that leaves you."

"So, he wants to kill me in order to take my birthright?"

He shakes his head. "No, he just wants you. You're worth far more alive."

"Then why allow Vincent to keep trying to kill me?"

"Because Dmitri didn't believe he could ever pull it off, and he was right. And if Vincent had ever come close to pulling it off, he would've been in a world of hurt." He raises himself up a bit, and I lean close until his breath is against my ear. "Don't let him take you alive. No matter what happens. Don't let them take you alive."

A shiver runs through me as I move back, looking into his eyes. I nod, scanning him over. "What's your name?"

"Erik."

"Pretend you're dead. Don't remove that knife. I'll come back for you."

He nods his head, and I rise, slowly moving around him and edging close to the chaos. The chaos has lessened, leaving me with a more ominous feeling of dread, like the calm before the storm.

There are dead and injured people everywhere. Matt and Tony are still cutting people down, and the whole place feels like a fucking clown car with the enemy seeming to come out of the woodwork endlessly.

At first glance, I don't see Darius or Agatha, but the closer I get to the far doorway, I see Agatha on the ground, with Dare kneeling over her. He's speaking to her, and she's swatting him away, so I keep moving toward the exit in search of Dmitri.

I skirt along the wall, around the ruckus, peeking around the doorway, then hurrying down the hallway. I turn the corner, and a small group of men are rushing toward me. They slow when they see me, and I stop, putting my hands up and waiting for them to approach. Luckily, they're stupid about it and don't approach me all at once, so I make quick work of the first one. The other two come at me a bit more aggressively, but I quickly disarm the one on my left, using the element of surprise to my advantage and then shooting his partner with the gun I swiped.

I'm facing off with the remaining man, and he curses me as he lowers his gun. I smile and laugh. "Can't just kill me, can you?"

He glares at me, spittle flying from his lips as he calls me every uncreative bad word he can think of. But I'm right. He really can't kill me.

Knowing there's an order to take me alive changes things. I step up to him, pulling my hand back and slamming the butt of my gun into his face. His head snaps back, but then he straightens, spitting blood, and we stand there staring at each other. "I need to know where he is."

It appears most of these men are here under duress. I'm sure there are a few truly loyal people, but this is where the idea of having a bigger army always backfires. The more people you work with, the more likely they don't want to be there. If they don't want to be there, they won't put their life on the line to protect you. He cocks his head at me, his mouth bloody when he speaks. "To what end? If it's not him, it's someone else. Do I want to go out there as a marked man?"

"Marked man or dead man. You decide."

He gives me an assessing look, then asks, "You're with Jayme, right?"

I frown, taken aback by his question, but respond, "I don't know about being with Jayme, but yeah, I know the guy. He's kind of a pain in the ass."

He curses under his breath, then spins around and moves back down the hallway, motioning for me to follow. He's muttering to himself as he rushes, and honestly, I'm not even sure he's leading me anywhere other than into a trap. I check what's left of my weapons, realizing a little too late that I should've grabbed more, but here I am.

He stops at the door at the end of the hall and turns to me. "As soon as we go through this doorway, he's going to see you. There's a walkway suspended across the middle of the room. I don't know where he is on it, but that's where he is. He's going to be in the middle of the other men, so honestly, you're better off just killing them all."

"And are all the men up there loyal to him?"

He shakes his head. "No. Only a handful. But you won't know who is or isn't, so I'll go in first, and you can kinda duck behind me. There's a slight chance we might at least be able to get underneath the walkway before he notices. It's a very slim chance, though, and the first thing they're going to do is shoot me to get me out of the way. They won't kill you unless you make them. If you have to choose between being dead or being taken, you want to choose dead."

This is the second time these words have been said to me tonight.

Apparently, this guy is a real piece of shit, or at the very least, has some real piece-of-shit ideas for me. I nod. "Will I be able to tell him apart from the rest of the crowd?"

"Yes. He'll be the only one over-dressed for the occasion. Are you ready?"

"Can I have your gun?"

He raises his eyebrows at me, his lips twisting. "You're right, you know. Jayme is a real pain in the ass. He has been since back before he found out any of this shit with his sister. Never would've thought I'd see the day that selfish bastard started jeopardizing his reputation for someone else, but here we are." He reaches inside his jacket, pulls out a pistol, and hands it to me. "Have one of mine. That's got a full mag. Don't waste them."

I give him a nod, and then he turns and slowly pushes the door open. I'm right at his back, and I peek around him, noting the walkway he spoke of and the cluster of men congregated there.

I put my hand on the man's arm, and he turns back to me. "I need him to move position. I'll never be able to get him up there."

He scowls as he considers his options. "How far are you willing to go?"

I consider his question for a moment, realizing there isn't any length too far if it means this will be over once and for all. And I can't wait and rally the troops because if I do, then Dmitri will be in the wind again, and we'll be right back to square one. "As far as it takes."

He nods again, then turns and takes off in the other direction. I follow, and we hurry to the other side of the warehouse, exiting out into the parking lot. He pulls out a two-way radio. "Mark is on the move. Current location: rear parking lot. Mark is alone. Repeat, mark is alone."

I can already hear the commotion in the building and people shouting. I have no idea where my people are, but I know what has to be done. I look at this man who helped me when he didn't have to and rest my hand on the shoulder. "You get out of here. Get out of here and get your family to safety."

He scoffs, then shakes his head. "No, I'll cover you. I can't just leave."

I bark out a laugh, shaking my head as I say, "There's only room for one death wish right now. We can settle up later; just find me."

He sighs, and I see the indecision in his eyes, so I continue, "Don't be a fool. You'll just get in my way, anyway."

His lips twist, but he nods without further comment, then turns and heads off along the building and disappears around the corner. The commotion is getting louder, and I take a deep breath in, then let it out before I break into a run across the parking lot.

I hear the door burst open behind me, footfalls pounding on the pavement as they give chase. I race across the parking lot, taking twists and turns until I find myself at a dead-end. I curse myself, recognizing what a completely asinine plan this likely was, but I know I'm out of options.

I whirl around just in time to see a group of men headed my way. They're walking now, the lot of them looking pleased with my current predicament. The group stops when they're only about ten yards from me, the few in the front pointing their weapons at me.

I toss my weapons to the side, putting my hands up. The group of men split down the middle, and then there's Dmitri, walking non-chalantly toward me. I'm watching the men more than him, assessing their demeanor to see who is invested in him and his mission.

Dimitri stops when he's only a handful of yards from me. He grins, but it doesn't meet his eyes. Everyone stops moving and stands there, staring at each other, no one saying anything. Dimitri has the most insufferable look of satisfaction on his face, so finally, I laugh kind of awkwardly. "Well, isn't this pleasant? As much as I'd like to stay and hang out, I should probably get going."

Dmitri raises his eyebrows and gives me an unamused look. "So, I guess the rumors about your jokes are true."

Now, I do smile. "Fuck, you've heard about my jokes?"

I hear a few twitters of laughter from the group of men behind him, but one glance over his shoulder, and they all fall silent again. "I didn't mean that as a compliment. Your inability to see the big picture is the reason you're in your current predicament."

I snort and then shrug. "Oh, that's not how I see it."

He takes a step toward me, but I stand fast. "Maybe you better enlighten the rest of us, because your situation does not seem ideal."

I scrunch my face up like I'm truly considering his words, then shake my head. "Nope. I'd rather not."

His eyes harden, his jaw clenching, as he takes another couple of steps closer to me until he's only a few feet from me. "I'm really looking forward to finding out what else that mouth does."

I close the distance between us, so I press my front against his. I tilt my head back and look him in the eye. "So many things."

He gives me a suspicious look, but he doesn't retreat. "Ready to get right to it. I can appreciate that. But is there anything you'd like to know first?"

I reach my hand between us, grabbing onto the waistband of his pants and tugging. "The only question I have is, what are you packing?"

His eyes widen, but he still doesn't back away. Instead, he pushes forward a bit, giving me the exact opportunity I'm looking for.

Because this arrogant piece of garbage forgot a critical rule of warfare: always pat down your enemy before running your mouth.

I do many things at once without breaking eye contact with him. I jerk him closer with one hand while my other hand disappears into the front of his trousers, the back of my hand brushing against his lower abdomen and dick.

One.

I smile up at him, laughing as he pushes his pelvis against the back of my hand.

Two.

He tries to grab onto my upper arms, but I tsk at him, and he drops them, eyeing me with interest.

Three.

Adrenaline pumps through me, and a maniacal laugh bubbles up and sneaks out.

Four.

I release his shirt, holding my hand up so he can see the pin from the hand grenade looped around my finger.

Five.

His eyes widen just in time for me to jam the pin into his eyeball as my hand twists on his balls.

Six.

He hunches over, grunting in pain, and I rear back, then smash my forehead into his face, pushing him down onto the ground. My hand that had been holding the lever in the grenade lets go, beginning the four-second countdown to detonation.

Seven.

I dive away, rolling as his men move toward me. I roll to my feet, scurrying to get away from them as I yell, "Grenade! Grenade!"

Eight.

I hear Darius in the background, bellowing for me, his fear reverberating through the parking lot.

Nine.

I try to move with the flow of men, but they're not moving fast enough, bouncing off each other in their panic. I quit trying to get through them, dropping to the ground and crawling beneath them as I also try not to get trampled.

Ten.

My name cuts through the frenzy, an agonized echo that cuts me to the core.

Boom.

Chapter Thirty

Dare

IT TAKES A FEW minutes for us to get control of the situation.

Vincent's men keep pouring in like rats from a flooding sewer. Most of them don't even appear to be fighting back, which is infuriating, given the kill-or-be-killed situation.

Then everything stops, and I look around, locating Tony and Matt breathing heavily and covered in blood and filth but otherwise, looking no worse for wear. Agatha is injured, but she shook me off earlier, telling me to mind my business, so I assume she's fine now. I look around, but I don't see Toni. "Anyone have eyes on Toni?"

Everyone looks around, shaking their heads, and then we hear the yelling and what sounds like a herd of people running past.

I move toward the doorway when I hear a shout behind me. I turn, and there's a man standing there with his hands up, approaching cautiously but quickly. He keeps his hands up, even as he is standing in front of me, and says, "She's outside. She's drawing Vincent's father, Dimitri, to her. She said she's going to end it."

I curse, the beast inside of me thrashing again. I turn away from him, ready to sprint to her aid, but his voice stops me. "No, you'll never get through that way. I'll show you the way."

The four of us look at each other, but it's not like we have any other option. "What's your name?"

"Anton."

"You helped her get outside?"

He nods as he says, "It was the only option that had any chance of succeeding. She insisted I leave, that I get myself and my family to safety, but I couldn't just go."

I look him in the eye, having no choice but to believe him. We always knew we might all end up dead after this. I guess now we're going to find out.

Anton spins around, running to the other side of the room, and we all follow. We go down several hallways and then come to an exit, and he puts his hand up for us to wait. He opens the door, peeking his head out, looking in both directions before moving to fully exit the building.

We pursue him closely, running around the building, stopping at the edge, and peering around. He looks back to us and whispers, "There's still many people in the way, but they won't be expecting you from this direction, so at least you'll have the element of surprise."

"Thank you." I grab his arm, drawing his attention before continuing, "If Toni said that you should go, then you should go. We got this."

Anton shakes his head. "No. Most of the men out there don't want to be here. They were coerced, forced, or blackmailed. If they see me on your side, they're more likely to fall back. No one wants to die for an unjust cause. It's meaningless to them. It has no actual point outside of someone else's desire for money and power."

That all these people have had their lives put on the line to serve the selfish desires of a madman makes my blood boil. Nothing else is said. We all turn and move around the building, Anton leading the way.

One person takes a shot at us but then does a double-take when he sees who's leading our charge. Around half a dozen men stand there, stunned, the confusion clear on their faces. A man in the back shouts orders, his gun coming up, but Anton takes him out first, and he drops to the pavement.

The men around him gape, their eyes wide with shock and uncertainty. Anton says something in a foreign language, maybe Russian. I suck at languages, so I have no idea what he's saying, but all five of the remaining men straighten their spines, their lips curling as they lower their weapons.

We keep moving, now with six of Vincent's men leading us to where the others are swarming. Anton says something else to them, and all of them reach into their gear, pulling out knives. They take off separately, obviously on missions of their own, and soon, I see they're singling out specific people.

There's a group of men up ahead, and through the path between them, I see a tall man standing near Toni. She steps in closer to him, and I increase my pace, running right into the crowd.

They pull out their weapons, intent on engaging me, but no sooner do they raise their guns does someone behind me takes them out. I hear Toni laugh, a strange, eerie one that sends a chill down my spine.

I push closer, and I hear someone shouting, and then some men appear to lunge forward before spinning around and running toward me. Above it all, I hear her voice over the crowd. "Grenade!"

The group of people suddenly disperse, everyone turning and

rushing in my direction. They're no longer trying to engage with us; they're running in fear, and I hear her voice shout one more time, "Grenade!"

I try to increase my speed, yelling for her, but my movement against the tide of people retreating in a frenzy is too slow. I hear Tony behind me, shouting for me to get down, then I'm hit from behind, my body connecting with the pavement a second before the boom.

The ground shakes, and then people are screaming. My ears are ringing, the surrounding noise muted as I push whoever tackled me off. I roll to my back and look over and see Tony. For a second, it looks like he's knocked out, but within a few moments, he gasps, trying to curse and breathe as he attempts to get back the wind that was knocked out of him. I blink a few times, then attempt to get to my feet, slowly righting myself and stand fully. I take in the surrounding chaos, not seeing Toni anywhere as I'm met with an ominous silence punctuated with random groaning.

I help Tony to his feet, and he grasps my shoulders as he says something directly into my face. I can't make out his words because of the ringing in my ears, so I focus on his lips, finally understanding when he repeats, "We'll find her. She's okay."

I nod in understanding and then turn back to stare into the carnage. Once I have my bearings, I slowly make my way in the direction I last saw her.

The closer I get, the more frantic I feel. I stop, standing in the middle of it all, and turn around in a full circle with my hands in my hair as I yell for her. A hand touches my shoulder, and I spin around, coming face-to-face with Agatha. She's pointing behind me, so I turn, looking in that direction. I move in what feels like slow motion until, finally, my brain and limbs sync, and I'm running, Agatha on my heels.

I stop at a pile of bodies, seeing a feminine hand sticking out of the pile. My stomach drops, and my heart stops in my chest as I stumble, but I right myself quickly. I rush the last few yards, then we work together to pull the bodies off.

Toni is lying face down, sprawled across two men, and suddenly, a memory of the darkness and the rain flashes before me. Once again, animalistic noises come from deep inside me, and I attempt to choke them back.

I drop to my knees beside her, my hands hovering over her, unsure how to proceed. Agatha comes up behind me, her arms wrapping around the front of me, holding me back, and I hear her saying, "We've got her. Just wait."

I sit back on my haunches and watch as Matt and Tony carefully lift her, rolling her toward me into my arms. Just like the last time, she's too pale, a limp ghost against me with her eyes closed.

Agatha leans close to her, putting her cheek against her mouth. She pulls back with a look of relief, and it sounds like she's saying Toni's alive. She's breathing.

Relief washes over me with such intensity I pause to catch the breath that was knocked out of me. A guttural sob rushes from me, and Tony says he called a bus, then the three of them take off to tend to whatever needs tending.

I adjust my stance so I'm sitting with her resting in my lap, her head supported in the cradle of my shoulder. I hear her groan, and she squirms. I whimper, looking down at her face, and her eyes flutter, then open, meeting mine. She stiffens, her eyes shifting around and then narrowing as they focus back to my face. "What happened?"

I clear my throat several times before I can get a word out. "Grenade."

She winces, taking a shuddering breath before speaking. "That explains a lot."

I tighten my hold on her, dropping my head so my face is pressed into her neck. "Are you okay?"

Her shoulders squirm, and then she's pushing me away. I pull back and look at her face, her eyes meeting mine, searching. "Who are you?"

My stomach drops. I let out a weird, whining noise as I process what she asked me. Like déjà vu, I have a hard time catching my breath, and I curse several times, staring up at the sky. Then her body shakes a little, and I look back down at her to see she's smiling and then she's laughing. My urge to shake her until her teeth rattle explodes. "You. Oh, I fucking hate you."

Now, she laughs outright. "The look on your face."

"You're lucky you're injured. I'll have to save your punishment."

She laughs for a few more moments, her body relaxing into me. "Did I get him?"

"Well, I don't see how you could've missed, considering you chose the most unusual, dramatic weapon."

"Pretty good, right? He never saw that one coming."

I shake my head, growling a bit as I think about what could've happened. "Yeah, don't worry. You're going to be punished for that one, too."

She laughs again but then winces, her discomfort obviously increasing with the adrenaline subsiding. "Do you think it's over?"

"For now."

I wish I had a more concise answer. I wish I could say that it was over, and we can move forward with our lives without worry. But evil will never "be over." People will always be drawn to money and power. There will always be people who will sell drugs, guns, and humans. People who will step over anyone and anything to gain whatever they feel is owed to them.

She's silent for a few moments as she stares up at me, and I get lost in the bottomlessness of her eyes. "I think Lilith would've liked this end. I mean, it's not as exciting as chewing out a throat, but it's not every day you get to stick a grenade in a man's drawers."

I grimace, and she laughs again. "I can't even imagine how you did that, but I'm relieved. I wish there was a way for you to promise me you would never put yourself in harm's way again, but I know that's not a possibility. Especially if you're going to continue on with The Dead."

"Oh, didn't you hear? Seems The Dead is in the middle of a change in management and decided to restructure and take the company in a new direction."

"You don't say?"

She nods, adjusting herself a bit in my arms as she explains, "That was Lilith's primary goal after securing my future. I don't think initially that was her plan, and her shift in perspective had more to do with meeting you than anything else."

I frown. "What do I have to do with it?"

"They led all of us to believe you were the evil in the world, but it turns out this was wrong. Once I took a moment to get a closer look, I knew it was a lie. While The Dead never worked for any one person, a lot of the cleanups they've done likely were unjust. This had already been happening less and less frequently once Lilith took over, but there were still the occasional problems, and she didn't want to do that anymore. She wanted to work for good, to stop doing the bidding of the powerful and start working for those who would be crushed by them. That's why she'd shifted the focus to where she was doing more protecting than killing. Most of those people would be dead or moved, but if she couldn't save them, then she'd do her best to offer sanctuary for their loved ones. It was a choice. We all have a choice."

I smile down at her, allowing a small trickle of relief to flood through me. While this new plan is not without risk, at least it's a risk for good instead of evil.

I glance around, noting the number of people rushing around, working together. A black van slowly pulls up, unable to drive all the way in because of the surrounding carnage. I adjust my arms and move to stand, but Tony and Matt are there. They take her from me, allowing me a moment to rise, and then they place her back in my arms.

She complains a bit, telling me she can walk on her own, but I shush her, carrying her to the waiting van. The medics have a board ready, and they take a hold of her, placing her on it while she continues to glare at me.

I turn back to Matt and Tony, who both followed us to the van. "You got us?"

They both nod, so I continue, "Give them a choice. They're welcome to go about their lives and pretend none of this ever happened. Or they can join us and start fighting for the other side. The choice is theirs. If anyone is scared for their family or has any other extenuating circumstances, we need to follow up on, make a note of it. We'll do what we can."

Toni interrupts, "There's a young man in the main part of the building with a knife wound. His name is Erik, and his favorite color is pink. Please make sure they tend to him."

They both nod again, then turn to continue taking care of business.

I take a last look around, catching sight of Agatha across the way, and she looks over at me, then waggles her fingers.

I shake my head, giving her an equally flippant wave.

Then I knock twice on the door of the van and step inside, closing it behind me.

Epilogue

Toni

I CAN'T DECIDE IF I have a stomach bug, food poisoning, or karma has finally come to kill me.

I'm on my third consecutive day of intermittently praying to the porcelain god, and I'm on the brink of madness. I can't think of anything worse than puking. Or maybe I can, but puking is high up there on things I never, ever want to do again.

I finish retching for the millionth time, then close the lid to the toilet and rest my head on it. I must've dozed off for a bit because I'm roused by a noise, and when I look up, Darius is standing there, giving me an oddly speculative look. I swallow painfully and ask, "What are you looking at?"

He raises a brow at me, then moves to sit on the side of the tub, giving me a small smile as he holds out a brown paper bag. I eye the bag suspiciously, glancing up at his face as I respond, "What is that?"

He gives me a patient look. "You've been ill for a few days now. Do you think maybe you've got something more than a stomach bug?"

My stomach twists again, but this time, it's not from any type of stomach issue. "What are you trying to say, Darius?"

He sighs, rolling his eyes as he waves the bag in the air and sputters, "Nothing, Toni. I'm not trying to say anything at all. I'm sure you're fine. Everything is fine."

My eyes narrow, and I'm working hard to suppress my urge to punch him. "Well, show me what's in the bag."

He gives me an impatient look, and for a moment, I think he might drop the subject and leave the room. But he doesn't. Of course, he doesn't. Instead, he keeps his eyes on my face as he reaches into the bag and pulls out a little box. He holds it out to me, and I eyeball it, my lips twisting. "And what is that for?"

He inclines his head at me and tsks. "Really? You know damn well what it's for."

"And why would I need that? Did you do something? Is there something we need to talk about? What have you done?"

His eyes widen, and his hand snaps back, the little box falling back into his own lap. "Um...how about accidents happen?"

I purse my lips and glare at him. "Accidents? Or one man's crazy possessive mission to get me out of fieldwork and into the kitchen?"

He barks out a laugh. "We both know the kitchen is the last place I want you."

I continue to glower at him. "That may be true, but you know what I'm saying. Do I need to remind you of what will happen if I find out that you did something intentionally to make something like that happen?"

He shakes his head and sighs again. "No, you made it perfectly clear that one time I had a laugh about that guy in the book who intentionally messed with her birth control and then gloated to his friends about it."

"Well, if not for subterfuge, why would I need that?"

"Toni, be reasonable. Occasionally, genuine mistakes happen. That's all. Most likely, you use it. It'll be negative—no harm, no foul. You carry on as you have been until whatever bug you've caught passes. But if it is positive, then you likely would require some medical attention, and I'd rather be safe than sorry."

I groan, the mere idea of that thing turning positive, making my skin crawl. I glance over at Dare, and he gives me a dirty look and then says, "Well, you don't have to look so completely disgusted by the idea of carrying my child."

"Don't take it personally," I say petulantly, my addled brain malfunctioning at the tiny chance I could be carrying Dare's parasite. "Children are gross. I can barely take care of myself. Never mind the fact that we don't exactly live a lifestyle that goes very well with child-rearing."

"Fair, but just humor me." He holds the box out to me.

I give it a dirty look but take it from him, saying, "Fine, but get out."

He doesn't argue; he stands and vacates the bathroom, closing the door behind him. I read the instructions about twelve times before finally accepting that it really is as simple as peeing on a stick and waiting. So, I do the peeing then wash my hands and quickly brush my teeth. I splash some water on my face, then exit the bathroom into the bedroom, where Dare is sitting on the edge of the bed on his phone.

I stare at him until he mouths that he's talking to Tony. I try to snag the phone from him, but he dodges me, moving off the bed and across the room as I yell after him, "*Where* is that guy?"

He shoos me away, continuing to walk away from me every time I try to follow him. I soon give up and sprawl out on the bed on my back, staring up at the ceiling. His footsteps move off into the bathroom, and I know he's going to check the results of the stupid pregnancy test. It's better he looks at it anyway because my initial reaction to a positive result will be complete anarchy, and I'm too tired for that right now.

I must've dozed off because I startle awake from a tickle on my inner thigh. I attempt to adjust my position on the bed, but I find I can't move my arms, and my eyes fly open to find Dare lying between my spread legs.

"What are you doing?"

He glances up at me, both of his hands stroking up my inner thighs and spreading them wider as he smiles. He tilts his head back a bit as if he's scenting the air, then sighs heavily and licks his lips. "Taking my turn."

"Not funny, Darius. I'm disgusting."

His smile widens, and he gives me a lazy shrug before his head falls forward, and he strokes my clit with the tip of his tongue, saying against my flesh, "You know I don't give a fuck."

I push down the moan, attempting to erupt from my chest, stopping myself from bucking my hips up, and instead, I manage to snap my legs together, squeezing Dare's head between them. He chuckles, the vibrations against my sensitive pussy sending a shiver down my spine as he croons, "That's right, baby girl. Keep me close."

"That's the opposite of what I'm trying to do. Now, get the fuck off me and let me go. At least let me shower first. And you have to tell me about your phone call with that fucker, Tony. He hasn't been in contact for weeks, and we really need to know what the hell he's doing. We promised Jayme—"

He shoves two fingers inside me, cutting off my tirade. Desire pools between my legs, my treacherous body begging me to give in. He adds a third finger, stroking in and out of me slowly, firmly, then he curls his fingers, pressing against my walls while his lips suck on my clit, his tongue swirling rhythmically.

I sob out a moan, my thighs falling open. I hook my feet over his shoulders for leverage so I can thrust myself up against his mouth. I know this is a trap. I know what he's going to do, but I can't stop myself. I buck my hips up faster, hoping to distract him from what I know is coming. I feel the pleasure building, the tension inside my body swirling, and I chase it, reaching for when it'll break.

But then he stops.

I scream in frustration, attempting to kick out at him as I curse a blue streak, but he's too fast in getting away. "You fucking prick. Get back here. Finish what you started."

He's standing by the edge of the bed, grinning down at me, and then his dirty chuckle washes over me. He avoids my thrashing legs, leaning near my torso to play with my nipple, giving it a good pinch.

"You better calm down."

I snarl, yanking on my bound hands. "You better get your shit together and finish what you started, or else I'll go out and find somebody who will."

All humor evaporates from his features, and his eyes narrow. He reaches out again, giving my nipple a slap, and I gasp. He growls. "What the fuck did you say to me?"

I give him a big smile. "You heard me. Fuck around and find out—right, baby?"

The growl deepens in his chest, and he climbs up onto the bed so he's kneeling beside me. Without warning, his hand comes out and slaps my pussy. I yelp in surprise. It hurts, but I can't decide if it's in a good or bad way.

I try to close my legs, but he leans on one, his other hand coming around to push the other one open, then he quickly releases it and slaps my pussy again, harder this time. I sob out a moan, and suddenly, my body is on fire.

I squeeze my eyes shut, breathing in sharply through my nose, then gasping as I push down another moan. I open my eyes, startled to find his face directly in front of me. He licks across my lips with the flat of his tongue, then presses kisses from the corner of my mouth along my jaw to my ear, where I feel his breath as he says, "Easy way or hard way, minx?"

I want to answer, but I won't. Instead, I snap my head forward, nipping his ear before he thinks to jerk himself back. He grabs me by my throat, squeezing my neck, pushing my upper body down on the bed, and cutting off my breath as his other hand touches his ear, coming back bloody. I choke out a laugh, and he tightens his hold on my throat. My eyes burn, tears tracking down the sides of my face and into my hairline. His eyes glow as he whispers, "That was a mistake. Now, you're really going to pay."

I want to deny it. I want to take it back, to beg and plead for the easy way. But I know it's too late. I also know that if I'd done that in the first place, he probably wouldn't have believed me. It would've been a trap.

He slides his hands under my arms, pulling me so I slide up the bed. He unhooks my wrists from the headboard, moving them higher and securing them so my upper body is suspended in the air. I feel the tension in my arms. He shifts up to the top of the bed so he's kneeling up by my head, and now he's gripping my hair, yanking until I drop my head back, so I see his muscular torso upside down.

He uses his free hand to unbuckle his belt, unfastening and un-zipping his trousers, pulling his dick out. He yanks my head back painfully, so my mouth falls open, and then he presses the tip of his dick between my lips. "You better not fucking bite me. Then you'll really see how a punishment feels."

I give him an upside-down smile, not making any promises, and then, with no hesitation, he shoves his cock between my lips, right into the back of my throat. I would've choked if I had any air to choke on, so I focus on not biting him as he starts to face-fuck me. He pulls out, and I gasp for breath, tears running into my hairline, drool splattering all over me as I look up, taking pleasure in the look of carnal satisfaction on his face as he stares down at me.

He sits up, leaning further over the top of me and reaching for something beside me. He nudges my legs apart, pressing something hard between them. "Squeeze your legs together, baby girl. Hold this in place." I do as I'm told, moaning loudly as it vibrates. Then his dick is back in my mouth, and I'm choking on my pleasure and his cock.

I can't breathe, the vibrations on my clit so intense that all I can do is moan around his dick in my throat. He pulls out without preamble, spit splashing all over my face as I cough and sputter through a moan, my orgasm right there on the brink. But then Dare reaches over, and the vibration stops, and I scream again. "You motherfucker. Oh, my god. I fucking hate you."

He's right in my face, his tongue against my skin, licking away my tears and saliva. I try to shake him off, but he grabs my head between his hands and holds me steady. "You fucking love me, and you know it."

I shake my head in his hands. "How could I possibly? All you do is torture me."

He gives me that dark chuckle that vibrates up from his chest, and I feel my insides flutter. Fucking asshole.

"Come on now, baby girl. Don't be like that."

I turn my face away from him, not wanting to give in too easily while also wanting to give in because I'm a pain in the ass like that.

He moves down, situating himself between my spread legs, and then his cock is pressing in exactly where I want him. I grab onto the ropes attached to the headboard, using them as leverage to get my feet under me, and I buck my hips, taking the tip inside. He leans closer, his upper body hovering over me as he brushes his lips against mine. "That's right. That's my good fucking girl."

I am a good fucking girl.

I moan in pleasure, adjusting my grip on the ropes so I have better control of my movements as I slide down on his cock. I release a panting moan, rotating my hips so I'm fucking him from below. He remains still, allowing me to use him for my pleasure, but I know it won't last. He wants me to think I'm going to get mine, and then he'll pull it away from me at the last second, like he always does.

I continue to move my hips, my feet bracing under me as I pick up my pace, taking him deeper, harder, and faster. I feel the tension in his body, see the look on his face, and know he's preparing to pull away, to control my response. I try to relax, to control my body and my breathing, but it's no use. I can feel it right there, and I want it.

His hands settle on either side of me as he makes a move to shift back, and that's when I yank harder on my restraints, my legs sliding down until I hook my feet around his thighs, and I pull him into me. "Don't stop. Don't fucking stop."

He smirks at me, a dirty chuckle vibrating up from his chest, sending my insides soaring. He drops his head closer to mine, and his lips press against my own, his tongue shoving in and stroking mine. He pulls back and presses his forehead against mine, his eyes boring into me as he says, "You gonna take what you want, baby girl?"

I buck my hips up, but I've lost most of my leverage in this new position, my range of motion restricted. I lick his lips, suck his tongue into my mouth, and sob in frustration. "More. I need more. Fuck me.

Oh, fuck."

He pushes his upper body away from me, and I whine at the loss, but then he reaches over me, releasing each of my wrists so my torso falls back onto the mattress. He leans back on his haunches, and I adjust my legs upward so they hook around his waist, my heels digging into his ass. His fingertips dig into my hips, and he uses both hands to pull me into his thrusting hips. "Touch yourself for me. Rub your fingers over that needy clit and come for me."

I move my hand down, touching myself as directed, and he fucks me with sharp, jabbing thrusts that hit the very end of me, then slide back out over my G-spot. He's grunting with effort, his teeth bared, and his wild eyes on my face as he watches me.

I open my mouth to speak as pleasure flows through my body, but nothing comes out but broken sobs and moans. He fucks me harder and faster, growling deep in his chest. "You want me to give it to you? Do you want your prize?"

I sob out a moan, my words breathless as I respond, "That's right. Give your good fucking girl what she deserves."

"Fuck. Fuck. Oh, fuck. You gotta come all over my dick. Come all over me. Take it. Take what's yours." His breathy shouts cause my insides to throb, and then he changes his movements subtly, my hand falling away as he drives himself against my clit with every inward thrust—measured, slow, and firm.

I focus on the slap of his body against mine, and my hands come up, reaching for him. He drops his face into my palms, and it's the look he gives me, those golden eyes boring into my eyes with lust, need, and love.

He pulls back, then shoves back inside with a slap of our bodies together, pushing in and in and in, grinding against my clit until the tension inside me snaps with a sobbing curse. My body trembles, and

I gasp for breath. "Oh, god. Oh, fuck. Yes. Do it. Fuck me."

He freezes like that, pushed deep inside, suspended over me with a look of pure euphoria on his features. He doesn't blink; instead, he stares right into my soul as his dick pulses inside of me.

We remain like that, our bodies connected, and eyes locked for a few moments before he adjusts his grip and lowers my hips to the mattress. He follows me down, his arms moving under my shoulders and his hands cupping my head as he drops his head and presses his lips to mine, kissing me deeply, languorously. Then he pulls back a bit, so his lips still brush mine as he whispers, "Tell me."

I smile, my hands reaching up to stroke through his hair as I say, "No."

He shakes his head at me, but he's smiling. "You're such a pain in my ass."

"Well, if that's your thing, I certainly could be."

He shakes his head again and places a last kiss against my lips before he pushes himself away from me, pulling from my body and then moving from the bed. He disappears in the bathroom and comes back with a washcloth, which he wipes gently against my forehead, then tracks it down between my breast, across my belly, and finally, between my legs. He walks back into the bathroom, and soon, water is running in the tub, and he's back, scooping me up and carrying me into the bathroom. He places me in the chair he insists on keeping in there, even though it doesn't match at all, and asks, "How are you feeling?"

"I feel okay right now."

"Do you want me to get you something to eat? Drink?"

"I'll take a drink, please, but no food yet." He nods, disappearing once again, and I know he's also giving me a moment to tend to my own personal needs. I'm back in the chair when he returns, a glass of fizzy water with cranberry in hand, which he gives to me.

I take a few sips as he turns the taps off, then sprinkles in some eucalyptus bath salts. Then he turns back to me, removing the glass from my hands and setting it on the shelf next to the tub before carefully scooping me up and placing me in the tub. I stopped arguing with him about whether I can walk on my own a long time ago. The fact of the matter is, he doesn't care, and it's not worth arguing about. I lean forward, and he climbs in behind me, pulling me back so I'm reclined against him.

His arms come around me, and I relax against him, a small sigh escaping. "I take it I'm not pregnant?"

"Well, you weren't."

I jab him with my elbow, and he laughs against my ear as I sputter, "You fucking stop that. It's not funny."

He laughs louder, squeezing me tighter. I squirm, attempting to elbow him in the gut as he replies, "It's kind of funny. But no, you're not."

I'm silent for a moment, but then he continues, "But would it really be that bad?"

I give a half-shrug. "I mean, if it happened by our choice or purely by chance, then fine. I guess. But to have it forced on me? No fucking way."

"I would never do that to you. I like my balls right where they are."

Fucking right, he does. I'll tolerate a lot of fucked-up bullshit from him, but there's a hard line there. I consider reiterating this, but decide to change the subject. "Did Tony say where he is?"

"No, which means he's likely up to no good. Which means I'll likely have to go find out what kind of fuckery he's up to."

"Do you think he found Carolina?"

Dare presses his face against my neck, licking my pulse point as he responds, "I'm sure he has. He promised he wouldn't kill her, but that doesn't mean he won't fuck her up in other ways."

"Do you think we should intervene?"

"Not yet. She deserves a little fuckery for how she played us. But I think Tony could learn a few things from her as well."

I agree. Carolina certainly pulled one over on us, but I also understand why she did it. Sometimes, you have to accept that things aren't personal at the time and move forward with the new information. That doesn't mean they're the enemy or that they're going to keep trying to come for you. It only means they're trying to survive, trying to protect the people they love. I know that feeling. Darius sacrificed himself for me. Lilith lost her life for me. So yeah, we'll sit back and let Tony have a little fun. At least we know he won't kill her.

I turn my head, wiggling my body around so I can kiss him on the jaw. "I love you."

He presses his face against the side of mine, his voice a rumble against my skin. "I know."

Not done with the Ends World yet?

Lucky you! I'm not either.

Get book 3, A Fine Line, now!

Well, I did it. I wrote two books. While I won't say it was easy, I will say it wasn't as difficult as I thought it would be. Also, I am certifiably insane, so...

No, for reals, though: writing is as traumatic of an experience as one can have without being physically near people who consistently make you laugh, cry, and scream, literally all at the same time. Sweat and tears, baby. Sweat and tears.

Here's just a tiny sample of all the people I need to thank:

To you, the readers: thank you for taking the time to read this book, and for taking the chance on a new author. Yes, I poke fun at negative reviews, but in all honesty, I know not everyone is going to like my books, or my writing style, or even me. And that's okay. Read what you love, love what you read.

My family: (you read it anyway) - for putting up with my self-imposed writing deadlines.

My Non-Book friends: (But mostly Jess) I'm still here. I still love you.

Layla Towers: over a year now and here we are, working on book 3. LY4E.

Jay: so glad you're still fucking around and finding out. ILY.

The Spicy Book Nook family: with extra shout outs to those who listened to me cry the most, round two—LA Ferro and LM Fox. <3

Still Censored: VR Tennent & Carolina Jax —*Someday* will be our *every day*. Lamp. ILY.

My KGQ family: Amanda, Dani, Heather— Love you, my OG bitches.

My Bookish Sisters: Issa Marie, April, Britt (888), Stef, Grace – wave those red flags

The Bookish Girls Services: Always a pleasure. Keepin' it classy...

Kayla: You're a magician & a professional bitch handler. Can't live without you. ILY.

vo.EROS & my Egirls: Tamora, Goldie (twinner), Katarina, Jane Apatova, Amy, Denise, Abby, Elle, LadyT, Erin, Candy, Kytana...to name a few. FFH. CHFM.

My CABFD crEw: Aimee, Ashley, Krystin, Mags, Manda–on those days where I barely survive, it is you all who hold on to my bootstraps. I'll never let go. ILYSM.

Big thanks to the BookTok/Bookstagram worlds for allowing me to continue to edge you relentlessly. Don't worry, I have more and more and more.

My ARC team: I know I play the strangest games of red light, green light, but y'all continue to humor me. No, I will not calm down. Appreciate you all so much.

Annette, Cami, Tabatha: Huge thank you for reading this fucking train wreck a million times to make sure I got it right and then again to make sure I didn't really fuck it up when I DELETED THE WHOLE MOTHERFUCKING DOCUMENT IN THE HOME STRETCH.

Kirsty McQuarrie with **Let's Get Proofed** for continuing to put up with my bullshit.

And to my brother, Jason.

I've got my cape out.

Now...JUMP...

I love you.

Made in the USA
Las Vegas, NV
26 December 2024